# Sunrise Surprise

Editors:
Mary Dillon
Leslie Chatwin
Dee Dee Richardson

Special Thanks:
Shel Weinstein
Tom Smart
Cha Cha Weller

Author photo: Kayle Matsumura
Illustrated by the author.

Published in the United States
by the Weller Institute
PO Box 518, Oakley UT 84055

ISBN:    Hardcover 978-1-7328832-5-3
         Softcover  978-1-7328832-6-0
         eBook      978-1-7328832-7-7

# SUNRISE SURPRISE

A MODERN WESTERN NOVEL

BY DON WELLER

A sunrise can reveal
a new shell on the beach,
or a decaying torso
in a tide pool.

A surprise comes
on its own schedule.

But a cutting horse ... well,
a cutting horse is a work of art.

*—An Outside Chance, by Thomas McGuane*

## Prologue

## December in the Cold Room

In an immaculate steel windowless room, a gray-haired gentleman pulled open a large drawer. The sound was crisp and metallic, like the bolt action on a big game rifle, a decisive click, under the cold florescent lighting.

The man brought a shiny rolling table next to the drawer, slid a tray supporting a dead woman's head and torso from the drawer onto the table, and pushed it into an area of intense light.

He was approached by a younger man, and together they stared at the remains.

"That's not something you see every day."

His nose twitched at the smell of ocean air, drying kelp and rotted flesh.

"I expect we'll get assigned to this one," the older man said, "and thought we'd better see it before the scientists start digging around."

The first man, Mikio Iwasaki, wore a slightly wrinkled beige suit, a dark blue shirt, and tie. Short, with an officious demeanor that hid a friendly spirit. He wore a bold moustache. His attitude toward the corpse suggested respect. He was 'kamaa, ina,' a local.

The other fellow, Clay Burnam, crossed his arms and shivered. He was casually dressed, curious and tentative in his movements. In his early thirties, three years out of the police academy, he was Honolulu's newest detective, a 'haole.' Taller than Mikio by six inches, he stood transfixed by the protoplasm languishing between them. It looked like Hannibal Lecter's science project gone horribly wrong.

Lying on her back, the head was turned left, showing the right side of a face that had probably been pretty once. Her hair was wild, still tangled with some seaweed and sand; her profile showed a perfectly chiseled nose and chin.

Her right leg was gone, torn off at the hip. Her left leg had been chewed away below the knee. The arms were at her sides and disappeared at the elbows. There was no color to her skin; in fact the artificial lights made her seem slightly green, altogether a ghoulish distorted mess.

"Where'd you find her?" Clay asked.

"Little kid, lives in Makaha, found her in a tidal pool, early yesterday. He was very excited. Told his mom, and she called us."

"So Mikio, you think it'll be our case?"

"I'd bet on it."

"Did you talk to the mother?" Clay asked.

"No," said Mikio." First it was some local uniforms. They said the mother was more upset 'cause the kid was skipping school than she had been finding shark bait on the beach.

"The cops got the medical examiner to pick up the corpse. She was heavier than you'd expect, they said. Probably messier and smellier too."

Clay bent down, trying to look into the woman's eyes.

"Shit," he said. "The other half of her face is gone."

"I think a shark that chewed off her leg, maybe, kissed her face goodbye." Mikio said.

"They don't usually come into the beaches, do they?"

"Not usually. Maybe she fell off a boat farther out?"

"Hard to tell how long she'd been in the water. I guess the lab will be able to tell us. And maybe DNA can show us who she is ... was."

"Would you guess two weeks in the water?" Clay asked.

"Maybe. Hard to know."

"How old do you think she was?"

"Hard to know in her puffed-up condition. Probably looked nothing like this when she was walking and talking. I imagine her kinda young ... twenties or thirties ... maybe. The fabric, what's left of the bikini top, suggests young. My wife gave up skimpy

< 2 >

attire in her twenties," said the experienced detective.

"Around her neck and shoulder hangs the remains of a T- shirt. All evidence for the lab rats to explore."

"Probably started swimming and overestimated her ability. Just ran out of gas or got a cramp or something," Clay volunteered.

"Or got drunk and fell off a yacht," Mikio said. "It happens."

"Guess we can check if anyone fell of a boat lately. See who got listed as missing," Clay suggested. "Or came on a plane and missed her flight home."

"But first we'll hope the lab can narrow down our timeline."

They continued looking and speculating, thinking out loud.

"Is that what shark bites look like?" Clay wondered.

"Consistent with what I've seen," Mikio said, "and I've seen a few."

He took off his suit jacket and pulled on a white lab coat, mask, and plastic gloves.

"Let's turn her over," he said, and when Clay was properly protected, they did.

The movement stirred up an awful smell, and the two men stepped back a moment.

Her arms had disappeared under her bloated body, but turned on her stomach, it was apparent the hands were fastened together behind her back with a zip-tie. The puffy wrists and the tight plastic showed they had been that way for a long time.

"Got a hunch we got a murder here," said Mikio, stating the obvious.

He went to a cabinet and came back with a camera. First, he photographed the hands, then everything else; the shark tooth marks, and the face ... both her good side, and the missing side.

"A murder," Mikio said.

"Our murder?" Clay wondered.

"Bet on it," Mikio said.

**Part One**

**Jake, Two Months Earlier**

It took more than a honeymoon to change some of Jake Oar's long held habits. Trying not to miss a single sunrise was one he clung to.

So, he squinted at the clock, and then reached into the blackness for the closest shirt. He felt for the fanny pack the hotel had presented at registration. It came with the room key and a tube of heavy-duty sunscreen. Jake added his cell phone and slipped quietly out the door.

In the predawn light Jake walked out of the hotel, passed the pool. An aqua rectangle lit from below, its surface moved slightly by a pathetic breeze. In the gloom he avoided chairs, lounges, and tables, all arranged carefully, ready for the new day's guests.

The tiki torches were dark, silent reminders of their flaming witness to the previous night's activities.

Jake stepped gingerly down onto the sand and took off his flip-flops. He tucked them carefully beside the low wall that separated diners from the beach. It was dark, but he could easily find them on his return.

The moon that had left a dancing silver trail the night before, was now far to his right, and the sea looked like oil rolling out of blackness.

Soft sand became solid as wet fingers toyed with his toes. The air was comfortable and smelled sweet and salty, of ocean and hibiscus. The water, warm and welcoming.

He waded in till his calves were immersed. Rising and falling, the gentle waves soaked his sweatpants above the knees. The tail of his shirt was threatened.

He walked slowly west as the sky lightened. Each step his legs

< 4 >

pushed against the moving water. On his right, the edges of tall hotels were becoming visible. Now and then a new light blinked on in a room up high.

When he reached the yacht harbor, Jake left the shore. The outgoing tide had left a line of little treasures; seaweed, a piece of plastic, more seaweed, some string, tiny shells, and a larger one. It was about the size of a child's fist, pointed at both ends, wrapped with bluish stripes. One end was open, once the entrance to a tiny creature's home.

Jake picked it up and slipped it into the maroon and silver fanny pack with his cell phone and hotel key.

He turned around to face the sunrise.

The sky lightened gradually behind the dark form of Diamond Head. Wayward backlit clouds began to perform in a slow-motion explosion of bright color with glistening edges.

Show over, Jake turned west again. The Hilton Waikiki Hotel and lagoon marked the end of the beach. He continued barefoot on cement past the expensive boats rocking at their moorings, and past others, out of the water on trailers or surrounded by tools, scaffolds, and ladders. Sailboats with their keels exposed, looking slightly embarrassed.

When Yacht Harbor Towers appeared on his right, Jake walked into Ala Moana Park, a long stretch of turf, palm trees, and flowers, separating the city and its traffic noise from the surf. Grass was between his toes now, grass and bird shit.

The coming daylight exposed seagulls, pigeons, and other stranger birds pecking around, checking snacks the tourists had left.

Jake was far from home and amazed by the tropics. Unusual birds, bold flowers, strange smells, the warm air so thick you could almost taste it. Exotic is how it felt.

Leaning against a tree, he stood looking at a little sailboat that seemed to be playing with the waves. Behind him the city was coming to life.

Forty yards away a solitary man walked toward a lonely bench that faced the sea. He moved slowly and stopped to feed a pigeon. He wore a baseball cap, a blue T-shirt and shorts. The gentleman appeared around Jake's age, early fifties, but seemed older.
It was as though he belonged to the park, yet something about him was familiar.

The fellow sat on the bench, leaned against the back, and surveyed the Pacific.

Jake pushed away from the tree, thinking it was time to drift back to the room. Vacation was a new concept for him. Existing without purpose.

Standing there, he looked at the seated man again.
There was a bothersome familiarity. Maybe earlier this week or last, they had passed each other, or spoken in a restaurant.

No, he thought, it was more important than that. The chance it was a friend from the mainland was possible, but remote.

What the heck. He walked toward the bench, thinking he would sneak another glance.

Closer he realized the man was no one he knew. A Dodger's cap, a short beard turning gray, and a ponytail. Nothing familiar. Yet there was something.

When Jake got near, the guy slid to the end of the bench as though making room. Apparently, he thought Jake wanted to sit. It was the only bench in sight. Though they did not make eye contact, Jake sat down. Independently, they both watched the tiny sail flirting with the sea.

"A Soling." the man said.

Jake froze, his mind spinning. He looked at the stranger, who continued staring at the ocean. It seemed impossible. Jake looked again, closely. He knew that voice.

"Wally?" he asked.

"Walter Abbott." The man announced staring straight ahead.

"Wally." Jake repeated. This time it was not a question.

"Do I know you?" the man asked, looking at Jake's eyes for

the first time.

Jake was sure. Dead sure.

"Un-fucking-believable! You Son Of A Bitch, Wally!" Jake spoke rapid fire, a verbal machine gun.

"I thought you were in prison for life. I never expected to see you again. Wally, this has me confused. What's going on?"

"I'm Walter Abbott. I don't know who you are, but you're crazy." The voice was cool and calm, matter of fact.

"Bullshit, Wally." Jake leaned into his face now. "This is pure bullshit. You owe me an explanation, damn it, Wally! We were friends until a Kevlar vest stopped you."

I'm Walter, don't you forget it."

"You are Wally Archer. Wally Fuckin' Archer."

"I don't know any Wally. I am Walter Abbott, Jake, don't you forget it. Shit. And it wasn't a fuckin' vest that saved your ass. It was a friendship. Shit."

"Well, this is amazing. You're amazing. Not in prison. Amazing."

They sat quietly a while.

"So, what the hell do we do now," Jake asked finally. "You gotta kill me for fear I'll tell the cops?"

"Shit ... I'm Walter now. I'm retired from crime. Witness protection program. I have a new life."

"Rumors back home, you went to prison forever and your wife divorced you. Sold all your horses."

"Well, she did, but you notice I'm not in jail. Gotta' new girlfriend. She doesn't know Wally, but she knows me, Walter Abbott."

The Soling was joined by two others just like it, and both men watched, but Jake's mind was not on sailing.

"This is no place to talk," Walter said at last. "And there's not much I can tell anyway. They couldn't prove much except shooting Prince, and I think they sort of thought I did them a favor there. I told them some stories and some names in trade to get them to stop bothering me. That's really about all there is."

"Wow." Jake said slowly. "Just wow."

"Shit," Walter said. "Why don't you come to our house for supper tonight?"

"No thanks." Jake said without a smile.

"You won't need your bullet-proof vest."

"No thanks." Jake said again. "Not ready. This is too much to process all at once."

He stood up then. "This has been the strangest conversation I can ever remember. I never expected to see you again, here or anywhere."

New people were meandering around, and the pigeons ventured closer. Walter pulled a handful of something and tossed it to the birds. It looked like grain, Jake thought. Wally's new life. Feeding pigeons.

Jake headed east into the sun. Thoughts and doubts were waltzing around in his mind.

Jake squinted and wished he'd worn his hat.

< 8 >

# Darcy Oar

The sun had climbed into a blue sky and spread brightness onto the steel and glass hotel room twenty-eight stories up. The room had blond wooden trim, an oriental rug, and floor-to-ceiling sliding glass, open to the sea breezes. A small balcony provided an ocean view and a glimpse of Diamond Head.

A splash of sunlight had reached the far-right corner of the rug by the time Jake arrived.

A huge bed dominated the room, dwarfing the woman lying there. She wore a carefully cultivated suntan, golden brown, about two weeks deep. Her feet were pointed south toward the view and the bottoms were pink, as were her nipples. Pink, centered in two white triangles.

She rolled onto her back as Jake moved to the coffee machine, showing a third triangle of white with a patch of brown that matched the hair she pushed out of her sleepy eyes. She looked at him. Her face was that of an angel, and the smooth skin belied her age.

"Good morning." Darcy said, through a generous smile.

"Howdy, Mrs. Oar," he said. "You're a sight for sore eyes."

He started the coffee, removed his damp salty sweatpants and lay beside her.

"Any adventures out there this morning?" she asked.

"You won't believe it when I tell you."

One hand was a gentle fist and he opened it exposing, the seashell, then placed it on her chest between the triangles.

"Beautiful," she said, looking down at the blue striped exoskeleton.

"No one's home in there, I hope." She was looking in the open end.

She turned toward him on one elbow and unbuttoned the top button of his Hawaiian shirt.

"Any plans for today?" she asked.

"Nope. You?"

"We could grab our snorkel stuff and try to beat the crowd to Hanauma Bay."

"Yep, we could."

"Then we could go to the mall and have a sushi lunch," she said, reaching for the second button.

"Sounds delicious."

"I'm thinking, start with misoshiru, then hamachi sashimi, and then seaweed salad." She peered into his eyes, and the third button was finished.

"Getting hungry just thinking about it." Jake said.

"If we go to Ichiban. Maybe Kimura-san could make us an order out of whoever lived in that shell you found."

The fourth button of his rather garish yellow shirt with the red and green flowers was open.

"We could have mochi for dessert." Darcy declared.

Hawaiian shirts, sometimes called Aloha Shirts, are an example of folk art and commerce in-breeding. The result is colorful, sometimes beautiful in the right setting, but bold and tasteless elsewhere.

Jake's was rather wild, screaming 'tourist' out loud, but really, didn't they all? With his cowboy hat, it was a fashion statement. His shirt was one of the cheaper styles, meant to be worn outside the pants, hardly any tail to tuck in. And it only had five buttons.

A small gray bird with a bright red head and white neck landed on the balcony rail and watched them as the last button was gone and the shirt was sent to the floor.

The little bird, a Rock Dove, was blown away by a gust of wind, and they spent the morning enjoying what is known in some circles as 'a roll in the hay.'

# Something Fishy Here

They left their snorkel gear in the trunk of the red Toyota rental, got out, and put on their hats.

Lots of hats are sold in Hawaii, but not many a real cowboy would wear. Theirs had come with them from home.

Her flat hat was vaquero style. His suggested rancher.

The Hawaiian sun was high and hot, but cooler under a hat.

In the hotel's fanny pack, Darcy had her timer, and a tube of skin protection that smelled like gardenia meets chemistry. Science and commerce working hand in hand.

Wearing T-shirt, shorts, and tennis shoes, Jake had given up on a tan. Where he had been brown, he was browner; other places were red and uncomfortable, but his forehead remained white.

After they were properly smeared and smelly, they walked to the drop-off, and looked down to the bay.

A half-circle of very steep green bank plunged to a quarter-moon shaped sandy beach. The bay was open to the ocean, where rocks in the water calmed the wild Pacific, leaving it quiet, calm, and shallow. The water appeared light blue, with dark aqua-green shapes of coral hiding just under the surface.

Some coconut trees hovered over the sand, pretending to provide shade. Their fleeting shadows flickered over the scene. Visitors came by the millions.

The attraction was the vast variety of fish that swam face to face with the snorkelers.

The honeymooning Oars looked down and saw the entire beach covered with towels and bodies. The water was alive with human backs, floating face down. People the size of kidney beans in a frying pan. They moved slowly, if they moved at all.

It was too late to get space down below, so they sat and watched.

"Well, we're alone, so let me tell you my big adventure this morning," Jake began.

"While I was sleeping?"

"Yup."

"How you got that shell?"

"That's only the beginning of the story."

"Okay," she said, "shoot."

She pulled her sunglasses lower on her nose and peered over at him. Jake looked into her curious eyes with a serious frown that got her full attention.

"Darcy, do you remember a guy named Wally Archer, from a few years ago?" Jake asked.

"I don't think I ever met him, honey. He was the murderer that was shot in the round pen. That guy?"

"His hobby was cutting horses, and his secret business was murder for hire. We witnessed one. He probably had legitimate work as well. I've known him on and off for thirty years, but didn't learn about his killings until the end."

"He was going to shoot you, but he shot a gangster instead," Darcy recalled.

"Well, this morning I took my early walk and I saw him."

"Get outta' here, Jake," she exclaimed. "He's in prison for life. You're seeing ghosts."

"No ghosts," Jake announced. "I saw him alive and well."

"How can you be sure?" She was incredulous. "Was he wearing an orange jumpsuit or something?"

"It was Wally. Feeding the pigeons, calm as you please."

Darcy stood up, took off her hat and scratched her head, and sat back down. Hat back on.

"Okay, tell me ..."

"I saw this guy, far away, and thought he seemed familiar. Got closer to check him out. It was Wally. He had a beard and a ponytail, and a stupid baseball cap. I sat next to him and recognized the voice and the eyes.

"Wally said his name was Walter Abbott now, and that he was in a witness protection program.

"Thing is, Darcy, I don't believe him. He's lived a lie all the time I've known him. Thirty years a murderer."

"You're sure it's him?"

"Positive." Jake said.

"That's an incredible coincidence."

"Yes, it is."

"So, what should we do now?" she asked.

"That's the question. I'm not sure."

"Do you believe the witness protection story?"

"I was starting to. He said he had a girlfriend. I think maybe he was trying to be serious ..."

Jake paused a moment. "Except if he broke out of prison, or jumped bail, or got abducted by aliens, I think we would have heard about it somehow.

"So, he's probably thinking, is stumbling into me gonna' cause him any problems? And I'm thinking, am I gonna' spoil his cover or cause him any trouble? How could I do that anyway? I have nothing but his assumed name to go by. So, he's safe. And if he wanted to find me, how could he do it?"

He glanced down at the silver and maroon hotel fanny pack and pulled out the sunblock.

"I guess we're both wondering if we pose a danger to each other," Jake said. "That we met was just the strangest coincidence I can imagine."

"How long has he been here, I wonder?" Darcy asked.

"Don't know, but his ponytail might be a clue. It's kind of short. Hair pulled back, a rubber band and about two inches hanging. Does that sound like about two years? Two inches of tail? Not yet enough to be proud of." Jake paused. "And as I remember, he seemed to be very well acquainted with the birds he fed."

"I think the pigeons are friendly after the first bite." Darcy said.

They sat watching the snorkelers. Knees up, red, but very well protected.

"My big question: is Walter ... Wally reformed? Or killer in disguise? I wonder."

Darcy was intrigued. "What was he like personally? How well did you know him?"

"Well, I knew him for a long time. He had a good horse and was competitive now and then. He was helpful if you asked him, and sometimes a jokester.

"Claimed to have been an athlete in his youth, a great skier in college, but I wouldn't know. When I knew him, he wasn't particularly fit looking ... actually, kind of pudgy. We lived too far apart to socialize easily, at least an hour and a half. Didn't talk with him outside of the horses, don't know anyone who did. A friend, but never close. He could ride a cutting horse pretty well though."

Jake paused. "Does that make sense?"

"Uh huh," Darcy said, thinking.

"I'll call Marv, our sheriff, when we get home," Jake said. "Try to get the story on Wally, witness protection, and all that. It just doesn't seem right to find him paying his debt to society in Paradise instead of prison.

"But I'm going to try to forget him for now."

From where they sat, they could see the foot traffic on the system of stairs and walks between the parking on the bluff and the beach below. Darcy noticed there was more traffic coming up than going down.

"Looks like the burnt ones are climbing out," she said.

"They're toast. Should we go down?"

"Let's."

Jake wasn't much of a swimmer, but he was a dandy floater. Face down, he breathed through the snorkel clenched in his

< 14 >

teeth. If his masked leaked or fogged up, he could stand up and fix it. If the water went over his head, a stroke or two in the right direction would give him footing.

The pattern of sunshine on the gentle waves danced with his shadow on the sandy bottom. Floating on his stomach, that was his view. That and the crazy fish.

The submerged coral reefs were surrounded by a circus of small creatures nibbling at the nooks and crannies. Nature's dinner guests at the Underwater State Park.

These fish tended to be thin when viewed from the front, but were comical little billboards when seen from the side.

One of them, who pecked her way around the reef, was a yellow and gray Triggerfish who aggressively chased others away. A territorial fussbudget, her face was almost human, mostly nose, with a tiny mouth at the tip. A nosy little librarian on patrol: 'Tsk, tsk, tsk, something fishy here'.

Others were Convict Tang, yellowish with prison bars on their sides, and Surgeonfish, black from the gill to tail, covered with white dots.

Looking like a mass of silver daggers, schools of Goatfish flashed past, or hovered, spinning, before zooming away all together like a glittering ball.

Butterfly fish, Parrotfish, and jellyfish were all on full display.

Moray eels hid in the rocks.

Altogether, a colorful crowd, an aquatic Disneyland.

When a new shadow finally joined his on the sand below, he knew it was Darcy.

His mermaid.

## Question:
## Can a retired murderer-for-hire
## find contentment in Paradise?

"Hey, Pinky, we gotta' do something. I'm going nuts on this damn island. Talk about gettin' Island Fever, it's driving me nuts."

Walter Abbott was speaking from the ugly couch, his ponytail bouncing with each phrase. The television was tuned to a game show, but the sound was off. The flat faces and animated mouths gave the room a sense of quiet desperation.

Pinky was a slim, tired-looking girl about half his age, in a faded pink tank top that seemed to accentuate her modest chest, sculpted shoulders, and neck. Her long blonde hair, combed and washed, fell straight to her waist. Thinking it was her best feature, she tended to toss her head a lot, like an unruly palomino.

"Watcha' wanna' do, honey?" she asked.

"Don't know. Goin' fuckin' stir crazy is what I'm doin' here. Can't stand it. Makes me wanna' kill somebody."

"Who ya' mad at?"

"Nobody," Walter admitted. "Just bored. Drivin' myself crazy."

"We could go to the mall, go shopping. Go for a drive. Go to the beach, watch the surfers. You never wanna' do much but lay around."

"Shit," Walter said. "I know."

"You never wanna' do what I wanna' do."

"I know. I'm sorry."

"We could lay on the beach with the tourists, maybe that would be fun?"

"Shit, you know I don't like the sun."

"Maybe just once?"

"I see enough beach in the mornings."

"Honey, you see nothin'. You're out before dawn and back

< 16 >

here before the tourists even get up. I could get you a bigger bag of corn and you could stay longer, feed more pigeons. Maybe even make a friend," she suggested.

"I met a friend, but I don't know if I can trust him."

"You can't trust your friend?" Pinky wondered.

"Don't know who to trust, is all."

"You can trust me," she said. "Me and the Lord."

"Shit, I'm fine. Just depressed is all. Depressed by the famous Island Fever."

"Let's go to Tahiti or Bora Bora or Kawai or Kansas for a vacation. That'll brighten you up."

"Take a vacation from my permanent vacation?" Walter asked.

She looked at him then, curiously.

"Honey, you know I don't like airports," Walter said, very sympathetically.

"I know, Wal, but you're so depressed. I'm just trying to help. You know the Lord helps those who help themselves. I'm trying to help God help you to help yourself."

"I appreciate it. Someday maybe I'll go to church with you. You'll see."

"I just hate to see you like this. Wanna' massage?" Pinky smiled.

Walter got naked and climbed onto the old aluminum folding table Pinky had found at a second-hand store in Honolulu. It was rather wobbly, but if approached carefully, it hadn't let anybody down yet. Just waiting.

He put his face in the flimsy padded ring and wiggled it around, trying to get comfortable. Pinky put a bath towel over his rump.

"The Lord and I think you need more exercise, Honey," she said.

# Aloha 'oe

Aloha 'oe, aloha 'oe     E ke onaona noho i ka lipo
One fond embrace,    A ho'i a'e au     Until we meet again

Farewell to thee ... farewell to thee ...
The charming one who dwells in the shaded bowers ...
One fond embrace ... Ere I depart ... Until we meet again ...
Sweet memories come back to me ... Of the past ...
Dearest one ... yes ... you are mine own ...

On the balcony high above Waikiki Beach, sounds were coming from a neighboring room, or possibly the floor below. It had been another nice day. Sliding glass was open to the warm breezes. Someone was struggling on a ukulele, wrestling with the Hawaiian lyrics. At every chord change, strumming and singing paused three seconds as sore fingers were repositioned.

The music was supposed to be Aloha 'oe, the most famous traditional island song. It had been recorded in hundreds of versions, featured in several very old movies, and murdered by millions of amateurs.

The sound wafted around the twenty-eighth floor before the trade winds took it away.

When they had listened to all they could stand, Darcy and Jake rode the elevator down to the pool.

The smell of Coppertone, bougainvillea, and chlorine welcomed them outdoors. They watched a bulky tourist paddling about, and a bronzed woman swimming laps.

Just inside the open-air bar, a musician was softly working a guitar in the style of the late Don Ho (Tiny Bubbles), whose songs used to melt widows' hearts when the cruise ships came to port.

This guy was pretty good, and since the sun was below the

< 18 >

yardarm, they moved into the bar and ordered two mai tais.

Their early supper in the bar consisted of shrimp and lettuce in a relationship with a very unusual dressing.

Darcy charmed the waiter and received a taste of Poi, but the small sample was more than enough.

Well after the cocktails were gone, but before their dessert, the singer took his guitar, stuck it into a case, and went to the bar to have a martini.

Outside, the tiki torches were being lit, and a band assembled on a little stage with the Pacific Ocean at their backs.

Boisterous, most of their music was modern Hawaiian with a throbbing beat, steel guitars, drums, and a lot of amplification.

Now and then they would play one with genuine Hawaiian lyrics. Unfamiliar words in a deep soft throat, sending up K's and A's to blend in sweet nonsense.

Like the aloha shirts, they sounded exotic, and just fine here in the islands, but goofy anywhere else. Unless, of course, you were in a South Seas state of mind.

After a set, the band took a short break and the Oars took a walk, out of the hotel and into the warm city night. They were in no hurry, perambulating in the dark, with lights of high-rise apartments blinking like low hanging stars.

Directly above, where real stars should have been, the sky was a midnight blue held up by the black shapes of palm trees, their elephant legs firmly planted in the earth.

Finally, Darcy and Jake found themselves in a large grassy park. Past some tennis courts and more palms, they were drawn toward a fire in a circular pit.

It was the center of a small gathering. People were on blankets or folding chairs with picnic leftovers nearby. It had the feeling of a neighborhood get-together or family reunion. No one looked like a tourist, and nobody was in a hurry, except some children playing tag off in the darkness.

Three fellows playing guitars were the center of interest.

One was just a boy, no more than ten, with an instrument that looked too big for him. But his skill and demeanor showed maturity.

Next to him sat a large man, referred to as Leonard, with a black felt hat and lots of yellow hair escaping in all directions. He sometimes introduced a song with a little story or joke.

And there was a weathered Polynesian in a white tank top with a neon orange towel by his side. He sat on the front edge of a plastic and aluminum lawn chair, so the arms wouldn't inhibit his movement.

On top of a battered guitar case laid a ukulele, the clown of the guitar family. Deserted, ignored, and alone. It was a piece of serious craftsmanship, but still looked like just a toy. Ukuleles got no respect.

Although the flames had pulled them there, it was the music that captivated the Oars.

The mismatched group performed together seamlessly. The result seemed effortless. No sheet music, just traditional songs, well-rehearsed.

The music was soft, and rhythmic. The audience, quiet and respectful.

Jake and Darcy stood well back from the fire, uninvited guests witnessing something special.

It had been over an hour when Jake sensed someone at his elbow. He assumed it was a child until she spoke. It was a petite Asian woman with a short haircut.

"Aloha, cowboy." she whispered.

A little self-conscious, Jake took off his hat and looked at her. She was very pretty, but no longer young.

"Slack-key guitars," she said. "Ever seen it before?"

"No, ma'am," he said quietly.

They listened and watched, and after another number or two, Jake noticed the small woman had gone. But she reappeared next to Darcy.

< 20 >

"Portuguese cowboys introduced Spanish guitars to Hawaii late in the 19th century," she said softly, "you like it?"

"Sure do," Darcy answered, looking into the lively dark eyes.

After another song the band stood up to take a break. The old member said he needed to pee. People smiled. He put his guitar down and walked into the shadows.

The woman explained a little about the music; that slack-key in Hawaiian was 'ki ho alu', which meant loosen the tuning key. It originated in Hawaii. She seemed proud of that.

"Most tourists leave Hawaii never having heard it live, and couldn't find it if they tried," she said. "Except on a disc in the malls ... or at the airport gift shops."

After fifteen minutes talking, they had become quite friendly. Curious visitors and this joyful Hawaiian lady chatting about the culture.

"Which is your favorite island?" Darcy asked.

"I love them all," she answered sincerely.

"Well, where were you born?"

"Hiroshima."

"Oh." Darcy said.

Jake's mind took a little flip, a very unexpected answer.

The musicians assembled again, tuned guitars and sat down.

The conversation was winding down, so the friendly lady invited them to an art show on Saturday night.

"That's tomorrow," she announced firmly. "Opens at five and there will be snacks and wine." And then she explained how to find the location.

She shook her black hair with a nod at them and smiled.

"I'm Suz," she said.

"Darcy, and it's Jake with the hat." Darcy said.

< 21 >

# Art Show

"Wow. That's a large woman," Jake announced. She would have been about eight feet tall if she stood up. But she was lounging on a couch, a big-boned handsome Polynesian with a pink flower behind her ear. And she was staring straight out at Jake, making unblinking eye contact.

She had been painted in bold flat shapes, her skin a golden brown and her hair black as night.

The huge painting was four-feet high by ten-long and dominated the white wall on which she hung.

Exploring deeper into the little gallery, Darcy and Jake found plenty of other South Sea maidens in more normal-sized frames. Most were in flowered mu'u mu'us or hiding discreetly behind ferns or flowers. A few were stark naked. Some were portraits. Usually there were flowers present, one way or another. The women all could have been sisters.

Jake was aware that their new friend, Suz, was there, but busy with some last-minute lighting problems, so he and Darcy looked around unguided. More people were arriving. Better to look now before the audience got in the way.

A Redbone Coonhound greeted every visitor. He bonded with Jake; two blue-collar types in a sophisticated setting. But with new arrivals, duty called. He returned to sniffing and wagging.

By five-thirty a pretty good crowd had arrived and was spilling onto the porch or pressing slowly through the house. Talkers competed with lookers.

The gallery occupied five rooms. A wine and tonic bar occupied a sixth.

A teenage boy and girl moved around with plates of 'Cheese Puffs' – bread coated with mayonnaise and cheese, then heated in a toaster oven. When served hot they were simply delicious, but cold, they were bad news. The hound provided cleanup.

< 22 >

With the lighting adjusted and the wine distributed, the tall, elegant gallery owner in a long tasteful dress and simple jewelry began striking a metal triangle hung from a string. "Tinkle, tinkle, tinkle," it went as she passed through the rooms, onto the porch, down the steps to the street and back.

Jake imagined a schoolteacher calling unruly children to order.

People followed her into the biggest room.

"Listen up," she said loudly.

Her crowd, a mixture of locals and tourists, had quieted down some.

"Welina mai kélá me kéia," she said. "Welcome everyone."

She looked around and continued. "Please enjoy yourselves. This is our fifteenth annual show for Suz Yamashiro, one of our favorite artists. She's been very busy, as you can see, creating the work for this show. It is a fabulous year's production. All new and never seen before by human eyes. The very first trip out of the studio for these lovely Hawaiian women. There are a few exceptions that you forgot to buy last year. But other than that, all new and all just great.

"I am so proud to present this work, and the artist whom you all know, except those of you who are new, or just passing through.

"Anyway, here she is now to say a few words ... Suz."

There was a little commotion as the diminutive Asian woman moved up beside the gallery owner.

Suz was dressed in tight black pants and a black long-sleeved T-shirt. She had a trim figure and a big smile.

"Thanks, Ann, and thank you all for coming. Aloha aloha a aloha mai."

"Hooray." someone said loudly. People chuckled, and glasses clinked.

"Makemake au e hó'ike i ka 'u mau ..." Her little speech drifted between Hawaiian, English, and just a touch of Japanese. "... My art explores the ancient bloodlines ... mo'omeheu a me ná kának a... I hope to impart ... me ka olioli a me ka uhane..."

She looked around shyly and seemed to change her tune.

"I let my paintings do the talking," she said in English.

The group erupted in a cheer and began moving around, looking and babbling. Apparently, she had many supportive friends in the gallery.

"Don't forget to buy," Ann announced in her teacher voice.

Jake looked at the prices and realized if they wanted one, he'd need to dig out his serious checkbook.

"Aloha, cowboy."

The gathering had thinned some, and Darcy was talking to a hairy tattooed fellow in a pink flowered shirt. Suz was at Jake's elbow.

"I see some red dots. It looks like you've sold some."

"Yeah," she said. "The little ones seem to go easier."

"They are all beautiful, Suz," he said. "How long does it take to do one?"

He knew it was an impossible question when he asked it, looking from the ten-foot-wide image to a twelve-by-eighteen-inch one.

"They are all different," she said. "And accounting for time, how do you figure in all the false starts and other ones that just don't work out?"

He appeared to be a serious guy, so she continued. "Artists like to say, 'a lifetime of work goes into each one'. So, from that perspective, I'd have to say these each took nearly seventy-five years."

Jake looked at her. Except for some wrinkles, she didn't look much over thirty.

"How do you stay so young?"

"Yoga," she said, "and the Aloha spirit."

"You must paint all the time. This is a lot of art."

"Well, Ann exaggerates how many of them are new. A lot of

< 24 >

these were here last year; only about two-thirds are new. Actually, a couple have returned three-years in a row, maybe more."

"That's still a lot," Jake said.

"I do paint a lot. But I can paint faster than I can sell 'em," she smiled. "And this is Hawaii, you know. Aloha time. Relax, there is always tomorrow. Nobody here works overtime. ... 'Surf's up,' and all that."

"So that's what you mean by the aloha spirit?"

"Yes, it is. Relax, be calm. It's okay to be late."

"In my life we call that procrastination." Jake teased.

"Where is your life, Jake? Your life with Darcy?"

There was a bit of a commotion then, as a newcomer pressed into the room.

It was really four folks, but they moved together like a wolf pack. The leader was a very fit-looking blond man, about forty, the kind of person who looks and acts important. Not obnoxious, but with a voice that commands attention and exudes confidence. He wore faded blue jeans and a white shirt, open at the collar, with a gold chain visible underneath.

There were two large men with him who could have been bodyguards or friends, and a rather glamorous woman, also blond. She might have been his sister, girlfriend, or wife. She didn't seem like a wife, though. Maybe his secretary, Jake thought. She referred to him as JP.

Something about them stopped conversations in the room.

With the area quieter the man stood looking at the huge painting of the woman on the couch. Two art patrons moved out of the way.

Jay Paul Gottlieb stood with his hands on his hips in a stare-down with the Polynesian princess on canvas.

Then he turned abruptly and said to the blond woman: "Get Ann."

There was a little fuss as the diversion departed, leaving behind whispers and conjecture.

An excited friend appeared between Suz and Jake.

"Bet you just sold the biggie," she said. "Congrats!"

Others were pressing up and Jake realized his conversation was over. He suddenly felt out of place.

Suz held Jake's sleeve.

"Why don't you bring Darcy to my studio tomorrow?" she asked seriously. Looking into his eyes, she handed him a little card with a painting on one side, her address and phone number on the other.

"Come for lunch?" she said.

About five minutes later a red dot appeared on the tiny, mounted sign that read: 'Kakahiaka (Morning). Oil on Canvas, 48 x 120 Inches. $28,000.

< 26 >

## In the Lobby

Cheese Puffs may have been the art world's idea of finger food, but it left some patrons with greasy fingertips and appetites aroused.

After the art show Jake and Darcy stopped for sushi, so it was almost dark when they arrived at their hotel.

The maroon and chrome lobby was busy. Huge ferns in giant pots, a few comfortable chairs, and a couch mingled with the visitors. There were conversations, but most of the individuals were headed for the restaurant, bar, or elevators.

Some guests were trying to register and pick up their little fanny pack with key and sunscreen.

In the elevator Jake pressed twenty-eight, and they held hands as numbers blinked the passing floors.

When they'd passed through the lobby, they hadn't noticed a bearded man with a short ponytail who had been pretending to read the *Honolulu Star*. They had been too tired, full, and focused. But he had watched them closely.

He folded his paper, stood up, looked around, and left.

< 27 >

## Leaning Windward

In 1795 King Kamahamaha invaded the island of Oahu. He landed thousands of men in war canoes at Waikiki Beach. After a vicious battle the King and his group drove the defenders up and over the cliffs to their deaths.

Today the Pali Highway leads travelers from Honolulu over the Koolau Range to Kaneohe, Maunawili, Kailua, and other locations on the east side of Oahu. At the top, tourists can view the legendary eight-hundred-ninety-five-foot cliffs of death.

The Pali isn't a long trip by mainland standards, but worth doing. Going up, the highway cuts through dense jungle; ancient trees with exposed roots, ferns, heavy foliage, and hanging vines. Exotic birds watch from the dark shade.

At the top of the Pali travelers can get off the highway and check the incredible views. There are three lookout points to see the cliffs and forest far below. And, of course, the ocean.

The wind is often blowing, and if it is, brave tourists can stand, feet firmly planted on the cement walkways, and lean into the howling air till they are at a forty-five-degree angle, their clothes plastered against their bodies on the windward side and flapping like a flag in a hurricane on the leeward.

When Darcy googled the address on the card from Suz, she noticed it was close to the Pali Highway, where the city ended, and the jungle began. It was a bright sunny morning with Waikiki visitors lying on their towels getting basted and wasted.

She suggested they drive to the Pali, lean into the wind, and examine the views before lunch with Suz.

Jake said he'd like to lean into a warm wind for a change, so they were soon in the red Toyota headed up the mountain.

As they left the city, the sky got gloomy. Through the dark

< 28 >

forest of mango trees and ferns, the clouds became black. By the time they realized there were no places to turn back the rain was pouring down in sheets.

Finally at the top, they pulled off at the viewpoint where they stopped and looked through the windshield, reminded of why most submarines don't bother with windows.

They headed back down toward Honolulu and the intense rainstorm became just a memory.

"That's the island for you," Jake said. "One side doesn't know what the other side is doing."

Since they had spent no time leaning on the breezes or looking at the view, and had no trouble finding the house, they arrived early.

"I had a coach in high school who said if you weren't fifteen minutes early, you were late," Jake said.

"Uh huh," Darcy said, "Suz could be on Aloha time … but let's risk it."

It was a small, neat structure with a wide front porch. Deep blue with white trim, it crouched at the jungle's edge, the drooping trees and vines sheltering it protectively. As they climbed the steps and paused on the stoop, they heard some old island song playing softly.

Before they could knock, the door opened, revealing a woman who looked familiar. A handsome Polynesian, she could have been the sister of most of the paintings they had seen the night before.

"Aloha. Please come in," she said. "I'm Keilani."

"Did we see you last night?" Darcy smiled.

"Only in some pictures," she answered. "It feels too creepy if I'm there. Sometimes her models go; they like it, but it makes me feel funny."

"Well, it was a super nice evening," said Darcy. "Really good to meet you."

Jake had taken off his hat. "I'm Jake and this is Darcy."

"Nice to meet you. Suz told me to send you out to the studio. It's out back."

She led them through the house and out another door, then pointed to a path that led into the jungle. Orchids, plumeria, and Bird of Paradise grew wildly among a festival of ferns and a huge banyan tree.

Seventy-five strides into the forest they entered the studio, a large room with lots of windows.

Suz Yamashiro stopped painting. She was wearing a white lab coat with colorful evidence of various accidents involving paint: spills, smudges, and smears. Colorful.

"Aloha," she smiled. "Look around and I'll wash these brushes."

She used a sink in the corner, took off the protective coat, revealing a black T-shirt and cargo pants, like to last night but barefooted. Her uniform.

She had a painting underway on an easel.

A large table served as a taboret. As well as mixed paint, it held a variety of artists' tools, rags, and cans.

Beyond laid drawings, photos, and other evidence of artistic endeavors.

A thick, stained rug rested in front of the easel. Nearby, a large model-stand was surrounded by benches, the type seen in art school drawing classes worldwide.

A spotlight on a stand with rolling wheels waited to be plugged in. A semi-full clothing rack stood at attention. A row of big windows filled the room with natural light.

This was a workroom. No apologies.

"Looks like you have the perfect place to paint," Jake said as he poked around.

"Thanks," Suz said. "Works for me."

"These are unusual, the wooden things."

"Those are benches for drawing. You straddle and prop your

< 30 >

drawing board against the high part."

"There's eight?"

"Well, most Tuesdays we have an uninstructed drawing group. We get a model and just draw. Some of my studies that survived the wastebasket are on that table."

Darcy looked.

"Mostly nudes. Beautiful drawings," she observed. "All ethnic types.

"We crave variety. On my own, the emphasis is Hawaii's heritage, the Polynesians. But drawing is drawing, and practice keeps you on your game. The way to learn drawing is to draw ... and Hawaii is a melting pot. It's where races meet and mix. So, it's easy to get any kind of model you want, size, shape, or color."

The door was pushed open and Keilani came in with a tray. It held three small bowls of misoshiru with tofu squares floating in them. She put it on a little wicker table.

"Would you like coffee or tea?" she asked.

## A Sandwich with Suz

Back in the house Keilani got out six thick pieces of white bread, added a slice of bologna to three of them. With a very sharp knife, she cut thin slivers of tomato. She flattened pieces of lettuce with a towel and her palm. Tomato and lettuce were stacked on the thin meat and the remaining bread slices went on top.

Three sandwiches.

She cut each into a perfect square and set the crusts aside. Then cut each one in half diagonally, from corner to corner, creating six little triangles. She stood them on edge, side by side facing opposite directions.

Three black plates, each with a tiny geometric sculpture; white with thin brown, red and green line running through it.

The chef then scooped up the discarded crust, lettuce edges, and most of the tomato into her gentle hands, then into her mouth.

Keilani delivered her treasures to the studio.

"Won't you join us?" Suz asked her.

"Sorry, no, sweetie. I gotta' go to the dentist and swing by the bank and laundry," she said. Girls gotta' do what a girls gotta' do. Nice meeting you, Darcy and Jake."

Out the door she went.

"I thought you'd enjoy a Japanese style sandwich. You can get good Japanese food on the island, but these traditional snacks are harder to find. Best we make 'em ourselves."

"Like beautiful little modern art pieces." Darcy observed.

"A lot of Japanese food is presented like art ... as though appearance is as important as the taste. And way more important than filling you up. ... If you're still hungry there is an Aloha Burger Shack, you'll pass on the way back."

"I bet we'll be fine," Jake said.

< 32 >

After the quaint sandwiches they relaxed with tea and coffee. The hostess seemed in no hurry.

"Do you need to get back to work?" Darcy asked.

"Nope. Show's over. Pressure gone. Think I'll enjoy a little burn-out."

So, they talked. It was a rolling conversation that moved seamlessly through many topics but since they were in the studio full of her art, it started there.

Suz's influences had included Paul Gauguin, a French fellow who got famous long after his death. He was a post-impressionist who painted women in Tahiti over a hundred years ago.

"So," Suz said, "in a way I followed him.

"In college, art was all about abstract expressionism. It wasn't really my thing, but I'm sure it was an influence. But the drawing classes were the most important to me."

Her current focus was specifically the early Polynesians because she sensed Hawaii was losing that pure blood. Her paintings celebrated the generations past.

Darcy had known of Gauguin in a college art history class, and the conversation drifted to her work with the Land Conservancy, trying to protect open space.

"At home the big ranches are under pressure from developers," Darcy said. "The land becomes too valuable and the price of cattle too low.

"Often the rancher wants to leave the place and lifestyle to his kids. Some children may want to stay and work the land, but others want a job in a city. Eight hours a day and weekends free. No heavy lifting. The kids divide it up and taxes force a sale."

"So that's my job in a nutshell and those are the challenges," Darcy concluded.

Suz was quiet for a moment. She sipped her tea and swirled the cup a little.

"You are a brave girl," Suz said. "You are a woman of the

< 33 >

future. Doing big things for coming generations.

"I heard you don't plant a tree for the shade, you plant it for your grandchildren. You are generous and unselfish."

A gecko scratched the window, and the sound caught their attention.

"Nature looking in on us," Suz said. "Sometimes Keilani leaves him a nibble there. So, he comes to check us out."

Suz looked straight at Jake.

"You are an interesting couple. What do you do, cowboy?"

Jake grinned. "Punch cows," he said.

"Only cow punching around here is on the Big Island, at the Parker Ranch. You don't look like you're one of them."

She sipped her tea again.

"What do they look like?" Jake asked.

"Rough around the edges, I guess. Mostly they're of Polynesian or Spanish descent. Burnt brown by the sun. They work hard, horseback a lot. I know one that plays the slack-key pretty well."

"If I put my hat back on, I'd probably look better."

He looked down at his aloha shirt.

"Guess I look like a tourist."

"That's right, but I knew there was something special about you two." She studied them a moment. "So, what do you do, Jake, really?"

"Actually, I do have cattle back in Utah, but emotionally, my inspiration, let's call it, came from history, too," he said.

"Do you know what cutting horses are, Suz?"

"Well, sort of. A friend on the big Parker Ranch is very interested in them, so I know just a little."

"West Texas," Jake said, "was once a fifty-million-acre unfenced pasture, with everyone's cattle mixed together. When they needed to be separated, they had to depend on a horse and rider.

"The tool they developed was a horse smart enough to 'read' a cow. That is; watch her eyes, ears, and body language and

< 34 >

anticipate her moves and be quick enough to control her. These 'cutting horses' were bred and trained for that job and were the pride of any ranch that had one.

"My interest is just that: breeding and training them.

"We can compete with the horses for sport or work with them as an art form. When everything gets right, it's like they dance with the cow."

"So amazing," Suz said. "You and I are clinging in our own ways to the distant past and we're fascinated by this girl of the future."

They both looked at Darcy.

"Well then, what you two doing so far from home?" Suz asked.

Darcy reached for Jake's hand.

"Honeymooners," she smiled.

Suz squealed and jumped up.

"I had hoped so! I had thought maybe that was it."

She took leis from the clothing rack and put one on Darcy and Jake and hugged and kissed then. She dropped one over her own head.

She had the biggest grin they'd seen in weeks. It seemed to consume the whole face, reducing her dark almond eyes to happy slits. All her teeth glistened brightly.

"We will celebrate now," she announced.

"I'll begin by showing you Oahu."

## Blue Monster Tour

Suz chose Keilani's extra car. Too big to park easily, it rested under its all-weather cover. It was called 'The Monster,' an old classic Chrysler. Light blue, it was so wide they all sat in a row on the front seat and traveled with the top down. Jake drove and Suz perched in the middle giving directions.

They sped up to Diamond Head and parked in the ancient volcano's crater. After climbing many wooden stairs and switchback they arrived at the bunker on top, a reminder of December 7th, 1941, when Japanese planes came out of the rising sun and flew over to surprise Pearl Harbor.

The views included Waikiki, Honolulu, and beyond. Glancing east they saw Koko Head and Hawaii Kai.

Back in the Blue Monster, they passed Hanauma Bay, and then followed the coast to Sea Life Park, their next stop.

On the road again, some white fences and horse trailers led them to a polo match in progress. Clacking and clicking of wood hitting plastic told the story of the game. The pounding of hooves and the odor of horse sweat made Jake feel at home. When the chukker ended, the small crowd of fans and families stomped around replacing divots the hooves had made, and Suz decided to continue the tour.

Up the coast they went, stopping now and then. They strolled on a beach, walked on a pier and into and out of a gift shop.

Finally, they turned around at the Sacred Falls and headed back. They drove west over the Koolau Range, found the Pali sunny and bright. They looked around and leaned into the wind.

The afternoon was gone when they parked the Blue Monster, put the top up and pulled the cover over it.

Suz summed up the day: "It is as if we've known each other a long time. ... It's a joy to be with you."

The Oars agreed, and they decided to meet for supper.

< 36 >

## Meka olioli a me ka uhane

W e're supposed to join Suz Yamashiro," Jake told the hostess at the dark little restaurant.

Suz and Keilani were already there. The artist was in black, and her friend in a tan dress. Jake found a safe corner for his hat, and he and Darcy joined them.

Suz's smile brought a waitress, who took their drink orders.

"I'm going to order a tonkatsu for the table. We can all share. Mainland visitors all love it, and I know cowboys go for it too. This is the best place to get it in all the islands."

"Do you know lots of hungry cowboys?" Darcy asked.

"Yes, I do. The Parker Ranch is stuffed with them, and some are my hungry friends. If your travels take you there, try to meet Jeffrey. He dreams about cutting horses and you'd like him. He might play you a song if he's not busy."

"I had tonkatsu once," Jake offered. "Breaded pork cutlet and cabbage. The sauce is so excellent that it's good on everything. I made such a fuss they gave me a bottle full. At home I put it on Wonder Bread. Made it taste like tonkatsu."

"Ugh." Keilani produced a Polynesian grimace.

She had a flower behind her ear but took it off and put it carefully on the table, like a precious centerpiece.

"You have sushi in Utah?" she asked.

"Yup." Darcy said, glancing at Jake. "He loves sushi but hates asparagus."

She looked at Keilani.

"What do Polynesian people eat?" she asked.

"Gosh ... we eat regular food, mostly. Burgers and fries, mac and cheese, Campbell's Soup ... you know. Regular.

"At family parties we have roasted piggy and poi. Start at the top, near the spine, and use your fingers to pull off the meat.

"But I usually eat what Suz eats ... Japanese, 'cuz I'm the main cook at our house."

"Where are you from?" Darcy wanted to know.

Keilani picked up the flower and sniffed it, smiled at Darcy, and shook her black hair. Then she scanned the purple and pink beauty with her wide eyes and took a big bite of it. She chewed a few moments before she spoke again.

"Born thirty-six years ago in Lahaina," she said with her mouth full.

They were all staring at her, Jake, trying to detect a sign. But her lips kept their secret. Truthful eyes hid behind lowered lids.

Jake caught the flower's smell, but wondered if tonkatsu sauce would have helped.

"But I've traveled some," she continued. "Raised up on Maui, of course, but I've worked on the Big Island for a few years, in Hilo, and at the resorts on the west side."

She paused to swallow the flower, but the act gave no additional clues. Stoic.

"I saw where the lava ran to the sea with steam coming up all around. Seen the ranch and everything."

She put the remains of the flower down and looked at them all. "I've been on most islands in the state except Kauai."

A blonde girl of high school age in a kimono brought their drinks. Suz smiled and said, "Misoshiru and seaweed salad to share as we plot out our order, please."

"Right away, Miss Suz." She smiled and darted away.

They were quiet a moment as they inspected the menu.

"So, Suz, earlier you said you'd seen polo in Santa Barbara. Do you know California well?" Darcy asked.

"I went to the San Francisco Academy of Art, graduated in painting. It was 1967 through '72. Pretty interesting years. Something of an adventure and an eye-opener. War protests and saving the whales. Haight-Ashbury, sex, drugs, rock'n roll."

< 38 >

They ate slowly as the conversation wandered, gradually swung back to art.

"What makes a good painting?" Jake asked, leading to a lesson on composition and value.

"What makes it sell?" brought up subject matter and color. And they were soon talking about the gallery show and the man who paid big bucks for the big painting of the big lady.

"Jay Paul Gottlieb," Suz said. "It's not much money for him. He's what we call a 'trustee' ... you know, like a trust fund baby. He collects art and, as luck would have it, he likes mine."

"He's a stud," said Keilani.

"We never see him alone. Always the little posse around."

"What do they do?" Jake asked. "The posse."

"Well, who knows? I think they're muscle, or business partners or just surf buddies. I don't always see the girl; she could be a secretary, or a girlfriend. She's smart when you talk to her. Not a bimbo, that's for sure.

"He's married, they say, but I've never met his wife."

The waitress deposited a bowl of cold mochi for dessert and Suz told her to put everything on her tab. Jake quickly protested, but the girl was gone in a swish of kimono and blonde hair. Jake sensed that Suz was used to getting her way.

"You met Suz modeling?" Darcy asked, turning to the younger woman.

"Uh hmm." She looked Darcy's way with her eyelids soft. A sultry expression.

"Suz had a note up in the market; 'Needed: a model', it said." Keilani's words were like smoke.

After a pause, Darcy said: "And?"

Suz was watching closely as Keilani spoke.

"She did some sketches and then I got undressed and she laid me on the platform to paint. And then I moved into our house."

"How long ago?" Darcy asked gently.

"Two years ago, about."

"Are you married?"

"Just good friends," Keilani said shyly.

In the parking lot, there were thank-yous and hugs.

"I really enjoyed getting to know you two sweeties," Suz said, holding their hands. "You are very special to me, and I love you."

Jake opened the passenger door and Darcy hopped in. He tossed his hat into the back seat, brim up, and slid behind the wheel. The door of the red Toyota closed, but the window was open to the warm night. Suz leaned in. As her mouth passed Jake's head, her tongue tickled his ear.

"I love you two. Darcy and her cowboy," she said softly. Then: "Watch for Jeffrey when you're on the Parker Ranch. Don't forget." She looked at him with serious eyes.

She stood up straight, leaving behind the smell of lilacs, and waved.

"Aloha," she said warmly. "Me ka olioli a me ka uhane. With joy and spirit."

## At the Gate

The Honolulu Airport was a nest of anxiety and confusion supported by a vast network of terminals, wiki wiki busses, escalators, long halls, elevators, and security checkpoints. It was a facility that took mango and drug smuggling seriously.

Changed gates, misinformation, and long lines produced worried travelers. They were rushed, and then they waited. Packed, ticketed, scanned, and bewildered.

Its gates were designed to cram mobs of humanity into jumbo jets who swallow them up, quickly and efficiently. Rush them in. Shut the door. Ship them home.

That's how cattle were loaded in Jake's home state.

By contrast the inter-island gates were smaller, the planes littler, the flights fewer. Passengers were quietly lured on board with smiles and glimpses of the Aloha spirit.

It was here Darcy and Jake sat waiting to fly to the Big Island. Relaxed. No hidden fruit. No worries.

Darcy was lost in a book. Jake, because the airport made him think of home, started a list of projects to tackle when he got back. They were early, the waiting area almost empty. They sat facing their gate.

Jake became aware of two men sitting directly behind him in seats facing the other way. He wasn't sure when they had come. The voices weren't particularly loud, but distinct, and a distraction from his list. It was hard not to listen. Apparently, they were businessmen from Honolulu going to spend the weekend surfing on another island.

"It won't be the Pipeline, but it'll be fun."

"Away from home. New scenery."

"For my money the best scenery is on Maui, if the scenery

you're talking about is skin."

"Dude, what else?"

"The smallest bikinis are sold on Maui, or so I heard."

"Eat, drink, and be Maui."

"Figure we'll prowl the beaches north of Lahaina. We'll be close when the surf's up."

As Jake listened, he tried to imagine the owners of the voices. There were two. He was thinking horny teenagers from their words, but the tenor of the speech suggested they were older.

"Did you bring somethin' to smoke?"

"Does a chicken have lips?"

An official announcement blocked the conversation for a moment. It ended, and the conversation resumed.

"What if we get white line fever?" A quiet question.

"Got an eight ball of blow in my crotch." Almost a whisper.

Something else was said, but the voices were too soft to understand. Jake wondered if they realized he was behind them. Time slipped away before one spoke again.

"How's your love life goin'? If you don't mind my askin'."

"It's quiet right now. She's on temporary duty in the states. Hopes to be back in a couple weeks. Delta stews ... it's par for the course."

"Any news from JP's big house?"

"Same as usual ... except I think Beth filed papers yesterday."

"Guess that was expected. How's he takin' it?"

"He wants out as much as she does, I think."

"Oh?"

"He said every time they're in the same room, they're screamin' at full volume. She's a volcano steaming inside, just hoping for something to set her off. One great weekend and two and a half years of hell ... That's how he describes it. Pretty much a direct quote."

There was a moment of quiet, and then the same voice said.

"He'll be glad when it's over."

< 42 >

"Dude, I bet."

More quiet time.

"A volcano?"

"That's what he said."

There was the sound of someone shifting around, changing position or fussing in a bag. Then:

"Does Carnation know?"

"About the papers?"

"Um hum."

"Probably. I think she opens all JP Gottlieb's mail. She pretty much knows what ever's going on with him."

"From my perspective, he shoulda married her if he felt the need to get married at all."

"Probably. I'd be surprised if he ever takes that leap again."

"That's it? That's the whole news?"

"That's it ... 'cept he told Jif he's gonna call John to figure which lawyer to use. He doesn't think it'll get too complicated. Only married two years and she never worked a day. He shouldn't get hit very hard."

They were quiet a while. Jake looked at Darcy, engrossed in her book. A simple gold ring on her finger. A solid marriage, no question. Darcy was a diamond.

He watched as a lighted sign announced their destination, Hilo. And at a gate behind him there was a similar sign that lit up marked 'Kahului.'

"Hey, we're at the wrong gate," one of the voices said.

"Finish your coffee and we'll wander over. I want a fresh cup and somethin' to read."

Jake stood up very casually, stretched, and sauntered off toward the men's room, sneaking a glance at the two fellows as he passed.

# Island Fever

"Hello," said Wally after he dug the noisy red cell phone out of a pocket.

"Walter Abbott?"

"Yes. This is Walter here. Is this you, Agent Polanski?"

"Yes, Mister Abbott, it is I. How did you know it was me?"

"Well sir, I don't get many phone calls, and I get none from the mainland, unless it's you."

"Are you well?"

"Yes sir, I am. And you?"

"Fine ... Mister Abbott, it is time I checked in on you. It has been two months since we spoke. I wanted to call before I go out for lunch. I hope I am not calling too early. Where are you?"

Wally could almost hear the gray suit in the voice.

"I am on a bench at the beach watching the sunrise."

"That must be pleasant." It sounded like a tall guy in a crew cut.

"It's okay ... beautiful, I guess. Beautiful yesterday, beautiful tomorrow, I suppose, but I'm gettin' Island Fever," said Wally.

"Explain, please."

"Well, trapped and bored, I guess. Feel the island closing in. Watchin' the TV is driving me stupid. Mostly it's bored, that I'm feeling."

Wally put the phone on speaker and set the little thing down on the bench beside him. There was no one around. Alone with this cold voice from far away.

"Well Mister Abbott, don't do anything illegal.

"Some people in your situation get a job at a grocery store or find a new career. Some might write a book ... idle hands can get into mischief, and we do not want that, do we?

"You could also look for a good psychiatrist," said the agent. "It's no crime getting professional help."

< 44 >

"I don't feel comfortable goin' out," Wally said. "There are Polynesians everywhere I look around here."

"Well Mister Abbott, I have some news for you on that front. The notorious Polynesian Band is no longer trying to kill you."

"Don't shit me, man!" Wally declared.

He sat up straight and stared down at his little phone on the seat.

"The Polynesian Band is out of business. Little Somba and Turd Bird were killed in a gunfight with police officers in Lehi, Utah, and Flexo was hit several times and is at the hospital in a coma. He will probably die. The other two members of the Band are in jail and will soon be in federal prison for killing a police officer."

Agent Polanski paused, then said: "So, Mister Abbott, if you keep your nose clean, you could probably feel pretty confident in getting a job or making new friends."

"Wow," Wally said, as he looked out at the sea.

"If that don't beat all, who else knows I'm here?"

"My partner knows, and one other FBI agent.

"Would you like me to tell your wife?"

"Shit no. We're divorced and she's moved on. I'd say just let her be."

A string of tiny clouds on the horizon was set on fire by the rising sun. They silently slid through a fan of colors, like slowly flipping pages in a painter's swatch-book. The sight was spectacular for several moments and then evolved into just another bright silver and blue day.

Wally sat watching the sky and ocean for a very long time before he noticed the flock of pigeons at his feet.

## New Walter Gets Clipped

"Honey, I'm home ... Sweetie Pie, Love Bucket, Sugar Lamb, my fluffy Nymph!"

"Wal, is that you?" Pinky looked up from her reading.

"You sound different. What happened to my Wal?"

"It's me, Pinky, a newer, fresher Walter," he said peeking in. "Sour, depressed, old-fashioned Walter has been replaced."

He did seem a little different, somehow. Same average height, still slightly pudgy, a middle-aged guy, but more upbeat, shinier, brighter. And where did that 'sweetie love pie lamb chop' greeting come from?

And late. He was never late.

Pinky popped over to where he stood in the doorway, faced him, and grinned a wide one.

Her long hair fell in one blonde braid down her back. She wore a white tank top and tan shorts.

She looked into his eyes as her slim hands gripped the tail of the shirt and she lifted its front above her face, showing him her ribs and soft chest. The view lasted only about three seconds, but it was a nice 'welcome home' for the new Walter, ... whoever he might turn out to be.

"Feeling frisky this morning?" he asked.

"Titties saying 'hi,' is all," and she gave him a quick little kiss. "You're an hour later than usual, sweetie. Were your pigeons sleeping in?"

"Huh uh ... got talkin' on the phone to an old pal in LA. He told me to cheer up and I took that to heart."

Walter flopped onto the ugly gray couch and smiled. She tossed her head. The long braid swept around, and she caught the end of it. Playfully she jumped astride his lap. They grinned at each other, and he raised an eyebrow. She looked at her hand holding the pale-yellow tail of hair. Her thumb was on the rubber

< 46 >

band, and she showed it to Walter.

"Your ponytail's never gonna' catch mine."

"Suppose not," he said.

"Well then, does the new Wal want me to give you a haircut?"

Walter considered the question. "I think he does."

The haircut turned out to be more of a harvest that left only stubble.

"My head looks like Kansas in the fall," Walter said.

Although he claimed to like it, he made her stop in time to save his beard.

"My new Wal," she said, admiring her work. "I hope it won't scare the pigeons."

"Guess I'll take a shower. Don't wanna' feel itchy after such a nice haircut."

"Maybe the new Wal would like to get rid of any loose hairs in the ocean?" she asked. And the new Wal surprised her when he answered, "I say yes."

"Waikiki?"

"Even the new Walter's not ready for those tourists. Don't you know some tiny remote secret place? You could bring your little surfboard, and I could lose this pale old Walter look."

Pinky did know of a rather remote beach or two.

They were above Makaha on the upper west side of the island. Just north of Makua, past Keawaula Beach, where the road dissolved. It's where most tourists decided to turn around. It had been a very long drive.

Pinky encouraged Walter to press on a little way to a dirt pullout where he could park. A trail to follow, a barbed wire fence in disrepair to cross, a 'no trespassing' sign to ignore, and thirty yards more of path through dense foliage.

Then they stepped out of the jungle onto a small bay with a nice beach.

Not another soul around.

Well, one more soul …

A scruffy little black and white cat had followed them down the path, staying safely out of sight. Near the ocean they looked back at the forest and the dark space where the trail emerged. There was the feline, waiting and watching.

"Let's not scare him," Pinky said.

"Little fella looks hungry. Probably hopes we're gonna' provide a picnic," said Walter. "We forgot to think about food."

Pinky dropped slowly to her knees.

"Come, kitty, kitty, kitty…"

"So much nature makes you feel close to God, huh, Wal?"

"Uh huh…"

"Here kitty, kitty, kitty…maybe the Lord wants us to love this little creature He created."

Walter hesitated for a moment, then knelt.

Pinky leaned forward and crawled slowly toward the cat. When it moved at all, she froze until it relaxed again. She murmured to it as she approached, "Kitty … nice kitty …"

After ten minutes she was about fifteen feet from the skittish animal. That was just too close, and it disappeared into the jungle. Gone in an instant.

"I guess if the Lord wanted us to comfort that kitty, He would have made it a little more friendly," Pinky said.

It was certainly a beautiful little place, dense green maze on one side, the endless ocean on the other.

The tide was coming in slowly. The procession of waves pushed teeny snakes of foam advancing as it ate up the beach, one bite at a time.

They spent two hours there, talking and looking at the sea. Walter took his new haircut for a short swim. This became their favorite beach for the next few days. They called it 'Oh Bee', short for 'our beach'.

But it was a long drive and as Walter got used to people, they

< 48 >

found sand closer to civilization. Keaau, Makaha, Lualualei, and others. By the time they got to Zablan Beach, Walter was no longer afraid of strangers.

With a towel, sunscreen, and a timer he worked on a tentative tan as Pinky searched the ocean for rideable waves.

On one of those beaches, between Makaha and Zablan, they saw an artist drawing.

At first Walter thought it was a child on a low folding chair; the kind that is very close to the ground, the occupant's bottom only two inches from the sand. The kid sat, knees bent, the drawing pad rested against his thighs. He looked focused and comfortable working like that. A little metal box of art supplies rested nearby.

As he watched, Walter realized the subject of the artist was not the seascape, but a Hawaiian woman in a boldly colored muu muu.

She stood at the edge of the rolling water, weight on one hip, casually looking over her shoulder. She stayed like that a minute or two. Then she would turn around and try something else, hold for a while, then pose again. Often, she'd be in the ocean up to her thighs, waves splashing her torso. She was like a stop-action dancer, making wide graceful movements, and then stopping, frozen again.

When the vibrant material got wet, it would stick to her body, defining the generous curves underneath. When she moved, she would sometimes pull the cloth away to make it billow out or fall differently.

Walter watched a while, before returning his attention to Pinky, further out there, trying to surf.

Finally, curiosity won. He got up and moved closer to the kid drawing. He realized then that it was an Asian woman with short hair. She was attractive and looked fit, but she did not look young.

< 49 >

Behind her and off to one side, he watched for many minutes. She was aware of him but focused on the nymph dancing in the sea.

"You are a very good drawer," Walter said finally.

She looked him in the eye. "Thanks," she said, and went back to her work.

Walter sat in the sand where he could see both the drawing and the model and watched for about an hour.

Finally, a thoroughly soaked Pinky came out of the Pacific with her board, and Walter got up to go.

Although they had not been speaking, he turned to the woman. "Thanks for the art lesson."

"I'm afraid I wasn't much of a teacher," she said.

"Your demonstrations were my education."

"Just a sec," she said, and got a tiny card out of her little tin box on the sand.

"Here." She smiled and handed him the two-by-three-and-a-half-inch card.

It was the first business card for the new Walter.

"I'll have to get a Rolodex," he told Pinky, as he put her surfboard under his arm, and they headed for their car.

# Davies Pacific Center

On the ground floor of Honolulu's twenty-two story Davies Pacific Center is a grand mural of a schooner's sails above some modern looking waves. It is a relief sculpture that appeared to be stone or tinted cement. Businessmen use it as a landmark meeting place. Parking is available below and several restaurants are within easy walking distance. It is east of Chinatown, west of the State Capitol, and stands a few blocks north of the harbor.

An agitated Jay Paul Gottlieb fidgeted under the sculpted sails. He was in a serious gray suit with a blue tie. Soon a heavier balding man in a dark suit approached.

"Jay Paul, good friend," said John Silverman, as they shook hands.

"John," said Jay Paul, "let's walk and talk."

It was early afternoon, and the lunch crowd was either back to work or drinking in a bar. They headed south on Bishop Street toward the harbor and the Aloha Tower.

"John, I've been in meetings all yesterday and again this morning with attorneys about this fucking divorce thing. She wants everything and is completely unreasonable. She screams at the drop of a hat. Even her attorneys know her demands are ridiculous and make no sense. She hates me, I hate her. But on her side, there is no communication. None.

"Basically, John, she wants to take everything I have, and if she can't get it all, she wants what's left to go to the lawyers. She doesn't care how long it takes or how much it costs. I want to move on, of course, but she doesn't. If it goes on forever, she's fine with that.

"A vindictive bitch. That's all she is. That's what she's been for two miserable years.

"It's just nuts. She wants to drag Carnation into the shit as

< 51 >

we go. Just pure hate. She wants my art collection, and she hates art. Why waste money on art when she needs more clothes and jewelry?"

"Divorce is often like this, at first," John said. "She will calm down and decide to move on by herself. It could get expensive, but in a couple of years it'll all be behind you."

"I don't think so. You haven't seen her. She is literally crazy."

"Really, I'd give it a few weeks. She's a looker; maybe she'll meet a guy."

"No chance. She's in a rage. It's been raging for two years and sure won't stop anytime soon. A fucking, raging volcano spewing hate and smoke and gas."

"Hmm ...," said John.

"A fucking volcano, erupting!"

They walked quietly a while until they neared the Aloha Tower and the harbor.

"She's Mauna Loa exploding."

There were no other pedestrians in sight.

"She'd be better off dead," Jay Paul said. "Better off for her and her hateful life. Give her some peace and quiet."

Jay Paul's voice was electric.

"Better off for both of us."

"Well," John said, "matter of fact, you can't kill her."

"Why not?"

"Well for one thing, big boy, it's illegal ... and for another thing, it's wrong."

"It would surely solve a lot of problems."

"Believe me, it would probably cause far more problems than it would solve. Two years from now you'll look back at this as just a rough patch."

They stopped. John glanced around, and then looked carefully at his friend.

"You've actually been thinking about this?" he asked.

"Uh huh ... sort of."

< 52 >

They stood looking at the water's reflection of rocking boats. The ocean smelled strong — dead fish, diesel oil, and salt. They listened to sounds of creaking boats pulling against heavy ropes that rubbed bumpers against a wharf. Seagulls called; little waves lapped.

"I suppose you could poison her Cheerios," John said, as he tried to lighten the mood.

"No," said Jay Paul, back on subject. "Thought I'd hire someone."

"I don't believe you're serious."

"I am."

A tour van stopped, and some noisy Japanese people got out, took pictures of the iconic tower, smelled the dead fish and oil, got back in, and went away.

"You could go to prison for life," John said, carefully.

"I know. That's why I'd hire a professional. He'd make it look like an accident and he'd not get caught. An accident. No crime."

"My advice is don't do it. And for Pete's sake, don't ever tell anyone you've been thinking this way."

Jay Paul looked at the silver belly of a dead fish floating in a little oil slick.

"You can't tell anyone," John said. "Why did you tell me?"

Jay Paul spoke thoughtfully. "You're the only person I know who might know how to find a professional."

"Oh shit," John said.

## Big Island, Big Plans

For Jake and Darcy, the huge island served as an emotional bridge to home. A first step in easing out of vacation mode.

Darcy's work focused on preserving open land, and though she was good at meetings, she most enjoyed seeing wide country and new landscapes. And that's what the Big Island represented.

Jake's life revolved around his cattle and horses. Cowboy culture. Although the styles and history were different, the Parker Ranch gave it a new twist.

Open ranch land dominated the upper middle of the island, and that was where they headed.

But it was impossible to ignore the mountains.

Mauna Loa, at 13,680 feet, commanded attention like a scorned woman throwing a fit, complete with smoke and flowing lava. Sometimes she appeared normal, but underneath there was all that hatred and heat raging, ready to blow at the slightest provocation.

Even though her partner, Mauna Kea, was 116 feet taller, he rested quietly, looking docile. And that's probably best when a wrong word could release an explosion from his steaming neighbor.

But for the honeymooners, whose plane landed near Hilo, the volcanoes were just a backdrop to their adventures. They planned to spend their nights on the western edge, where the resort hotels blossomed next to the sea. Sunsets on the beach, mai tais and guitar music, naked nights on hot sheets, cooled by the ocean breeze, the smell of gardenias. How a wedding vacation should be.

As usual, Jake was up before dawn walking south on the beach. He hoped to get far enough that the hotel wouldn't block his view of the sunrise over the mountains.

Later, after breakfast, he and Darcy headed toward the historic

< 54 >

130,000-acre Parker Ranch headquarters near Waimea Town. They were looking for land and cattle, but what they saw were tourists, a heritage center, historic buildings, real estate offices, tour vans and busses, an empty rodeo arena, gift shops, and a coffee shop.

"Where's the actual ranch?" they asked at a gift shop.

"You're on it," was the answer.

Similar scenarios played out at the restaurant, gas station, and the heritage center where they learned the proper name for cowboy was paniolo. That cheered Jake up a little. He felt like they were gaining ground.

Finally, back in the rental car and searching, they stumbled into a tourist who knew where to rent a horse. That led to a kid who guided the visitors on horseback and wished he were a cowboy. He knew where some paniolos might be.

He gave careful directions and wished them luck. Best time, he thought, would be before supper. He wanted to go with them but had to lead a new group in about an hour.

Jake and Darcy followed the directions carefully and arrived early. The buildings, pipe fences, and a deserted tack room with a few saddles missing, gave them hope.

Sure enough, at about three-thirty they saw riders. Three men with jangling spurs, flapping leather, and thumping hooves, arrived in a little dust cloud. Jake and Darcy smiled, causing "Alohas," all around.

The paniolos stepped down from their sweating horses with grunts, creaks, and a snort or two, in that careful way that often follows a long ride. A dismount that asks: 'are my legs going to work now that I need them?'

Jake moved toward the oldest man, guessing he might be the one in charge.

As the fellow flipped the stirrup over the saddle's worn seat and reached for the latigo, Jake stepped to the other side and grabbed the cinch when it swung loose. He gathered it with the rear one and hung them on the saddle's leather 'keeper.'

That simple act carried a wordless message: a familiar little chore, and a willingness to help. It saved the paniolo a trip around the horse's tail, and back.

"Gracias, Señor," the grizzled fellow said, looking across the saddle at Jake. "May we help you?" he asked.

"I'm Jake and this is Darcy."

"I am Polo, like the game, sir. Nice to meet you ..." He looked at the others, unsaddling, and exchanging bridles for halters.

"These are Little Juan and Dixie."

Dixie grunted through his beard, and Little Juan smiled at Jake and turned to Darcy. "Holla!" He tipped a soiled hat that had been over many a prairie and under a few greasy tractors.

Jake was ready to assist, fully aware these men had their own routine, and a helpful stranger usually got in the way.

When the saddles and bridles and horses were put up, they sat on a bench beside the door of the shed.

"We hope to find Jeffrey," Jake said. "Do you know him?"

"Si," said the old one.

"Sure," said Little Juan. "He's boss of the horses. You are his friend?"

"Well," Jake said, "not yet. How do we find him?"

"I'll call him for you, Señor." And he did.

Jake overheard half of a conversation, partly in English, partly Spanish. Then it paused.

"Is your name Jake Oar?" Juan asked.

"It is."

There was a little more to the phone call and then Little Juan hung up.

"He wants to meet you sir, at the Starbucks in Waimea in about an hour."

It was nearly an hour before Jake and Darcy were in the coffee shop wondering what this would be about. They didn't

< 56 >

wonder long.

"You're Jake Oar," the cowboy said as he entered. "And you must be Darcy." He tipped his hat.

"Aloha, Jeffrey," Jake said looking for eyes behind those aviator-style sunglasses. Dark mirrors. Jake saw Jake.

They all sat around the little table, Darcy and Jake with lattes as Jeffrey took off his glasses.

He looked much more like a mainland cowboy than the paniolos had.

"My name's Jeffrey McCumber," the man said. "Originally from Texas but I've been here long enough to lose most of the accent. I'm the main horse guy here."

"I guess Suz must have called you, that we might stop by. She sure can create a warm welcome," Jake said, although it was her goodbye that came to mind.

"We've known Suz a long while. She's pretty neat."

"Yes, she is," Jake said, and Darcy nodded agreement.

"Well, she said you-all were a cutter, so we looked you up on the internet." Jeffrey smiled. "You're not just a cutter. You're an especially good one."

"Oh yeah?" Jake said tentatively.

"The National Cutting Horse Association website says you've won over two hundred fifty thousand dollars so far."

"A lot of that was amateur and non-pro," Jake said.

"You were in the top ten at the big Futurity in Fort Worth several times as an amateur and Non-Pro reserve at least a couple times and once you were the Open Champion. Winning the Open means you are a legend."

"Mostly luck," Jake said.

"More than luck, my boy. For someone who's not a professional to win the Open; it's almost never been done."

"Spencer Hardon and Allan Hamilton come to mind," said Jake. "Where's this all going, anyway? You have cutting horses on this ranch?"

< 57 >

"Not really, but we're thinking about it," Jeffrey said. "If you and Darcy don't have plans, we'd like to take you to supper tonight, or tomorrow, if you'd rather. There's someone who wants to meet you, so the sooner the better."

"If we gotta' dress up," Darcy replied, "we could meet at our hotel about seven thirty. Or if you want to eat early, we can go dressed as we are."

Jake flinched and looked down at his flowered shirt. "I don't feel like a legend dressed like this," he confessed.

"You-all 're in Hawaii so you're just fine.

Jeffrey made a couple of cell phone calls, and they all took a short walk to a restaurant one block away. During cocktails, they were joined by Jeffrey's wife, Allie, a younger woman who had definitely not lost her Texas drawl.

Their short conversation was soon interrupted as Bob Claymore, the ranch manager, arrived.

The conversation touched on the honeymoon, Suz and her art career, Angus and Charolais cattle, and the ranch: one of the largest in the United States, founded in 1847, years before the earliest Texas ranches. Parker Ranch pride was in evidence.

A waitress said the table was ready and the conversation turned to food and then to cutting horses, the ranch horse program, then back to cutting.

After dinner Bob offered cigars but got no takers. Over Grand Marnier, Bob got serious.

"We are proud to welcome you to the Parker Ranch and if there is anything we can help you with, just let us know. Horses to explore on, a private tour, anything. Jeffrey plays a serious slack-key but mispronounces the Hawaiian lyrics. Anything, just ask," Bob said.

A friendly little speech.

"But let's talk a moment. We raise some horses here. We've had racehorses and more trail horses than I can count.

"We've talked recently about having some cutting horses to

< 58 >

raise, train, and show. The foundation that owns the ranch has agreed to our proposal, and we have some money budgeted toward it.

"Of course, we'd start small and kinda grow into it. The serious cutting contests are on the mainland, so the best horses would have to be there, and we've figured on that.

"For several years we've been doing our due diligence. Jeffrey and I have been to the Futurity for the last four years and talked to everyone. We understand the expenses and think we're ready for the next step."

Bob leaned forward and seemed to sit taller.

"We're looking for an advisor and show-man. Of course, all the good advice we get is to hire a trainer in Texas or maybe California, and give him a big pile of money.

"But what Jeffrey and I see is a crapshoot. We'd be just another client for those trainers. They have a barn full of prospects, and many assistants who sort through them during the training process, looking for the two best they'll take to the Futurity in Fort Worth. The rest end up going home, to the small futurities, or get sold to team penners.

"We understand how this all works," Bob paused here and looked around. Then he focused on Jake.

"So, in our naiveté Jeffrey and I are tossing around the idea of approaching it differently.

We see that sometimes a talented horseman raises and trains his own horse and wins the Futurity. Not often but it can happen. Instead of picking through hundreds to find the best, his entire focus is on only one or two horses. No distractions.

"A special horse and horseman. No back-up plans. No assistants. One focus from start to finish. What a concept that would be." Bob sat quietly, pausing a moment.

Then Jeffrey spoke. "If we imagine the odds of any specific horse entering a trainer's collection at, let's say, as a long yearling or just turning two, versus the same horse entering the guidance of a gifted amateur who will ride only this horse. Well, you-all, I think the odds favor the gifted amateur's horse."

"Jake," Jeffrey said, "you made the case when you listed Spencer Hardan and Allan Hamilton. I think Bob Byrd did it too. Sandy Bonnelli and Phil Rapp were Non-Pro Champions who trained only their own horses. You did it and won the Open. There may be even more. You all started with only one or maybe two horses and focused on it for over a year and a half."

Jeffrey was looking at Jake and sat quietly, resting his case. Jake took a deep breath.

"The problem," Jake said, "is a non-pro or amateur will lose their card if they ride your horse. If they get paid, they are professional whether they like it or not. Everyone you mentioned owned the horse they competed on."

Bob stubbed his cigar into the ashtray. It had gone out anyway, leaving a blue curl hanging in the air.

"That's why," Bob said, "we need a talented amateur who wants to slow down, tired of dominating some local area, who is willing to give up his Amateur-Non-Pro card and move slowly into the big time but is not interested in the rat race a trainer's life becomes.

"One client with deep pockets, who understands the odds and is taking a chance. Enjoying the process. No expectations. No pressure."

"Maybe," Jeffrey said, "there's a talented fellow who's won everything and has nothing left to prove, who loves cutting horses for the horse more than the glory. Perhaps on his honeymoon and is thinking of spending more quality time with his new wife."

Jake looked thoughtful and then offered another idea.

"You could, of course, buy the best horse you can find and get a trainer to show it all year to qualify for the World Finals. They have those finals in Fort Worth, during the NCHA Futurity."

"We could," said Jeffrey," but nobody cares. The Futurity is in the Will Rogers Colosseum, packed to the roof with screaming

< 60 >

fans and a huge purse to split up. The World Finals is a marathon trailer race with nobody watching. The finals is in the Watt Arena with mostly friends and family cheering. We've seen it. It's good watching, but nobody cares."

"Your idea is interesting. Let me think about it," Jake said.

"You'd have a Parker Ranch beach house any time you came to visit us," said Bob. "Want a cigar?"

Even as they walked to their various vehicles, Jake's mind was working overtime.

# Art Lesson

A glamorous woman in a hostile mood jumped out of her Porsche 911 Carrera S Cabriolet and slammed the door. The top was down, and her hair was wild. She could have been a model, high cheekbones and full lips. Her skin was flawless, except for a rather large ripe pimple on the side of her excellent chin.

She stood on the sidewalk considering a note, then wadded it up and flung it on the grass. She looked at the porch and house. A tasteful sign announced "Ann Korigan — Fine Art."

She stomped on the steppingstones that led across ten feet of cut lawn to the porch steps.

Ann's Redbone Coonhound had wagged his tail as the silver car parked in front, but as the woman started to approach, he quietly rose, backed a few steps, turned and slunk away.

Up the steps she came and flung open the door. She stood staring at the huge Polynesian woman staring back at her. There was the hint of a smile on the classic islander and a serious frown on the newcomer. The two were alone for a minute assessing one another. Finally, the bad hair day spoke quietly.

"Fucking ..." she hissed.

"Good afternoon," said the voice of Ann from the back room. "Please look around and if you have any questions, feel free to ask."

"This big painting," she called loudly. "This is the one Jay Paul bought?"

"The four feet by ten with the red dot? 'Lady on a Couch,' that's the one."

Ann was on her feet now, coming into the room. "We have similar ones, but smaller. Nothing nearly that big, I'm afraid."

"So, this is Jay Paul's now?"

"Yes, he bought it at the opening. Caused a little commotion. He's sending someone to pick it up this afternoon or tomorrow."

Ann smiled. "You sound like a knowledgeable art patron. I'm so glad you got a chance to see it."

Without looking at Ann, the woman stepped to the painting, reached into her small handbag, fumbling there a moment before coming out with a switchblade knife. She popped it open and stabbed the painting near the flower in the black hair.

Ann screamed.

The visitor made four slashes, essentially cutting the face out of the canvas. It hung by a few threads at one corner.

The woman turned and walked away, closing her weapon and returning it to her purse. It had been very sharp.

At the door she paused and looked at Ann for the first time.

"Tell your mister Jay Paul, how does he like his expensive art now?"

The hound dog came to Ann and nuzzled her calf. On the porch they watched the silver car slip into the street and slide away. Ann headed for her desk to write down the license number. It belonged to Beth Gottlieb.

Later Ann went to the studio and told Suz about the incident. The artist was silent a long time, thinking.

"The paintings are like my children, sort of," Suz said quietly. And she sat down.

## Royal Treatment

For the rest of their vacation, the honeymooners' days were filled at the Parker Ranch. Jeffrey was their personal guide, in ranch vehicles, riding their best horses, guiding hikes, and giving a tour in the Ranch 2010 Bell 407 helicopter.

Sometimes Allie joined them, and when she did the conversations became a bit rowdy. Her accent flew in the face of communication, but a lively spirit and Texas pride worked wonders.

While exotic drinks and seafood had dominated their meals on Oahu, the menu turned to burritos, steaks, vegetables, and whiskey.

Bob joined them twice for a breakfast of steak and eggs — once in Waimea, the Parker Ranch town, and the other in Kapa'au on the North Shore.

Bob was a great source of information on land, real estate, the Parker Ranch Trust, and how they were developing bits of their holdings. He and Darcy were finding a friendship and mutual respect.

And he knew all about raising cattle on the island, grasses, seasons, market prices, and the weather. Everything.

On their last day on The Big Island: Jeffrey dropped them at their hotel earlier than usual and played a little slack-key, sitting under a palm near the entrance. Three songs and he had drawn a little crowd.

Jake and Darcy knew they had been courted and had fun with it. And the Ranch was giving them all the time needed to think. No pressure. Just think about it.

They agreed a vacation that had started rather touristy had ended up educational, with unexpected royal treatment. But finally, that was over, and they were back in their beach outfits one last time.

< 64 >

They walked on the sand again, along the comfortable edge of the ocean. The heat of the day had cooled to a sultry tropical evening. They had mai tais, and fish for supper.

Over the water the sun seemed to crunch quietly into a far-off cloud bank, lighting the sky on fire and then disappearing in an orange wall that slowly darkened. They watched the whole show from their third-floor room. The glass door was wide open, and seductive ocean air from the Orient moved the curtains that framed the sea.

< 65 >

# A Murderer's Tracks

Back home in northeastern Utah, Darcy and Jake had no time to decompress.

Buster was beside himself, perhaps the happiest dog on the planet. Even the cats that had become strictly outdoor creatures, quickly resumed their prior status.

Darcy's assistant at the Summit County Land Conservancy met with her for six hours reviewing areas of progress and new opportunities. The business moved in spurts and stalls. Success came in slow motion until it changed to fits and starts. Darcy, back in her element, had a full calendar by the end of her first day home.

Despite the time change, Jake had been up before dawn doing the chores. Then he met with his neighbor and employee, Simon Banuelos, who had kept things running.

Everything was pretty much as he had left it, ready for winter. Hay in the barn. Tools and machinery put away. The previously slick horses had haired up, and now looked fuzzy. Mud season had arrived, and an early snow was on the ground.

Most of Jake's cattle were spending the winter on the desert west of The Great Salt Lake, and he planned to go out and take a look before the serious winter set in. His replacement-heifers were in a ten-acre lot eating his hay.

After he'd reviewed everything and laid plans, Simon headed out to feed and Jake went to the Kamas Kafe to meet an old friend for an early lunch.

At five after eleven, Trixie greeted Jake at the little cafe on State Road 32. She parked herself in front of him, a hand on each shoulder and looked in his face.

"Good grief," she said," I never expected to see you again."

"Oh yeah?" Jake smiled. "How's that?"

"You've been gone so long I forgot about you. Three years

< 66 >

gone by my estimate, and my memory just ran out."

"It's only been three weeks," Jake said, innocently.

"Hell sakes," she said, flabbergasted. "I'd have thought it was a lot longer. Well, you gotta' admit you sure looked at least thirty years older. I assume you've seen a mirror. You can't have aged that bad in just a month. Poor tired old man. Looks like you been rode hard and put up wet."

She gave him her sweetest smile and a wink.

"Thanks, Trixie."

"Well," she said, "your sheriff's waitin' in the back booth. I hope he can recognize you. Coffee?"

"Sure."

Trixie and her white uniform disappeared.

Marvin stood when Jake approached. The two old friends smiled as they shook hands.

"You look young and invigorated," Marvin said. "The honeymoon did you some good."

Trixie came with the coffee, wiggled her ample bottom at them and disappeared.

"Any excitement while I was gone?"

"You missed football season. South Summit was good, but not that good," said Marvin. "How was Hawaii?"

"An exotic paradise, about like you'd expect."

"Never been there," Marvin said, "don't know what I'd expect. Palm trees and beaches, I suppose. Everyone mellow, probably no crime. Do I have it about right?"

"Pretty close," Jake said. "They say 'Aloha' a lot, which explains everything. You know, like tomorrow is soon enough. It was exotic, and an adventure.

"Get Kay and we'll meet you for supper and tell you about it sometime. We have a disc with some music for you."

"You're on," the sheriff said.

"How about next weekend at a sushi place in Park City?"

"I'm worried about raw fish," Marvin said, making a little face.

"Will you teach us what's edible?"

"Sure. Darcy's busy right now so I'll ask her to check her schedule and call Kay and make a plan. Probably Friday or Saturday."

The white uniform popped into view, hovering at the edge of the booth.

"Late breakfast or early lunch? Suppose you'll need a menu, bein' gone so long and all," Trixie said, looking at Jake.

"Nope. Eggs, toast, and orange juice please," he said.

"Sheriff?"

"Pancakes. I'm feeling a bit exotic today," Marvin said.

Waitress gone; Jake leaned forward looking at the sheriff.

"So, Marv, here's my question.

"Do you know what ever happened to Wally Archer? I was under the impression he was in prison somewhere."

"Last I heard was about three years ago," said Marvin, "a couple months after Ray Whorton was down here and tossed a knife into your irrigation ditch."

"Yes?"

"Wally's investigation by the law in Fremont County, Idaho, had wound down. Wally's file was thick but was finally turned over to other investigations. The Feds, I think.

"Various jurisdictions were fine tuning the evidence against him, but I hadn't heard if it had gone to trial or whatever. I am kinda' curious now that you bring it up. I can't remember if he was in jail at the time, or out on bail. He was out of the hospital, I'm sure."

"Well, you won't believe this," Jake said, "but I stumbled into him in Honolulu, sitting on a bench staring at the ocean, feeding pigeons."

Marvin stared at Jake for a long moment.

"Not likely," he said.

"I couldn't believe it either. But it was him, in the flesh. He denied it at first, said I was mistaken, that he was Walter Abbott.

< 68 >

But it was our Wally.

"I told him I thought he was in prison, but he said he was in a witness protection program with a new name, a new social security number, a new ponytail and a beard. Feeding birds.

"He said he had a girlfriend. Wally. Our Wally. Can you believe it?"

Marvin thought about that.

"I don't think I believe him," Jake continued "He lived a lie for thirty years; I hesitate to believe him now. He might have jumped bail, or climbed over a wall, left everything, and split."

"I'll call our friend in Idaho and find out," Marvin said.

Their booth was quiet then.

Two thoughtful old friends were looking at each other, their hats on the seats beside them, coffee cups in between.

Over breakfast they discussed other things — the weather, crime, the illegal drug business, cutting horses, life in general, and mutual friends.

In his office, Marvin grinned at Molly, his deputy and dispatcher.

"Is Jake glad to be home?" she asked.

"Think so. He looked rested and happy. A little sunburned on his forehead," Marvin said. "He had sold some of his horses and says he wants to slow down some. Spend more time with Darcy.

Sounded like he made some connections on the Big Island, and he is thinking about an opportunity there."

A pause, and then he asked:

"Molly, would you get detective Ray Whorton on the phone for me?"

Ray was out fighting crime, but he finally got back to Marvin at eight-thirty the next morning.

< 69 >

# The Murderer's Trail

There was about five inches of old snow on the ground, soft and melting fast. Above, a dark ceiling with some gathering cotton wads under it suggested rain. The snow would probably be almost gone by tomorrow.

While Ray Whorton was on the phone with Marvin, Jake was touring his property on horseback. He was checking everything, making notes. Buster was Jake's guide, and a gray gelding, his transportation.

Jake was near the back of a large pasture when he saw the sheriff's car winding past the willow trees marking his long driveway. He aimed for his barn in a hurry. Speeding through the heavy wet white stuff caused the action to be more like leaping lunges than a comfortable gallop. Snow flew airborne in chunks, the horse breathed loudly.

Although he tried, Buster couldn't keep up.

"Hi Marv," Jake called as he swung off.

They walked together to the barn and put the steaming gelding in a stall. Jake let him drink a few sips, tied him and loosened the cinch three holes.

They left their muddy boots on the porch and wiped the dog's feet. Inside Jake made more coffee and they sat in his office.

"I talked to Ray Whorton and got Wally's story," the sheriff said, as he shed the official brown and gold coat and sat on the big leather couch.

"The investigations were deep and complicated," Marvin said. "Some of the files are still open, but not active. It's become an almost seven-year project — much more if you start counting with the hunting 'accident' in the Wind Rivers.

"The murder we saw him commit has gone unpunished, 'cause the guy he killed was a drug kingpin, and so he did

< 70 >

everyone a favor. Wally had good attorneys and claimed it was self-defense, and maybe, in a way, it was. So that was that.

"But they were pretty sure he was responsible for the hunting accident long ago, and at least five killings since. Probably more. Ray thought maybe up to twelve victims, most all drug related.

"Meanwhile, poor Wally had a long period of waiting to be arrested, with attorneys talking all the time. Tons of evidence was collected. Investigators wanted to talk to Wally, and some of them did, with his legal team present."

Buster appeared then. Since Jake's feet filled most of the empty space under his desk, the dog settled near Marvin. The sheriff was deeply committed to the comfortable couch, but he reached for the dog's ear. It was out of range, so he scratched Buster's back with a toe instead. The tail wagged.

"Some folks wanted to arrest him," Marvin said, back to his story. "Read him his rights, and then lock him up, for fear he'd flee. Others knew they had circumstantial evidence only and couldn't hold him for long. They needed something rock-solid on which to build a case.

"During all this, Wally did give them some names, very carefully, with attorneys present. Names that proved useful in other cases. But nothing that would incriminate himself. The names were traded for various little deals between his lawyers and the prosecutors.

"But those names came back to haunt him, when everyone found out that a dangerous little gang of killers called the Polynesian Band had been hired to shut Wally up permanently. They were from South Salt Lake City, Lehi, and Spanish Fork.

"With these no-nonsense killers after him, his attorneys wanted Wally in protective custody. That probably sounded a lot like jail to him.

"But protective custody never happened.

"There was some effort to get him in a witness protection program, but for some reason, that never happened either.

"Various new investigations led to fresh murders they liked him for, and the District Attorney wanted him safely locked up somewhere, so that when they found one they could really prove, he'd be handy.

"Whorton said these were kinda' long shots, you know. The DA grasping at straws.

"Finally, as they were about to move on protective custody, Wally disappeared. He left his wife, horses, skis, home, and simply vanished. The law made a stab at tracking him, but it may have been half-hearted, probably thinking they'd let the Polynesians Band handle what they couldn't accomplish."

"Wow," Jake said.

"I was on the phone about an hour, but that's it in a nutshell," Marvin said. "Wally's gone, but the killing continues."

"Except one more thing. Ray Whorton thinks some law enforcement agency is keeping tabs on Wally, off the record.

"That's not a common way to do it, but it's done sometimes. Somewhere between protective custody and witness protection. Pretty much unofficial, but if he keeps in touch, they let him be. Any new name is his own invention.

"Wally, out in the ozone, but not completely."

"What happens now?" Jake asked.

"Ray will snoop around. These deals are not public and even law enforcement is on a need-to-know basis. Someone might be interested in your story, if one of the cold files warms up." Marvin rested his voice and looked out the window.

"I'll think about it," he said, "but unless Wally's name comes up in a new case, things will probably remain as they are. I am curious about the Polynesian Band. Maybe it has roots overseas. Although it sounds like it's strictly a Salt Lake phenomenon."

After they said goodbye and the patrol car rumbled down the driveway, Jake collected the gray gelding and rode back into the soft snow. Wise to do this today. The sky was getting even darker.

< 72 >

## Tattoo Parlor

In 1769, James Cook and his crew on the HMS Endeavour were sent south of the equator to observe Venus moving in front of the sun. Travel for science.

And there was a secondary mission: to find the rumored Southern Continent. For commerce, and perhaps, conquest.

They circled New Zealand, visited the Great Barrier Reef of Australia, and made other discoveries. They included the Hawaiian Islands, where Cook died at the hands of tattooed natives in 1779.

Early drawings and etchings of the South Sea Islanders showed fierce folks with highly decorated bodies. The stylized designs, when completed, could be read like a visual language. Beautiful as well, if your taste leans that way.

Nowadays, with more Hawaiians examining their history and culture, body marking is making a comeback. For the purists who have been trained by the old masters, it is done with reverence and care. Tapping to the rhythm of a beating heart. It is slow and painful, but the results can be stunning.

Lying still for hours, day after day, getting tattooed with handmade tools, presents an adventure nearly identical to what one's forebears experienced centuries earlier. It's a unique and personal connection to one's ancestors.

The designs were a serious way to share beliefs and lineages. Adapting the traditional patterns, and understanding their meaning, made it an important rite of passage. The participants find the experience can be life changing.

These traditional marking are only for those with the appropriate bloodlines, culture, and the time to spend.

Tattoos for the tourists were completely different and could be found in Honolulu's Chinatown at Sailor Jerry's.

< 73 >

There you could pick what you wanted for your vacation souvenir — a cute hula dancer, for example, or an anchor. Here your artist would wear plastic gloves and use a buzzing electric machine. An angry hornet on your arm or butt.

Fast, and you don't miss your airplane.

When Jay Paul went to prep school on the mainland, tattoos were far from his mind, although he had seen tattoo parlor signs in the dirtier corners of a couple of America's big cities. And although he'd never entered one, he and his friends could imagine what it would be like inside.

'Where will I find the scum of the earth?' he asked himself. 'Where will I find a professional killer?'

For some reason the image of a tattoo parlor presented itself.

One sunny day Jay Paul and three friends were headed to Honolulu's Chinatown for dim sum.

Walking past the sign for Sailor Jerry's, on a whim, he stuck his head in. It was not what he had pictured. Comfortable looking lounges, neat with lots of light, and youthful artists with plastic gloves. Observable cleanliness.

Two blocks later, however, he saw another sign over an ugly little yellow door. The window was plastered with aged photos of tattooed body parts. Squinting between the pictures, it looked more like what he had imagined.

"Go on, you guys. I want to look in here a moment," he said.

"Hey Dude, no sweat, we'll wait."

"No, I'll just be a minute or two." He sounded serious. "Go on. Get us a table."

Jay Paul entered cautiously. It was rather dingy, and the proprietor was resting on the well-worn lounge chair. It was centered under a fluorescent ceiling light suspended on wires, low over the recliner.

"Come on in," the old fellow said.

< 74 >

He got up slowly as Jay Paul approached. He had a full beard and long hair, combed and moussed into a flamboyant greasy sculpture.

A wrinkled sleeveless shirt and shorts revealed a body entirely dedicated to art. A walking catalog of tattoos.

"Have a seat, young man," he said. "What can I do for you today?"

Although there were a few dusty chairs in a corner, the artist motioned toward the leather area he had recently occupied.

"Just want to ask a question or two."

"Well, you came to the right place. I'm one of the last holdouts."

When the grizzled fellow spoke, his lip ring seemed to dance around the words. A touch of gold hiding under the gray moustache.

"Sailor Jerry's pushing everyone else out. Not many of us real artists left. You came to the right place," he repeated.

"I'm about half the price of those goofballs. And I can do that cute shit they do even better.

"I'm damn good at specialized lettering, and about anything else you want. And my spelling is pretty good.

"I'll do those traditional patterns and designs too, with modern, safe tools. Can you imagine the infection from the old way? Bet most of those natives died of skin infection. Now we got a new batch of artists, quote, un-quote."

He held up two hands, fingers wiggling.

"Polynesians, looking for their roots, doin' it the ancient way. Go figure. Layin' on a filthy rug all afternoon in somebody's carport gettin' poked with sharpened rusty nails day after day. Patterns supposed to tell your history that nobody can read. Shit, no wonder they're dying out."

The elderly proprietor looked Jay Paul over. Dressed in a green polo shirt with red trim and faded jeans, he could be anybody. There was a clean-cut look about him, and not a tattoo in sight. Fertile ground? Maybe.

"What kinda' art you like?" he asked, squinting his gopher eyes at Jay Paul.

"Well, I don't want art," Jay Paul said, "just maybe ask you some questions ..."

"Doesn't need to be art. Sometimes just designs are better. Sometimes just lettering, a name or statement or slogan. How about a catchy phrase or something else?"

"No, I want to talk business for a second," Jay Paul said.

"Okay, talk. But I got a client coming in a couple hours."

Jay Paul seemed a little hesitant. So, the artist continued:

"We're like barbers, we can talk and work at the same time. Here, sit down."

He patted the seat where he had been sitting. He took the stool while Jay Paul tentatively tried the lounge.

"Lean back and relax. Nothing will hurt till I turn on the machine."

"Umm ..." Jay Paul said.

"Go on, son. There is nothing I haven't seen or heard before."

Jay Paul did lie back. It was sort of like a psychiatrist's couch, but not so clean. The smell of rich leather was long gone, traded for stale smoke and rank sweat.

"It's for a friend of mine," he said, looking at the lip ring.

"Oh yeah?"

"My friend needs to find someone to do a job."

"I know guys outta' work. Sometimes I can do an odd job now and then myself."

"Well, it's kind of a special job." Jay Paul was trying to relax, but it wasn't working.

"How special? Is it dangerous?"

"Dangerous for an amateur, but a professional would have no trouble."

"Is it illegal, that's why you're whispering?"

"I guess so," said Jay Paul, a little louder.

< 76 >

"You're an undercover cop. Shit. I smelled you from a mile away. My answer is no. Actually, it's fuck no. Get out."

Jay Paul didn't move. He looked at the beard and said, "I'm not any kind of cop."

"So what'cha want then?"

'I just want to find someone who will do a professional job."

"An illegal dangerous job. Who are you anyway?"

"It's not for me, it's for my friend."

"Yeah, I bet. What's this so-called friend want done?"

"My friend," Jay Paul said carefully, "wants a woman killed."

The artist got up. "Is there a tattoo involved?"

"Nope."

"Not interested."

Jay Paul swung his legs toward the floor and sat up. They looked at each other for a tense minute.

"I didn't expect you'd want to do it. I'm just looking for suggestions. How to find the right person."

"Hey, Buddy, I don't know any murderers. Hell. Just hang around the Ninety-nine Street Halawa Mob Crips, watch 'em play B ball, and ask which is the meanest of the bunch. Go talk to him."

"I thought they were all about graffiti and giving other gangs the finger ..."

"Make sure to talk to one of the guys selling drugs. They're the businessmen. They'll be the meanest and smartest."

There was a pause that seemed to end the conversation.

"If you think of somebody, how can you let me know?" Jay Paul asked.

"Gimme' your phone number, of course. I'll call you. But don't hold your breath 'cause I don't hang around with murderers."

"It's not for me, it's for my friend, and he doesn't want anyone knowing who he is."

"Fine. Give me your number then."

< 77 >

"Me neither," Jay Paul said.

The tattoo artist thought about that for a moment.

"Does this job pay?" he asked.

"Yes, it does," Jay Paul said looking at the older man.

"Yeah?"

"Something in the high five-figures," said Jay Paul.

"Wow ... This woman wanna' tattoo? I could work on her, and you could stick a little arsenic in the ink as I work. We could split your friend's money."

"Arsenic?" Jay Paul said. "There's an idea ... But I doubt she wants a tattoo ... We'd have to catch her and hold her down and drug her ..."

"Works for me," the lip ring said. "Figure out the details and get back to me." His tone was flip, not particularly serious.

Jay Paul thought a moment. "Well ..." was the best he could come up with.

"Well ... if I think of something, I'll stick this picture outside on the doorframe and you can stop in," said the old guy. "If I'm workin' come back later."

He held up a small illustration of a hula dancer, an old decal. An instant tattoo for a young child that would last until the first bath.

"I'll pin it above the door ... if I think of anything."

Jay Paul got up and said thanks and goodbye.

He headed for the dim sums down the street.

# Arsenic

Arsenic, a natural component of the earth's crust, is a metalloid. Its primary use is in alloys of lead, but it has many other applications, including the hide tanning process and, sometimes, murder. It is most toxic in its inorganic form. Arsenic trioxide, white arsenic, is deadly in small doses and is a powder easily served in hot soup.

Jay Paul googled arsenic on his iPhone as he walked to the restaurant.

In the Golden Dragon they chatted about the food that came by on carts. Char siu bao, cheung fun, shrimp dumplings, naiwong bao, and hot and sour soup.

A Chinese waitress would snare the desired little morsels, put them, two by two, on small plates and hand them over. Impatient, almond-eyed girls with black hair and tongs.

It was cart after cart, waitress after waitress.

Gradually their hunger was abated, replaced by the stack of empty dishes. Small plates. And soup bowls.

Jay Paul looked thoughtfully at the soup bowls.

Across the city someone else was googling poison.

Beth Gottlieb, angry and steaming, had typed in her computer: 'Arsenic as a murder weapon.'

Her index finger pressed 'enter.'

< 79 >

# Fargo

Jay Paul's Doberman had been his companion for six years, and he loved the dog. A friendly pet when the master was home. But when he was away, Fargo was guard of the yard. A rather nasty presence on the other side of the iron fence. He was a black as death, with brown edges and a slick coat. A canine storm trooper. Long and slender. Aloof and dangerous.

When Beth moved in, Fargo accepted her warmly. All three slept on the big bed together ... for a while.

When the fighting started Fargo remained neutral through the yelling stage, past the months of screaming, and into the desperate time of dishes and lamps breaking.

When Beth moved out of the big house and into the beach bungalow, the dog seemed to miss her. Beth had wanted to take Fargo with her, but Jay Paul said no and had the locks changed.

While he surfed, relaxed, met with divorce attorneys, and made love to Carnation, Beth seemed to spend all her time focused on revenge.

That was what led her to park the silver Porsche behind some bushes where she could see the black Caddy full of surfboards pass as Jay Paul went to pick up his buddies.

After two years of marriage, she knew his routine.

Sure enough, she didn't have to wait long. He passed and she started the ignition. Up the curving driveway she went, stopped at the top, got out and went to the fence and greeted Fargo, slobbering and wagging, whimpering with delight.

"Nice to see you, too, old friend," she said sadly.

Beth offered a raw wiener through the iron bars and the dog said thanks by wiggling his black body and long tail. She scratched his ears before she left.

He was dead before she got down the hill to the first stoplight.

# Fatissimo

Detective Clay Burnam was poking around to see if there were any donuts left from the morning. He'd found a house to buy and was thinking mostly about the mortgage. He was settling into life on the island. Sinking roots.

"Hey, Burnam, I've got something you might need to hear," said a voice from the doorway. "You got a moment?"

"I do," Clay said. "What's up, Mack?"

"We're interrogating one of our favorite gangsters and he has something you probably should hear."

"Oh yeah?"

"Is Mikio around? He should hear it too."

"I think he's across the street in a meeting with the DA about some doggone thing or another," Clay said.

"So, our boy sold some fentanyl to Hal who was working undercover. Hal's probably the only officer who didn't know him personally. Him being our perp named Big Fatissimo. His brother is Little Fatissimo, by the way."

"Anyway, after that he and Hal became pretty good pals and so Hal bought some cocaine as well. The friendship grew and the kid upped the amount. All this friendship lasted about an hour, then Hal cuffed him, and the friendship started to sour."

"I don't think I've ever met this famous Fatissimo." Clay admitted.

"You're one of very few. Mikio knows him; he could tell you tales about the Fatissimo brothers."

They had been walking as they talked and stopped at the door of an interrogation room.

"Here we go." said Mack.

The room had a table and behind it a prisoner who looked rather hostile. His head had been shaved but showed a dark shadow suggesting about a week's growth. He was a big guy,

< 81 >

tattooed. Probably in his mid-twenties, in a clean white T-shirt and baggy shorts. The arrest must have gone smoothly by the look of the shirt. Not a wrinkle or smudge.

Hal sat across from him, and Clay and Mack stood.

"Gentlemen," Hal said.

"Fatissimo, this is officer Burnam," said Mack, real friendly.

Clay said hello and Fatissimo grunted.

"Tell Clay what you told us," Mack suggested.

"My attorney ain't here yet," Fatissimo said.

"We're not lookin' for new news," Mack said, "and nothin' to do with your drug problems. And your attorney is coming. He's on his way. Just tell Clay about the guy. Okay?"

"Well shit," the gangster muttered, "he was just a guy." Fatissimo looked at Clay. "Came on kinda' nervous like, hinting around about where somebody could get something, opioids or cocaine ... like he wasn't sure what he wanted or how to get it.

"He looked too rich to be that stupid. I thought he was an undercover cop, but a lousy one if you ask me. I sure as hell didn't know what he was.

"I played along with him, 'cause what the hell ... he probably had money. He had a gold chain.

"So, we're dancin' around like that, talkin' shit, me knowin' he wants somethin' but not knowin' what.

"Finally turns out he wants to hire somebody to kill somebody. Of course, he says he's looking as a favor for a friend.

"I know that's bullshit. It's not for no friend, it's for him."

Mack opened the door and dragged in two chairs and he and Clay sat down.

"Did he identify himself?" Clay asked.

"Nope."

"Did you get any idea who he wanted killed?"

"Sounded like it was some woman. We were sort of chatting and I was playin' along because I had nuttin' else to do. I got the feelin' he wouldn't mind if the lady got hurt in the process.

< 82 >

Seemed like he hated her."

"Any ideas how he wanted it done?" Clay asked.

"Nope," Fatissimo said. "Didn't mind if it was painful. Said he wanted a professional job, whatever that means. Probably so nobody takes the fall for it. He wanted the bitch gone with no loose ends."

"Anything else you can remember about the guy?" Clay asked.

"Not really. He was kinda old. Not real old, not a grandpa or like that, but older than any of you. I'd guess mid-forties or more. Looked to me he was too old to be wearin' a gold chain. Did look rich though. Acted rich and kinda' important if you get my drift."

"Unusual features?" Clay asked.

"Nope, pretty regular. Woman might think he was a stud, but I thought he was sort of a pretty boy surfer type. Like he usta' surf and talk big but now he's old, the big walls scare him, and he mostly talks."

"You got to know him rather well?" ask Clay.

"Wasted an hour with the fool, I did. But when he left, I watched him a while 'cause I still thought he might be a cop, and so I saw his car."

"What kind?"

"Don't know. I was too far away. Cars all look alike nowadays. Designed in a fuckin' wind tunnel. Takes all the personality out of 'em. Recent model, I'd say."

"Any license number?"

"Nope."

"What color?"

"Black," Fatissimo said. "Coulda' been a Caddy. Shit, they all look the same."

"How did you end your conversation with this guy?" Clay wanted to know.

"Told him I didn't know any professional killers. He said it would be worth a lot of money. I said I didn't wanna' hear the number, so he left. He gave me a card with a phone number on it, though."

"Can I see the card?" Clay asked.

"Nope. I threw it away," said Fatissimo.

"If I give you my card, will you throw it away or call me if you think of anything else about this?" Clay asked.

Fatissimo grinned at him, showing some teeth.

Mack stood up.

"Thanks," Mack said, "We'll get outta here so you can get your story ready for your attorney."

"Nice to meet you, Mister Fatissimo, and thank you," said Clay as he stood.

In the hall Clay looked at Mack. "Quite a story."

"Fatissimo is a character," Mack said. "As a kid he was always fun to arrest, but tough if he wanted to be. He has some serious scars under that shirt."

"I thought the little snake tattoo on the forehead was a nice touch," Clay said.

"The Honolulu law enforcement community has known him since he was twelve. His sheet is long. He was very active in the 99th Street Halawa Mob Crips. They used to have major combat with the Samoa Crips, probably where he got most of his scars," Mack said. "That's most of his rap sheet too; fighting and graffiti. Quite a criminal. I don't think they've got him for anything too serious.

"Oops, they did; joy riding. Guess they call it grand theft auto on the mainland. Anyway, he's a convicted car thief, and probably pretty soon he'll graduate to drug dealing."

"Glad I got to meet him," Clay said. "Now I'll try to track down Mikio."

"Ask Mikio about Fatissimo. He knows him as well as anybody."

"Man, I love Hawaii," said Clay.

< 84 >

# Livin' the Life

*Let's go surfing now*
*Everybody's learning how*
*Come on a safari with me*

W e're really living life," Jay Paul said from the couch facing the big window. A few roofs and palm trees, and then the ocean filled the view from where he sat. If he stood up and walked to the glass, he would see more houses and streets below, but the Pacific would still go edge to edge.

"There is nothing like the sound of the Beach Boys to put me back in California."

"Dreamin'?"

"Back when surfing was imported. It was an art-form then, not yet a sport."

"You were there as the Beach Boys pushed the dinosaurs off the sand?" Buddy asked. "Can't believe you're that old."

Jay Paul let it go. He wasn't really there at the beginning, but close enough. Certainly, he was the oldest in the room.

"Corny as the lyrics sound, it's the rhythm that carries my life," Jay Paul said relaxing deeper into the couch. "Rhythm of the Beach Boys carries me horizontally; the ocean out there carries me vertically."

"A philosopher?" said Jif.

"Did you know the Beach Boys didn't surf?" Jay Paul asked.

"Get out."

"I heard he wrote it in high school music class and got an F. Then in a couple years it got famous, and the school changed the grade to an A."

"Who wrote it, JP?" Jif wondered.

"Brian Wilson and Mike Love, I think."

< 85 >

"Which one got the A?"

"Dunno ... look it up."

"Where we goin' today?"

Buddy's question came from one of the stools at the island in the big kitchen and was aimed at Jay Paul.

"We should be close to a full moon," he said. "Did Carnation have a chance to check the tides?"

"I'll ask her," Buddy said. He stretched and stood up.

"What are we lookin' for, JP? Rollers? A tube, what's your pleasure?" asked Jif from the other couch.

"I'm in the mood for a big drop," Jay Paul said, "if I take my new camera stuff. Otherwise, I'm mellow. You guys with me?"

"That might be too scary for Carnation," Jif said. "Is she comin' today?"

'Don't know." Jay Paul said, "And wave wise, I imagine we'll have to take what we get. That's a lot of surfing; plannin', watchin', waitin', and takin' what she gives you."

"She?"

"The ocean. Our mother the ocean. She gives, and she takes away."

Idle surf talk floated around the living room and kitchen on most days. Tired clichés. Exaggerated memories.

Big surf with long lulls ... Broken boards and rocky shores ... When in doubt, just opt out ... No place to park a car ... no place to paddle out ... got it all to ourselves ... Jet ski lifeguards ... Razor rocks ... Face as big as a garage door ... on and on.

"Come on baby, surf with me." Jif, quoting in a singsong voice.

"I guess those lyrics do sound a bit lame," said Jay Paul, the dinosaur. "Sorry, Jif."

< 86 >

# Private Dick

Jay Paul lived in the grand home of his childhood. Except for prep school and college, and some travelling, it had always been home. Remodeled after his mother passed away, it retained its classic architecture, but the spirit inside was more like a university frat house.

It now contained his office that looked out — over lawn, flowers and gardens — at the glimmering ocean. There, as he sipped his coffee, he picked up his phone.

"Hello," he said when the ringing was answered, "is Sam Waterford there?"

"Just a moment sir," a female voice said.

Then, "Sam Waterford." Deep and husky.

"Good morning. This is Jay Paul Gottlieb. John Silverman suggested I give you a call."

"How is John?" Sam asked, with his up-beat voice.

"He's fine. Wants me to tell you hello."

"Okay ... how can I help?"

"Well, I suppose we should meet," Jay Paul said slowly, "But briefly my problem is that my wife has filed for divorce and is trying to make it as difficult for me as possible. I just want to get it over with, but she wants to drag it out and take everything I have."

"You're contesting?"

"I want the divorce as badly as she does, but she's got her lawyers going after me like hungry sharks. We've been married for two miserable years, and she's done nothing but spend my money. She hasn't worked or contributed anything and now she wants it all. She's not reasonable and her attorneys know it, but there is no communicating with her. She's completely nuts."

"So how can I help you, Mister Gottlieb?"

"Well, basically, maybe you could track her, watch her, find

< 87 >

out what she's up to. Anything that could help my case."

"Do you think she's having an affair?" Waterford asked.

"I don't really think so, but who knows? If she was, that would be good news, I think.

"She is doing things to hurt me, and if I had any warning, it might help."

"Things?" the detective asked.

"For example, she poisoned my dog, and sunk one of my sailboats. She ruined a piece of art I'd purchased."

"She's angry, I guess," Waterford offered.

"Shit, yes."

"Well let's meet then, and I'll draw up an agreement. You can talk to me about her habits, and her friends. Car license number. Names and addresses, please. I can do some things that the police can't. I can put a tracking device, like an Apple Air Tag, on her car or in her shoe. I can do it, but illegal for the real cops.

"Anyway, when would you want to meet?"

"ASAP," said Jay Paul.

"Gather names and addresses for anyone relevant and come over. I could see you after three today, or sometime tomorrow. My secretary will give you the address."

"See you at three," Jay Paul said.

"Okay. Hold on, Lillian will give you the particulars ..."

The bedroom next to Jay Paul's office had been converted into an office for Carnation. Her actual bedroom was upstairs near the library.

She was a tallish blonde woman with a can-do presence, an understated elegance, and smart. A looker, certainly, and three years older than her employer.

She was usually available if Jay Paul was between girlfriends and if they were both in the mood. Sometimes it seemed like romance, other times more like lust. If he was lonely or blue, and she felt motherly, it could be a 'help me make it through

< 88 >

the night,' affair.

But whatever it was, both understood the parameters and were comfortable with it.

But whichever bedroom she came out of, her days had focus. She handled Jay Paul's day-to-day events, the bookkeeping, and his schedule. She was the brains balancing his spur-of-the-moment life. She usually knew what he was up to before he did. If knowledge was power, Carnation held the key. So, they both knew he had been contacting a private investigator.

Buddy, a childhood friend, had a bedroom in the house as well. With no official title, he served as surfing pal, errand boy, and muscle. A big guy, he had been a linebacker in high school football. Being a tough guy was a seldom-needed talent in his life with Jay Paul, but it was the job he liked best.

They both had been relaxing, Carnation with an accounting spread sheet open on her computer screen, and Buddy sitting on the corner of her desk, absent-mindedly swinging a leg. They had been discussing lunch and listening to Jay Paul's end of the conversation in the next room.

When Jay Paul ended his conversation, they were quiet a moment before Carnation called out.

"Hey, JP, we're talkin' about lunch at Hungry's. You wanna' go?"

"You guys go, I've got to gather some stuff and make some notes before I go meet this private dick at three. Maybe bring me some onion rings if you think about it."

After Carnation and Buddy got their food, they found a shaded private bench outside.

"I feel sorry for JP," Carnation said. "That woman is merciless."

"She's a headache for sure. The world would be better off without her."

"It really would."

"I think she's really dragging him down. We've lost our

carefree leader," Buddy said.

"Yes," Carnation agreed. "Wish I could help him."

"Me too."

Buddy looked thoughtful.

"Seems like you could write her a big check, payable when she gets her ass to Paris or somewhere permanently. New York or wherever she wants. Give her a pay-day and get her gone," Buddy said. "JP found her with nothin'. Seems like she wants to leave paradise well paid for her two and a half years."

"JP couldn't approach her about that. They'd be screamin' at each other in two seconds," Carnation said.

They thought quietly and ate a little. Except for the pigeons they were alone, under the palms.

"He couldn't talk to her, but maybe we could," Buddy suggested.

"I suppose she hates us, too," Carnation said, "we are his family ... that's the reality."

"Yeah, but we got muscle, we could force her to listen."

"What do you think JP would pay her to disappear?" she asked.

"Shit, Car, you're the bookkeeper ... maybe half a million? Maybe a quarter mill? A whole million?"

"I suppose ... we'd have to ask him."

"Just thinking out loud ... maybe it's better if he doesn't know ... give him deniability. You know, if something goes wrong. He's innocent because he didn't know."

They worked on their lunches then, thinking, and they rewarded the birds for waiting. The shadows of palm trees, enlivened by tropical breezes, danced on the pavement with the pigeons and the onion rings.

The two friends got up and walked. There was no rush to go back to the big house. They were mostly quiet.

At last Carnation said, "We're not plotting here, just talking; but if we did it, say we went to the beach house, knocked on the door and she invited us in, and we explained our idea, and

< 90 >

she agreed, we'd give her a big postdated check.

"When she's disappeared, we'd tell Jay Paul and we could all relax ... but," Carnation continued, "what if she says no?"

"I bet she'd say yes."

"Yes, that's what we hope, but what if it's no."

"Well," Buddy said, "we've got her on the couch ... maybe we cause her to disappear another way."

"Kill her?"

"Well, that's something that's been on Jay Paul's mind," Buddy said.

"I don't think so." Carnation sounded amazed. "You can't just kill people because you don't like them."

"I know it's crossed his mind." Buddy said.

"It has?"

"Yes."

They got quiet when pedestrians passed. As they talked it was mostly conjecture and imagining, but sometimes it seemed serious. Finally, Carnation confronted the most serious question of all.

"So, Bud, suppose she says no ... how ... how do we disappear her?"

"We take her for a ride in my fishing yacht, out on the ocean, but she doesn't come back.

"Divorce proceedings go permanently into limbo. Her lawyers can't find their client." Buddy smiled. "Lost at sea."

They walked a block in silence.

"I could get somebody at Wilcox and Stevens, probably Robert, to prepare a document for her to sign when we give her the check. That would be the good ending," Carnation said, looking at Buddy.

"The other ending, the hard one," Buddy said, "we knock, she tries to shut the door, gets all hostile, I grab her in a bear hug and push her into the room. You slam the door. I'm holding her arms behind her back. You're wearing your baggy pants with all the pockets, and you pull out a twenty-inch zip-tie already in a big loop, pop it over her hands and pull it snug at her wrists. Then we push her onto the couch, pull up chairs, and say we want to talk.

"If she gets crazy, we have a syringe, and you give her an injection. If she gets loud, you have a little bottle of chloroform and a rag. If worse comes to worst, we take her to the garage and stick her in the trunk of the Porsche.

"I'll have my fishing boat close, maybe at that little dock in Malakole Harbor, near M Dock. Usually deserted, but for sure after sunset. There are no lights, and we can park right next to the boat. We'll have a heavy chain and an extra anchor on board.

"That would be doing it the hard way," Buddy said.

"Bud, you're starting to scare me. Have you been thinking about this before?"

"A little, I guess."

"We're just talking, imagining. We're not planning anything. Right, Bud?" she asked.

"Uh huh … just talk."

"You realize your idea of disappearing someone is actually murder?"

"Wrong," Buddy said. "Only if we get caught. Otherwise, it's an erasure."

"Let's remember we're just friends talking. We are not criminals planning anything."

As they started back, they realized they'd fed all Jay Paul's onion rings to the pigeons.

"Oh well," said Carnation, "I'll make him some peanut butter crackers when we get back."

< 92 >

## A Fifty-Foot Hinkley

"A sailboat is a hole in the ocean where a rich man can throw his money." Someone said that a lifetime ago, and it's probably still rings true.

The sleek beauty at a slip in the Ala Wai Harbor was a fifty-foot Hinkley that had been built in Maine over half a century ago. The Sou'wester fifty was a powerful yawl based on designer Bill Tripp's original Hinkley-forty-eight. She was a big cruising and racing machine and sat on a ten-thousand-five-hundred-pound keel.

Floating quietly, she looked slender, fast, and graceful, like a fashion model lounging on her side in a lingerie ad. Her white reflection gleamed seductively in the dark water.

On her deck everything had been designed for efficiency. Varnished teak wood trim, metal fittings, rope and wire prevailed. Below, carefully finished teak reigned, with brass detailing and navy-blue cushions.

She was re-named 'Aloha Spirit' after Jay Paul got her. Six previous owners had loved her and left her. She had been up and down the Atlantic Coast, hung out in Florida several years, visited the Keys and the Caribbean Islands, and explored the Panama Canal.

She had been to Seattle and the San Juan Islands before crossing the Pacific to Hawaii with the man who sold her to Jay Paul. His last words to her as he stepped off were: "I surely love you, baby, but I never, ever, want to see you again. Thanks for the memories.

She was Jay Paul's favorite possession.

Aloha Spirit was a patient but neglected mistress.

< 93 >

Sailing her properly required a crew of at least two or three knowledgeable helpers, plus the owner, and Jay Paul used her mostly tied in her slip, for meetings or entertaining.

The boat was a chick magnet.

Maintenance and slip rental were costly, but those bills always got paid quickly.

When John Silverman stepped on board, Jay Paul was already there, waiting.

Bloody Marys from the little galley were offered and accepted. Then they relaxed on deck a while, making small talk and just reminiscing.

"A sweet boat," John said. "Bet it gets admiring glances."

"Every time we go out, people look. I truly think I'm on the prettiest boat in the harbor."

"I think you are," said John sincerely.

"That's how I usta' feel when I first met Beth, like I was with the prettiest girl at the dance ... that was 'till I found out what a horrible creature lived behind that glamorous face."

John was an old pal who had known and advised Jay Paul since he was fifteen. Before his mother died, she hired John, a lawyer and accountant, to take care of the boy. John knew his finances, his various other attorneys, and his legal situation. He handled the trust fund and was his very best friend.

They sipped their drinks and enjoyed the restfulness a marina and boats provided. Ambiance that included ocean smells, the sound of gently lapping water, and the calls of gulls.

"Let's take a little boat ride," Jay Paul suggested.

John didn't know sailing, but he knew Jay Paul wouldn't try to sail the Aloha Spirit alone.

"I thought you used your small boat if you sailed without a crew," John said.

"I've got some problems there. I'll tell you about them.

"We'll just motor out and have a little talk and a little cruise

< 94 >

with no sailing," Jay Paul said, as he got ready to cast off.

The eighty-horsepower Lehman Ford diesel rumbled to life somewhere deep below, and they passed out of the harbor smoothly.

There was none of the excitement of sails taking hold of the wind. No leaning into waves, no sea foam over the bow. No gathering speed and building excitement. Just the steady sound of the engine pushing through the water and the excellent fresh air coming from somewhere over the horizon.

"This is certainly a good place for a private chat," said John.

"You asked about the thirty-foot Newport Mark II, said Jay Paul. "Well, I can no longer use her. She sank in fifteen feet of ocean water."

"Oh yeah?"

"Beth did it."

"How do you know it was her?"

"Couldn't be anyone else. She went on the boat with a chainsaw and cut a square hole in the bottom, then climbed out and let it sink. Right there, tied to the dock."

"Sounds pretty drastic," John said, looking at his friend.

"She is an explosion of pure hate," said Jay Paul. "My divorce lawyers are meeting with hers all the time and nothing gets resolved except the bill that keeps going up. She and I can't talk at all.

"She's in the beach house currently and the locks on my doors have been changed, so she can't get in to kill me. She is trying to hurt me every way she can think of."

"She really sank your boat?" John was still trying to process that one.

"Sank it and left the chainsaw inside when she got out. It's inside the boat, ruined.

"She also ruined a thirty-thousand-dollar piece of art I bought. Ruined it at the gallery before I even got it home. And she poisoned my dog. I thought she loved that dog, but

< 95 >

apparently, she hated me more.

"And she worked over my Caddy while I was surfing. Took a hammer to it, all over. Broke every window and light. It looks like a pile of tin cans. The doors are hard to open, but it still runs."

Jay Paul was quiet then for a while.

Finally, John asked, "How come she sank the little Newport instead of this boat?"

"Who the fuck knows the mind of that crazy bitch? It was easier, I guess. The Ala Wai Harbor is busy and has security. Lights stay on all night. I kept the little boat near the beach house at a tiny yacht club, and there's usually nobody around."

"Did you ever talk to the police?" John asked.

"I did after the first episode, when she cut up the art. Ann, the owner at the gallery, saw it happen, even got the license plate number. They asked if I wanted to press charges, but that was shortly after the divorce papers, and I didn't want to piss her off. Thought it wouldn't be such a huge deal. Simple divorce. I thought maybe we could still be friends.

"The other stuff, how do you prove them? Fingerprints on a chainsaw ten feet under water? The dead dog? I just got the feeling the cops had more important work to do."

They were making lazy circles in a rather calm sea.

"Can you steer this thing, while I'll make us another drink?" Jay Paul asked.

"Seriously?"

"Just steer it like a car. Don't do anything radical."

When he came up, they traded seats again. Jay Paul took the wheel, and they went slowly in the direction of Pearl Harbor.

"John," he said, "I have to kill her. She's never going away. The smoke and sparks have matured into a full-fledged eruption. It's not gonna' stop till she dies of her deadly hatred."

"Problem is you can't just kill somebody."

"But John, it's done all the time. There are millions of unsolved murders every day. They solve 'em on cop shows,

< 96 >

but on the news, the real ones are mostly unsolved."

John was looking at the ice cubes rocking gently in his Bloody Mary.

"Maybe we should head back; my stomach feels a little woozy," he said.

Jay Paul turned the wheel. "If I could get her on this boat, I'd fasten the anchor chain to her ankle and go out about a mile and push it overboard. I bet she'd be a missing person, never a murder victim. No crime, just gone missing.

"What ya' think, John?"

John watched the shoreline, focused on it. The only thing not moving.

"I think my stomach feels weird," he said.

Jay Paul secured the wheel, disappeared below, then returned with a little pill container. "Dramamine," he said, and gave the older man two pills.

In a few minutes John didn't look quite so green, and about twenty minutes later he dared to take his eyes off the horizon and look at Jay Paul.

"Just thinking," he said, "the shit she's putting you through, what it adds up to, makes a problem for your plan. If she were to disappear, it focuses on you as the guy with a motive. They'd look at you awfully closely, and especially at your boat."

"Hmm ...," said Jay Paul.

"That's my worry," said John.

"Or if I could find a professional hit man," Jay Paul said. "Is there any hope of that?"

"Shit, Jay Paul, I was hoping you were not serious."

"I am serious, John. I am deadly serious. If you can find any way to help ... please. Serious. Deadly serious," he said again.

The Aloha Spirit was rocked gently by waves caused by a huge container ship headed into the Honolulu Harbor. John twisted in his seat, half-stood, leaned, and vomited over the side.

# Fledgling Artist

"Happy Birthday, honey," Pinky said.
It wasn't Wally's real birthday, but it was the birthday Walter celebrated; the date he arrived in Hawaii.

"What we got here?" he asked as she handed him a little package.

It was a small tin box, a kid's watercolor set, a sketchbook and three soft pencils. HB, 2B and 4B.

"Aw, Pinky, you shouldn't have," Walter said, sarcastically, but with a warm smile.

"Now you can use your Rolodex and take art lessons."

"Thanks, Honey. Where did I put that card?"

"It was in your sock drawer. The Lord led me to it."

She pinched his cheek. "You know," she said, "talking Rolodex makes you sound old fashioned. Your phone has an app for that."

"I know honey, but I like the card. It has a painting on it."

That's how Walter ended up at Suz's studio on a Tuesday evening for an uninstructed drawing session, with his metal box and book of empty pages. Counting Walter, there were six people.

Although there was no teacher, Suz gave Walter some advice.

"Save your little box and book for sketching on the beach. Use one of our drawing boards and this conte crayon and draw on these big sheets of newsprint.

"Walk around now and then, see how other people are approaching it. You'll see gesture drawings, contour drawing, smudgy approaches with light and shadow, and scribblers. You'll find your own way.

"Ask questions; we're all friendly and no one will bite," she said. Then she introduced her friends.

Promptly at seven, Suz took command and they all focused.

< 98 >

The benches were claimed, and the rolling light turned on. A Chinese woman in a kimono stepped onto the stand and the colorful silk came off and was tossed aside. She stood stark naked and bold in the spotlight.

Walter, speechless, watched as the light was moved around, creating shadows and highlights that exaggerated or minimized the human form.

Various preferences were made known; benches were moved. When everyone had gotten adjusted and satisfied, talking stopped and drawing commenced.

Walter sat and looked, unsure how to start. Glancing around, he started to do what others did. Tentatively.

In ten minutes, an alarm went off; the model stood and changed her pose.

There were times she sat on the chair, or stood by it, straddled it, or simply stood alone. And drawings were produced one after another.

Sometimes an artist made three drawings in ten minutes. Other times someone worked on the same drawing long after the pose changed. Everyone was quiet and once and a while, there was the sound of crumpled paper and a muffled grumble as an unsuccessful attempt bit the dust. That usually causes smiles of understanding and sympathy.

Although the model was the same, the drawing styles were all different. Walter was too intimidated to ask any questions, but he was getting an education.

There was a break at eight. They gossiped and walked around looking at each other's work. And there was a large commotion when someone saw the huge painting of the woman with her face cut out.

"Oh Suz, no! What happened?"

"A collector named Jay Paul bought it, and apparently his wife didn't like it. Now that it's worthless I got it back," Suz explained quietly.

"Honey, that's terrible," and she got a hug from a shy brown-haired girl, and sympathy from everyone.

"What can you do with it?"

"Well for now I'm going to leave it there and see what I can learn from it. The whole experience is trying to teach me something. I'm trying to be receptive, but not overthink it."

Then she changed the subject. "Let's draw."

After three long poses they stopped shortly after nine.

The Chinese woman was back in her kimono, and they all chipped in to pay her. Artists gathered their stuff and rolled up their drawings.

"Aloha," Suz said as they left. "See you next week, same time, same station."

She pulled Walter aside as the others departed.

"Did you learn anything, Walter?"

"You can call me Wal," he said. "I learned I've got a lot to learn. As an artist I'm a primitive."

"Don't worry, even Grandma Moses had to start somewhere.

"Are you comin' back next week?" It was a question, but also maybe a command.

"Yes, I think maybe I will," he said.

< 100 >

# A Hand Off

"Hello," said Walter, clutching his red cell phone. He was with his pigeon friends on a bench in the park, looking at the post-dawn ocean.

"Walter Abbott?"

"Yes. This is Walter here. Is this you, Agent Polanski?"

"Yes, Mister Abbott, it is I. How are you doing out there in the ocean?"

"Just fine, sir. Just fine."

"I believe you were suffering 'Island Fever' when we last spoke."

"No more, sir, feeling good. No fever."

"Well Mister Abbott, I can give you an update on your Polynesian Band friends who were looking for you."

"You can?"

"Flexo was in a coma two weeks and died. Turd Bird and Little Somba died at the gunfight with the police in Lehi, and they're still dead. The other two, Slick Mick and Jacko, went to prison, and Slick Mick was knifed, throat cut, about three days after the door slammed shut. So that leaves only Jaco to bother you, and he's in for sixty years for shooting a police officer. You probably don't need to concern yourself with him for about forty years."

"That's great," Walter said.

There was a long pause, and Agent Polanski cleared his throat.

"Mister Abbott, I will be handing you off to an agent in your city, to allow closer scrutiny of you and be around if you find yourself battling 'Island Fever' again. I think this will be better all around."

"Whatever you say, sir," Walter said. "It's okay by me."

"Were you able to get a job, mister Abbott?" he asked.

< 101 >

"I'm a starving artist now." Walter smiled to himself.

"Well, keep your nose clean, Walter, and good luck. An agent named Clay Burnam will contact you shortly."

# Beach House

The button on the beach house front door presented a semi-melodic buzz when pressed, and Buddy pressed it twice.

Beth anticipated a visit from her nearest neighbor, same road but about a hundred yards west. A friendly gray-haired specimen who loved to commiserate on reckless husbands, the glories of divorce, and the danger from careless skateboarders. This was a little early, but visits could come any time. So, it was a cheerful voice that sang "Come on in," to the ringer.

But the tone quickly changed when Beth realized who was pushing their way in.

"Get the fuck out now!" she yelled. "Shit, get out now! Damn it, Bud, don't fuckin' dare touch me!"

His arms had her wrapped up in a hug, his hands grasping for her wrists. Carnation was closing the door behind them and began to reach into her pockets.

"Get out right now, both of you!" Beth screamed. "Let me go, you rotten motherfuckers!"

She was stronger than Buddy expected, and he was having difficulty getting control. He had one wrist up behind her back but the other was thrashing wildly.

"Freeze everyone!" A new voice.

The bedroom door had slammed open, and a large man stepped forward. "This is a pistol, folks, so nobody move." The voice of authority.

Buddy looked. It was an olive pistol, a military issue, held in a large hand. The voice was deep and sounded very firm. Its owner was in a tight white T-shirt, and stood in camouflage fatigue pants and shiny black brogans.

Buddy was big; this guy was bigger.

Everyone was quiet.

"Stand over there," he said, pointing toward the couch.

"Who are you people, anyway?"

"These are a couple of JP's asshole friends," Beth said. "The big guy is Buddy, and the bitch is Car. JP's lover, I think; one of 'em anyway."

They looked at each other wondering, how to proceed.

"So why are you here?" the armed man asked.

No answer.

"Come on, you must have had something on your minds."

Finally Carnation spoke. "We wanted to talk to Beth," she said.

"You came in awfully rough for people who just wanted to talk," the stranger said. "Are either of you armed?"

"No," said Carnation quietly.

"You?" he looked at Buddy.

"No answer? Okay, put your hands on top of your head and lace your fingers.

"Beth, pat him down, empty his pockets." He pointed the gun at Buddy, the muzzle about two feet away from his eyes.

There was a gun, and Beth found it. She turned it over in her hands, examining it carefully.

"Bud, you are a true piece of shit," she said.

"Take it to the sink, Babe ... or better yet, put it in the freezer." The stranger looked at Car.

"Empty that lady's pockets and we'll see what she brought."

Carnation was frightened, but she let Beth forage through her pants. Beth put everything on the coffee table.

"Interesting. You came to talk with a weapon, an unmarked envelope, some zip-ties, a bottle with something that smells like chloroform, a rag, a syringe with a amber liquid loaded with a fresh sharp needle ready for action in a protective plastic tube with cap, a set of car and house keys, and a boat key attached to a little float." He spoke slowly, giving dramatic meaning to each item.

< 104 >

"Babe, take one of those zip-ties and fasten Car's wrists together behind her back. Make it snug but don't cut off the circulation." Then he pointed to the couch.

"Sit," he said.

"Now Buddy, you're next."

"Wait a minute ... "Buddy started to say, but the newcomer smashed the heel of his boot down on the arch of the deck shoe and kicked Buddy's legs out from under him. He looked up, wild-eyed.

"On your stomach."

On his stomach he let Beth connect his wrists.

"All right, now, let's talk," the big man said. "We'll start with Car."

Carnation explained their idea of a settlement that would be nice for Beth. That JP had not sent them. How the envelope contained an agreement to sign and information about how the payment would work.

When Beth heard the proposed amount, a quarter of a million, she threw a fit.

Apparently, that wasn't nearly enough to get her attention. She pointed out that the beach house they were currently in was worth five times that amount. No ... Beth wanted a lot more — and most of all, she wanted JP to suffer. She hoped he would be broke and broken by the time she was through with him. All this she explained in rough, colorful language.

And finally, they got around to what would happen if Beth said no to the agreement.

"Well then," Car said, "we simply walk away, and the divorce process will continue."

"Now that's the part that makes no sense," said the man with the pistol. "Let me mention I am Beth's brother, Fletch, a retired Army Master Sergeant and here to help my sister through this shit-storm. And it looks to me like you two came to talk but weren't planning to take no for an answer.

"The evidence is on the table. Zip-ties, chloroform, and a needle full of something. Keys to a boat. And the gun in the fridge."

Carnation, sitting on the edge of the couch, hands fastened behind her back, said nothing. Her eyes had filled with moisture.

Fletch put his pistol on the coffee table with the evidence. He bent and rolled Buddy onto his back. Then he took him by the shoulders and pulled him into a sitting position, his back against the couch, legs out straight on the floor.

"Okay Buddy Boy, what have you got to say?"

Buddy had nothing.

"Where's your boat?" Fletch asked, looking down at Buddy's sour face. It reflected the pain of a damaged foot.

"Shit," Buddy said, so Fletch kicked the crushed arch.

Buddy yelped. "You can have the fuckin' boat. It's yours."

"Where is it?"

"Tied to a little dock just west of Ko Olina's M dock, Malakole Harbor."

"Great," Fletch said sarcastically. "You know where that is, Babe?"

"Sort of," Beth replied. "I think so."

"What's in the syringe?" He was looking at Carnation.

'I don't know," she answered. "Makes you sleepy or something, I guess."

"Well let's find out."

He sat next to her and looked into her eyes full of tears. She was wearing a loose white T-shirt over a bikini top. Taking the sleeve in his two hands he ripped it, exposing the shoulder.

"Beth, would you hand me that syringe, if you please?"

< 106 >

## Part two

## Big Surf

On the walls of Jay Paul's foyer, left and right of the door, were two huge images, leaving no doubt to the owner's passion.

One was a giant sepia-toned photo of Duke Kahanamoku standing on a beach in front of his solid redwood surfboard, twice as tall as himself, taken in 1921, the year after he won two Olympic gold medals in swimming.

The King of Surfing and his long board.

And directly across from the Duke, and about the same size, hung modern surfing's iconic image, the poster for the 1966 film, Endless Summer, a line resolution of a surfer with a short board held on his head. The background showed a huge yellow sun in an orange sky sinking into a hot pink sea. A simple graphic statement designed by John Van Hamersveld.

The history of surfing precedes the earliest history books. The Polynesians were surfing when early European sailors stumbled onto them in Tahiti in 1767. It was an important part of the Pacific Islanders' culture. The best surfers became the community leaders. It was their tradition.

In the early 1800's, missionaries came to Hawaii and began to discourage the native culture, surfing included. By the 1900's there were few surfers and scarcely anyone who knew the traditional methods of making a surfboard.

So, credit the Duke for keeping the old ways alive, where the ocean is life. Where the ebb and flow of water is the breathing of the sea. And where riding the wave is a spiritual connection to the culture and the history. A sacred ritual.

< 107 >

And credit *Endless Summer*, the Beach Boys music, and the California waves near places like Del Mar and Dana Point for the new breed of surfers. With boards made from styrofoam, resin, and fiberglass, shorter and lighter, surfing blossomed into a sport. It was the late 1960's and the 'Surf was Up.'

Jay Paul himself learned on a short board and loved showing off on California's waves. He followed the waves to Oahu where his mother and the big waves resided.

With maturity and a broken nose, some cracked ribs, and episodes of reef rash, he began to respect the Polynesian history and Zen-like quality, where surfing was more about bonding with the ocean and less about competition and cheap tricks.

For the really big waves he took pictures.

Photographing surfers became his new hobby. From the beach he shot a Cannon EOS 5 on a heavy tripod with a long lens. The biggest was a 600mm, his pride and joy.

In the water he used his Canon in a LiquidEye housing with the pistol grip, or his Hero 5 Go Pro waterproof camera designed specifically for surfing. After a few hard knocks he wore a helmet when he bobbed among the surfers, looking through his camera.

Jay Paul's private challenge was to get one of his photos on the cover of Surfer Magazine.

That, and resolve his frustrating marriage problem.

"So, JP, where are Car and Buddy this morning?"

"I sure don't know," Jay Paul said. "Car's been talkin' about going to see her mom in Kansas. Maybe she went, but I don't remember her making any specific plans."

"And Buddy?" It was Sammy asking. He was staying in a spare bedroom with his girlfriend. They had come for a week's vacation but extended it to a month. It had actually become three months so far.

"Buddy may still be asleep," Jay Paul said, "or last night he

< 108 >

may have slept elsewhere. I haven't talked to him either."

"Were they here yesterday?"

"Now you mention it, I don't remember ... we all had breakfast ... maybe that was the day before?"

"Anyway, they'll show up soon," Sammy said. "Always do."

It was early, shortly after dawn, and Jay Paul had eaten his banana and cereal, and had finished a second cup of coffee. The TV weather had predicted twenty-five-foot waves on the north shore for an early surfing contest. It had lured some big wave surfers world-wide.

For inspiration, the screen in the living room was playing the movie Blue Crush and Jay Paul had fast-forwarded to one of the good parts: a green swelling ocean, rising into a blue sky, almost filling the screen. At the top the monster began to curl over. It was as though you're looking into a throat full of water with foam teeth closing in on a tiny surfer racing across to avoid being swallowed up.

Finally, the curl closed over him and exploded into a sea of froth.

Jay Paul stood up. "That's enough incentive for today. Let's go surfing."

"Surf's up," Sammy said, trying to be cool.

"It won't be the huge walls yet, too early. You'll see them in December and January if you're still here. But it should be good.

"Your girlfriend coming?"

"She's still sleepin'. We'll leave her. She'll read or go shoppin'."

They were moving faster now, with purpose.

"Takin' the Caddy?" Sammy asked.

"Still in the shop," Jay Paul said. "Our boards are on the Subaru. Our pretend Woody. Camera gear is all loaded."

With Jay Paul in the driver's seat, they backed out and headed down the drive.

"Grab my cell and call Jif. Tell him we'll pick him up in seventeen and a half minutes."

< 109 >

"He'll meet us at the curb," Sammy reported, "wants to know if we're bringin' boards or just watchin' the contest?"

"Tell him, bring a board, in case we want to get wet. Caddy's still in the shop. Have him watch for the maroon car with the wooden doors. We'll be there in a minute."

Sammy hung up and, in a few minutes, the three friends headed to the North Shore.

< 110 >

# Coffee Break

Jake came back to Hawaii. It was for a serious meeting with Jeffrey McCumber and Bob Claymore at the Parker Ranch. Since Darcy was busy at work, he decided to make it a quick trip alone.

From Utah he flew to Seattle, slept in a motel, and got an early flight to Honolulu. Because of the time change he got there about mid-day.

After hours trapped in the seat-in-a-tube, the landing was applauded, and people began to stand.

"Please remain seated with your seat belts fastened until we get to the gate and the captain ..." flight attendant white noise.

The moment the door actually opened; the human crush began. Smell of warm, humid, floral Hawaiian air brought the knowledge that freedom was just twenty-six rows away and drawing closer.

Free at last, Jake stood in the airport lounge, wondering what to do. He had arranged to have supper with Suz and buy a small painting for Darcy that the gallery would ship. He had reservations for a morning flight to Hilo tomorrow.

He stared at the TV news playing in the corner.

Mainland winters meant snow, but on Oahu it brought world-class surf to the North Shore.

On the screen the news covered weather reports, and this time of year it began to include information on tides, phases of the moon, ocean currents, and anything else they could think of, information wise, concerning big surf. Besides sun and rain, the weathermen predicted the size of waves at the legendary beaches – Pipeline, Sunset, and all the rest.

Following the weather came a bedside interview with a surfer who had just broken his back, crushed between a big wave and

< 111 >

the sand ... He couldn't wait to get back on his board.

Just like skiers and bull riders back home, Jake thought. Youth ... so much to learn.

The television mentioned an early season surfing contest, happening today, followed by an interview with an Australian champion in town for the winter of big waves. Today they suggested 20 to 30 feet. The giants would come later; 40, 50, or 60 feet high.

Why not rent a car, drive north on the Veterans Memorial Freeway and take a look, Jake decided.

When he got to Haleiwa, the ocean was right in front of him. He turned into ponderous traffic. Going up north looked easy enough but coming south it was jammed. Apparently, the contests and the best waves were over.

In no particular hurry, Jake pulled into a parking lot and walked into a coffee shop.

He passed displays of packaged coffee and desserts on his left, little tables, stools, patrons, and windows on his right, as he went to the back of the room. There he ordered a chai latte, paid, and moved to the pick-up counter near the entrance.

There were several other people. One was waiting to place an order, others drinking, talking or watching the traffic outside.

Jake waited as a young woman with a fresh face made drinks.

Soon she announced: "Jake."

As he turned to pick up his order, he heard a commotion outside. There had been sirens and some shouting above the background sounds of too many cars and too many people. But now the loudest noise was very close. Just outside.

The door banged open, and a young man burst in. He had on a gray motorcycle helmet and an olive T-shirt.

"I'll shoot the first asshole that moves," he screamed. "Sit where you are, get on the floor ... you fuckers are hostages!"

He was extremely agitated, looking frantically at the startled customers. Waving the large Glock 21 almost carelessly.

< 112 >

He seemed trapped and confused.

Making his plan as he went. Playing it by ear. Desperate.

Jake was at the little counter near the door, directly behind the man. The store employee was in back of the counter. The latte, forgotten.

The gunman's attention was on his hostages. Clustered between chairs and little tables, they looked anxious and scared.

"Get the hell down," the helmet yelled, "right now. Be quick or I'll start shootin'."

He was shouting at people too frightened to move. Frozen.

Without thinking clearly Jake stepped beside the man who started to turn his way. Jake crouched slightly and hit him with all his might in the solar plexus. Fist slamming into lower abdomen just below the belt. Illegal in legitimate boxing, but effective none the less.

Surprised and stunned, unable to breathe, the fellow doubled over and sank to his knees. Jake pushed him onto his back on the floor.

Jake straddled him, pinning an arm down with his leg and body weight. The gun was still in his hand and Jake grabbed the weapon in one hand, the wrist in the other, trying to twist it away. But the pistol was held in a death grip.

Gasping and getting his breath back, strength returned fueled by adrenaline. Jake's adversary was presenting a major challenge. They struggled on the floor. The fellow was on his back, his mouth snarling and grimacing inside the helmet. His eyes were hidden behind a plastic bug shield and dark glasses.

Jake was still on top, but the element of surprise was long gone, and he was fighting a much younger man.

If he had another hand, he could pull those sinister fucking glasses off and smash that nose. Anything to get the rascal's attention off the gun.

I desperately need some fuckin' help here, he thought.

The customers had vanished out the door, but Jake was

< 113 >

not alone.

A Starbuck's green apron appeared over his shoulder and moved around trying not to get hit by the thrashing legs and elbows. She was young and quick with a coffee pot in her hand. Jake thought she was going to break it over the helmet.

Wrong.

She tried to pour it into the face, twisting side to side, a moving target.

She splashed it on a cheek, and it ran toward his ear. His face was rolling back and forth as she sloshed coffee on his nose. Hot coffee with that fresh roasted odor. Then coffee on his glasses and some more good, rich, Starbuck's coffee into his gagging mouth. He screamed, a horrible bubbling sound.

He released the weapon, and it clunked on the floor. Jake let him grab at his face, the gun forgotten.

The hostage taker was desperate to get his helmet off and Jake watched, stood up carefully, and with his toe slid the pistol far away from the spilled coffee, over to the wall behind the counter.

"Nice job," Jake said to the girl.

"That was six cups he got," she said. "... Well, I guess half of it went on the floor."

"You're quick and brave," Jake said. "My favorite waitress from now on."

"Not a waitress." She grinned at him. "I'm a barista. Lots of cowboys know that."

"Oops," Jake said. "Nice to meet a barista — my first and my favorite. I'm Jake."

Jake touched his hat brim.

"I'm Isabella but nobody ever calls me that."

"Oh yeah?"

"Usually they call me Honey, sometimes Izzy."

Their opponent started to gather his feet and get up, but Jake kicked his legs out from under him and he sat again, back against the counter. His butt in the coffee. He said nothing.

< 114 >

"Stay put," Jake told him, and Izzy handed him a towel.

"Blot, don't rub," she advised.

They were the only three in the room, but not for long. Outside a small crowd had collected, along with a couple of police cars.

It had been less than two minutes since the gunman entered and in two more seconds the door whipped open and a plain clothes officer arrived, gun in hand. He paused outside, peeked in, then entered carefully, pistol first.

"Is this our man on the motorcycle?" he asked quickly.

"He came with a gun and the helmet," Izzy said pointing at the man on the floor. "So, I guess so, your cyclist."

His helmet was nearby on its top, retaining about three inches of coffee.

A closet door opened in the back and another bright green apron cautiously emerged. She was another young woman who looked relieved and confused. She noticed the mess and went to get a mop.

Things had calmed down, but Jake's heart rate was still lively. The gunman was left sitting on the floor in the coffee, his hands cuffed behind him. He was smelling good but looking bad.

The little store filled rapidly with cops. The helmet and the Glock went into evidence bags.

The customers were now witnesses, being interviewed outside on the sidewalk. Names and phone numbers were written down. It was crowded out there with law officers, reporters, photographers and sight seers.

But inside Jake and Izzy were on stools talking to the officer who had been first to arrive.

The center of the ruckus was still on the floor, with his grey helmet gone, his red hair was exposed. His face had turned red and was getting even redder.

And his rights had been read.

When an officer squatted and invited him to explain things,

< 115 >

he said he wasn't ready. Getting his breath back and thinking more clearly now, he seemed rather belligerent.

Some medics helped him to his feet and took him to a chair where they spread goo on his face. He still declined to talk without an attorney, so one of the officers took him to a patrol car with a screened back seat and left him there to reflect on life's twists and turns.

With the medics and the perp gone, the crowd dispersed. And the police weren't far behind. They had another crime scene fifteen minutes away, up the highway, toward Pipeline Beach.

So, when his interview with the police was over, Jake sat and tried to calm himself, gather his wits, and drink his latte. Izzy had given him a fresh one. Said it was on the house.

His hat had received some coffee stains in the scuffle, and he was appraising the damage when two new detectives came in.

The younger one was in an aloha shirt and shorts. The older, an Asian man with a gray mustache, wore white shirt and slacks. Both wore clip-on identification and badges.

"Mind if we drink with you?" the young one asked.

"Have a seat," Jake offered.

This Starbucks was temporarily closed, but Izzy delivered some coffee like a real waitress. She had told her story to several officers and two reporters. She seemed to enjoy reliving the adventure, so she pulled up a stool and told the story again.

"What you did probably saved lives. That guy was wired crazy, and it easily could have gotten very bad," the young detective said.

"We wanted to say thanks. You're heroes. Mister Oar and Izzy Ward."

Jake winked at her. "She poured the coffee so Isabella is a barista and a hero."

She smiled at Jake, and then at the two detectives.

"I'm Clay Burnam and this is Mikio Iwasaki. We're from

< 116 >

Honolulu, on loan up here for crowd control, watching for trouble ... Where are you from, Mister Oar? You don't look like a surfer."

"No sir. Call me Jake, I'm from Utah."

"That hat suggests you are a rancher or horseman of some sort," said Clay.

"That's good detecting, detective." Jake said.

Clay had been raised in Elko, and they talked a little about his mainland roots. The subject rolled into horses and then to his love of Hawaii. Single and buying a home, he was settling down.

"Well, it's been an unusual day," said Mikio. "Guess we could check out and quit for the evening. We've been goin' since before dawn."

"I suppose," Clay agreed.

"Where are you stayin', Mister Oar?" Mikio asked.

"Motel in Honolulu. I fly away tomorrow."

"I have what might be an idea," Clay said. "We'll radio in and I'll check out, and you," — he looked at Mikio — "can fight this traffic jam over the mountain to supper with your wife. I'll buy our hero a beer and let him drive me to Honolulu and my car in the Federal Building garage."

"He knows me pretty well," said Mikio, glancing at Clay, then looking at Jake. "Not much for nightlife anymore. Maturity has made a homebody outta' me."

Do you have plans tonight, Jake?" Clay asked.

Jake smiled.

"I'm going to have a beer with you, then go by an art studio, select a painting on her computer, then meet the artist for supper at a Japanese restaurant.

"I could drop you off any step along the way. You could join us for supper if you like. The food and the painter are extra special."

Clay looked thoughtful.

"I don't want to mess in your romance," Clay said.

< 117 >

"No romance," Jake said. "You'll like her, I think. Old enough to be your grandma."

Jake smiled at Detective Iwasaki. "You and your wife could meet us for supper, too."

"Thanks, but no thanks," said Mikio. "You young folks go on and have your fun. We'll be in bed before your seaweed salad is gone." Mikio smiled. "I'd bet on it."

< 118 >

## Assassination Attempt

With beer on the monkeypod wooden slab bar in front of them, the two men talked, relaxed, and shared stories.

Clay had been dating stewardesses, a popular pastime for single men of marrying age on Oahu.

"Mostly," Clay said, "they're looking for a Delta Captain, but they're usually fun. Dating stews is almost a cliché over here. Romance is in the air every evening, and if one gets tired of you, she'll hand you off to a girlfriend."

Jake said, "Oh yeah?"

About twenty years older than Clay, romancing stews had never been on his radar. He thought, he probably had more in common with the older detective, Mikio, the homebody.

"How old do you think she was?" Clay asked.

"Who?"

"Your barista at Starbucks."

Jake thought for a moment. "Hmmm ... good question. Early to mid-twenties, I guess. A barista in full bloom."

"Was she wearing a ring?"

"Look at you, lonely old detective. You rascal," Jake grinned.

"I'm probably too old for her."

"Well, I got to know her pretty well," Jake lied. "Her being my barista and all, and she said she was definitely looking for a handsome detective to marry."

Jake gave Clay a self-satisfied smile.

"Seriously, did you see a ring?"

"Nope. And I bet one of the interviewing officers has her phone number."

They moved on. Clay talked about his youth in Northern Nevada. Some of it had been on horseback.

Jake talked about horses, explained cutting horses, the Parker Ranch, and the men he was meeting there.

Finally, Jake said, "Well, let's go check the traffic."

Once they were on the highway, Clay said, "Let me tell you what you'll see on the news tomorrow."

"Okay."

"When you wrestled that guy, you might have been surprised at how fast the law showed up," Clay began. "They had been chasing him.

"Because of the surfing contest, things up here were packed. Always are for the bigger surfing events. We saw thirty-foot waves earlier, or at least they seemed that big to me.

"Besides the people, there were extra cops, ambulances, medics, and news folks, cameras, and plenty of beer. By the time of your involvement, the mob was headed back south, cars inching along. Everybody going one way. Windows open, elbows out in the sun. That, or sealed up, with the air conditioning on.

"This motorcycle comes alongside these cars in the opposite direction, going north, in the open empty lane. Wearin' his helmet and a little mask, you know, like a Covid mask.

"When he gets to this one car, he stops and says a few words to the driver, who's sittin' there stuck in traffic. Then the guy sticks a pistol into the open window, starts shooting, inside the car, then speeds away.

"A bold assassination attempt, right? Lots of witnesses, but they're all stuck and can do nothing. He's goin' the other way with no traffic. Gone before anyone can react. His bike, nothing special about it. Gray helmet, face mask. Bug shield and sunglasses. Just another motorcycle in Hawaii. We got millions. Free — and gonna' be famous.

"A legend without a name."

Clay paused his story and took off his sunglasses.

"But what actually happened," Clay said, "a little way farther up, a frustrated motorist is maneuvering his car around trying to get loose of the traffic, wants to go back north, the other way.

< 120 >

And he gets his nose into the open, backs up a little to get a better angle, then pulls into the empty road ahead of our shooter.

"A lot of screeching and swearing and more witnesses. Scratches on the car and a bent fender. Our excited biker changes plans and escapes back down the empty lane goin' the wrong way. South.

"With all these witnesses, each with a cell phone, and lots of law around, and plenty of cameras and newsmen: well, that's the parade of sirens and cops that ended up at your Starbucks."

Jake took his eyes off the road and focused on Clay.

"Holy cats," he said.

"Mikio and I saw none of this. We were too far north, but when we got the call, we raced to the murder scene in time to see an ambulance loading the shooting victims. Found out it was no murder, only a murder attempt. We got some witness names, enough to keep us busy for a while. Then we heard about your adventure with the perp, and we rushed to your Starbucks."

Clay paused, then: "That's what you'll see on the news tomorrow."

Jake looked at Clay again, the jungle flying past behind him in the early evening light.

"Hawaii's idea of road rage?" Jake asked.

"I expect tomorrow Mikio and I, and probably others, will interview the young chap you punched."

"Guy so mad he just decided to shoot people? Pick a car, any car?" Jake guessed.

"Well," Clay said, "it could be exactly like that. But it was a distinctive car. A specific car. A maroon Subaru that looked like a woody. A rather new car, fit with clever decals making it look kinda' like a 1948 Ford surf wagon. A woody. It looked like the doors and back end were wood, but they weren't.

"Shooter that hates wood? A tree hugger? That's nuts."

"Lots of possibilities. It's all conjecture now, but this is what keeps the job interesting." Clay said.

< 121 >

# Keilani's Test

After a quick stop by the studio at the jungle's edge, Clay and Jake saw Suz, and selected a small painting for Darcy. Then they followed Keilani and the artist to a hidden Japanese sushi bar famous for tonkatsu.

All four ate the tonkatsu hungrily. It was Jake's first meal since breakfast in Seattle, a stingy snack somewhere high above the Pacific Ocean, and some pretzels with Clay. This was the first of that delicious pork cutlet and cabbage since he was last in Hawaii. He hoped he wasn't making a pig of himself.

Keilani looked great in a white silk shirt and a long-flowered skirt. A pink flower rested in her black hair, zaftig and exotic. A Polynesian princess. She smiled easily, often aimed at Clay.

She looked at Clay. "You like it?"

"Delicious," Clay said.

"I'll order some more," said Suz. And she did.

"You like sushi, Detective Clay?" asked Keilani.

"Sure," he said, carefully ... "depends ... sushi was something I'd never tried till I got here."

"Well, ladies and gentlemen," Keilani continued, "Let's test our guest on unagi."

"Two orders will give a piece for each of us." Suz said and nodded at someone, and the blonde waitress appeared.

When the unagi came Clay took his piece and caught the Polynesian woman watching him. Juicy eel sleeping on a bed of white rice, a tiny seaweed safety belt holding them together. It was one bite for everyone but Clay, who took his in two.

"Sweet and delicious," he said, and Keilani gave a little squeal. "Don't tell him what it was," she demanded.

Clay had several exotic culinary experiences that evening. The last one was uni, a soft mushy yellowish thing fenced in by

< 122 >

a dark crunchy green wall holding the sticky rice that supported the meat.

"Take it in one bite," Keilani ordered.

Clay did and smiled at the taste.

"That's the final test," Keilani announced. She stood up and, with a rather sultry grin at Clay, reached somewhere, maybe a pocket in her skirt, pulled out a card, and handed it to him.

"Congratulations," she said.

It had one of Suz's painting, and on the other side, some lettering that read, 'ARTISTS MODEL', over very small type: 'nude or otherwise'. And there was a phone number.

Clay turned it over and looked at the painting again. It was Keilani, of course, naked, with a flower in her hair. Clay didn't know what to say. After a moment he said, "Thanks."

They discussed food, and later Clay told of the motorcycle-riding shooter, his capture, and Jake's heroics at the North Shore coffee shop.

"I'm sure there'll be more news after the investigation," he said.

"You said the car had wooden doors, like an antique?" Suz asked.

"We'll track it down," Clay said. "The fake wood looked like a decal designed to fit the shape of those particular doors and back end. It was cleverly done."

Later, in the parking lot, they split up and said goodbyes.

"Jake," Suz said, "I'll call Ann tomorrow and the painting you picked will be on its way to Utah. Thanks."

There were hugs and kisses.

"I love you, cowboy," Suz said. "Bring Darcy next time. Don't forget."

As they drove away Clay asked, "By the way, Jake, how old do you think that Keilani girl is?"

"Gosh, I think she's just right." he smiled.

< 123 >

# Hospital Interview

Jay Paul Gottlieb was sitting up in his hospital bed looking perky. The top of his shoulder and the side of his neck were wrapped with a bulky padded bandage that restricted some movement. Breakfast had been eaten; the tray pushed aside.

"Morning, Mister Gottlieb, how are you feeling?" Mikio said.

"Pretty good, considering. My shoulder hurts a little."

"I'm Mikio Iwasaki, and this is Clay Burnam. We're detectives investigating your ... incident."

"I thought you guys might be doctors. The nurse thinks I might be going home today."

"Well, we talked to one of your doctors who said you are doing okay. The bullet missed any bone, just tore muscle and may have hit a nerve. You might need some rehab later. He'll talk to you about it."

Mikio took off his necktie, folded it carefully, and put it in a jacket pocket. "Would you like more coffee?" he asked.

"No thanks, I'm fine."

"We're here to talk about what happened. Do you feel like talking?"

"Sure," Jay Paul said. "I'm a bit drugged up on meds, but I can talk. You can call me JP."

"Take your time and tell us the whole story then, please."

"Okay," Jay Paul said. "Here we go ...

"We went early to the big wall surfing contest, and I set up my stuff and took pictures. They hyped it as big wall, but it wasn't really big. Garage door size. Really big surf comes next month.

"My pals, Sammy and Jif, watched a while. None of us got our boards wet. Unusual, 'cause we do surf a lot.

"The waves were big at first, I think maybe nearly twenty-feet. And, except for at the contest, there were too many people in the water. Tourists, amateurs, haoles, goofballs fighting for the next

< 124 >

wave ... then too scared to take it when it came. A traffic jam of wanna-be's bobbing on the ocean like ducks.

"So, we just watched surfers, bikinis, and waves. With my long lens, it's almost like being out there with 'em anyway."

Mikio seemed to think this might be a long story and asked, "Mind if we sit down?"

"Sure, guys." He pressed a button on a white cord.

The head of a nurse popped in with a bright expression.

"Nurse, could you get these gentlemen some coffee and another chair?"

In a moment the detectives were seated, sipping and listening. The remains of Jay Paul's breakfast had disappeared.

"So anyway, you know, we had some beer and hot dogs for lunch. The real pretty early light was gone so I kinda' sat with those guys in the sand watching. And it was good watchin', too.

"But about one-thirty we got to thinking, the biggest waves were gone and maybe we'd beat the crowd back to the city. I gathered my camera stuff, loaded, and off we go. But everyone else had the same idea at the same time.

"Contest was at Pipeline, and so when we realized traffic was so bad, we could have stopped and surfed at Waimea, Kawiloa, Hale'iwa, or anywhere in between. Hell, we could've done anything and probably missed gettin' shot."

The detectives nodded to that.

"Uh huh," Clay said. "Probably right."

"So, we're sittin' in shitty traffic headed south and this motorcycle is comin' slowly north. Not real slow, but they usually go zippin' along; this one is just comin' regular speed and slows down and starts lookin' at our car. Then he glides to a stop and looks in.

"Sammy's drivin' 'cause I've been studying the pictures on the back of my camera. Some of the ones with the early light are beautiful and kinda' unusual.

"The camera's over there in that bag in the corner. I can show you a couple if you're interested. They really are worth a look."

Jay Paul looked at his visitors.

"Maybe later," Mikio said.

"Okay," Jay Paul nodded. "Anyway, this guy looks at Sammy and says, kinda' quiet, 'You Jay Paul?' And Sammy says 'Huh,' you know, surprised at the question, and I look over in time to see his pistol as he shoots Sammy right in the face. Then it was like once he's shootin', he can't stop and real quick shoots me and then shoots a bunch into the back seat."

Jay Paul looked at both detectives.

"That's the story," he said. "Want more coffee?"

Always the good host.

"Well," said Clay, "guess it wasn't random road rage."

"No road rage about it," said Jay Paul. "I can save you guys some time. I know exactly who did it."

"Exactly who?" Mikio asked.

"My wife."

"You're sure?" Clay wondered.

"She hates me. Married two and a half years. She wants a divorce and so do I. Two weeks of passion and two years of hell. Divorce is fine with me, but with lawyers charging by the hour, she wants to drag it out till I'm broke and dead."

The same nurse came in then, with more coffee.

"Aloha," Clay said as she handed him a fresh cup. Her smile was generous, and he tried to guess her age.

"Tell us about the divorce," Mikio asked.

"Well, the woman is completely unreasonable, so she keeps the lawyers busy trying to settle, trying to draw everything out. The attorneys on both sides know she's batshit crazy, but she won't let it stop.

"And she's making a career out of hurting me every way she can. She poisoned my dog, sunk my boat, cut up my art collection, till I changed the locks at home.

"Her hate has made her nuts," he said, winding down.

< 126 >

"Now she's shot my friends."

"You're saying she hired the motorcyclist that shot you?"

"Yes I am. Can't be anyone else."

"Any idea who the actual shooter was? The guy she hired?" Clay asked.

"Fuckin' asshole was an amateur. Little black mask like he's still scared of Covid. Shit. She probably found him in a hole somewhere. Under a rock. Amateur. Bet she didn't pay much. Bitch loves to spend my money, thinks she knows quality when she sees it, but she really doesn't know shit from Shinola."

"How do you suppose he knew what car you'd be in and where and when?"

"I've been thinkin' about that all night. It's easy. She knows me and it would be a good guess I'll be at the big wave contests. She knows my cars. She ruined my black Caddy with her hammer a while back, so the choice was the Ferrari or the Subaru Woody. She knows I never put the roof rack on the Italian car. She knew it would either be Buddy's van we'd go in, or the Subaru.

"My driveway curves down through trees and bushes, and there's a place she could sit in her car and look down through the trees and see cars leaving my house. I can't see her 'cuz she's on the road above me behind the bushes and I gotta be lookin' at the sharp curve.

"The Subaru has an unusual paint job that made it look like a forty-eight Ford Woody, so it would be easy to spot. She could report it to her assassin, and he could watch for it.

"Another way could have been a little Apple device planted under the car that tracks it and tells where it is, but I'm thinkin' she's way too fuckin' dumb and crazy to do that.

"Ugh ... worst marriage in history," said Jay Paul.

"We'd better talk to her," said Mikio. "How would we find your wife?"

"The bitch lives in my beach house and drives my silver Porsche, so she should be easy to track down. Her name is Beth, but that's not what I call her.

"I have a private eye supposed to be watching her, but I guess she slipped through his fingers. For names and phone numbers you can call my secretary, Carnation. If you call my home, she'll answer, or call you back. She may be out of town, but she's probably back by now. Never stays gone too long.

"You can get me on my cell unless I'm doin' something. You guys can take one of my cards. They're in the little pocket on the side of the smaller camera bag, over there." He gestured with his good arm. "I could show you a couple pictures?"

When they were outside the room, Clay looked at Mikio. "Man, Royal Hawaiian treatment. Hospitality like a grand hotel. Nurses serve coffee. I'm a long way from Elko. ... Aloha."

They headed for lunch, and as they walked out the main door Mikio said, "Over here, Clay," pointing to a huge plaque honoring hospital donors. One of the large names near the top was Henrietta and Jay Paul Gottlieb.

"Well, that explains something," said Clay. "I suppose Henrietta is his mother?"

"Bet on it," said Mikio.

Sammy and Jif shared a hospital room just down the hall from Jay Paul. After lunch, the detectives interviewed Jif, who had been dodging lead in the back seat during the fracas. He'd been struck by three bullets, one in the thumb, one in the ear lobe, and one near the elbow. But he couldn't add much new information to Jay Paul's story.

And then they saw Sammy. The bullet went into his mouth and out his cheek. It broke his jaw, so he could only grunt at their questions. He would need dental surgery, as well as everything else. His head was so bandaged he looked like a mummy.

Nothing new there.

< 128 >

## Good Cop, Bad Cop

Clay and Mikio had the red-headed man, Alfred McGriffin, and his rap sheet. There had been drug arrests and convictions, and he'd served time. Also, grand theft auto, and some misdemeanors.

"Put your hands through here," Clay said.

He stuck his hands through the opening, and Clay cuffed him. The three of them started down the hall.

"Where we goin'?" Alfred asked.

"Interview room to talk to your lawyer," Clay said.

He opened the door and pushed the man in. Mikio shut it behind them with a metallic click.

"Ain't talkin' to you, peckerhead, nor that yellow nigger neither."

"Sit over there behind the table," Mikio said quietly.

Clay glared at him for four seconds before he said, "Sit."

"Put out your hands in the middle of the table please."

Clay sat opposite and reached for the wrists, staring into the hostile eyes, unblinking. He brought out a key, unlocked one wrist, passed the empty cuff through a big steel ring bolted between them, and then re-cuffed the hand, all without looking anywhere but into those stormy orbs.

The detectives left the room and tickled a computer until their prisoner appeared on the screen.

"I don't think playin' good cop bad cop is gonna get us anywhere with this guy," said Clay.

"Bet you're right," said Mikio. "Think I'll focus on bad cop all the way."

"I guess what we really want to know is who hired him," Clay said.

"And all the details," said Mikio. "But I bet his defender won't let him talk ... at least not yet."

Mikio proved right. They learned nothing. After the lawyer left, they took him back to the holding cells where a young uniformed officer said, "I'll take care of him from here."

Mikio shook his head. "I got him, want to tell him aloha."

Alone with the prisoner outside the cell, Mikio said quietly, "We don't use racial slurs in this building," and they stepped together into the cell. The red headed prisoner held his hands out and the older man removed the handcuffs.

"Nice talking to you, fuckhead yellow nigger," he said, rubbing his wrists.

Mikio hit him so hard and fast his legs melted.

Later that day Mikio called the Honolulu DA.

"When you talk to the public defender in the case of Alfred McGriffin vs humanity, you'll hold all the cards. We'll have his fingerprints on the gun, ballistics, and eyewitnesses from the shooting scene, eyewitnesses to the bike hitting car fiasco, eyewitnesses to the hostage situation at the coffee shop. So, there's not much they can negotiate.

"But what we need is who hired him to kill Jay Paul. Anything you can find out in that regard would really be appreciated."

When Mikio hung up, he was hopeful. Then he called the guys going over the vehicle.

"Funny they got shot in a car with a wood decal on it," the lab officer said. "Pretty unique.

"We're not through with it yet, but we found four slugs, 45 caliber, and we discovered an Apple Air Tag under a floor mat. We'll buzz you if we get anything else interesting, but I think that's mostly it. Some blood, of course, and the blood types match the victims. We dusted for prints around the driver side window where the shooter stuck his head in, but got nothing good."

"Well, now I bet we probably know how the shooter knew when and where to find his target," Mikio said.

< 130 >

## Clay's Responsibility Now

Mikio and most of the department had signed out and gone. Clay remained to clear up a couple of things and in twenty minutes he was done. His desk was clean except for one piece of paper.

'Walter Abbott' it said and included a phone number.

Clay picked up his phone.

"Walter Abbott, please."

"This is Walter here."

"Walter, this is officer Clay Burnam from the Honolulu Police Department."

"Been expecting you'd call," Walter said, "Polanski told me you'd be handling things from now on."

"I guess I'll be your local contact," Clay said. "Sound okay to you?"

"Sure. It's not really up to me, you know. I'm just trying to live a simple retirement in paradise. Less connections I have with the past the better."

"Well, Polanski said I should help you if you need it, steering you on the straight and narrow. This is new to me, outside anything I've done or heard about, so I guess we'll learn together.

"He said you'd been suffering 'Island Fever.' That might have been why he thought a local would understand better. They don't catch that in LA."

"It passed," Walter said. "it's gone. I'm well now."

"So how shall we proceed?" Clay asked.

"Well," Walter said, "you could call me in about ten years, and I'll tell you if I got the fever or not. How about that?"

"I had the feeling Polanski wanted a little shorter leash than that." Clay glanced at his holster and pistol hanging nearby.

"Suppose I buy you a beer and we meet somewhere?" Clay said.

"Let's have lunch on your expense account," Walter suggested.

"All right. Are you free tomorrow?"

"I'm always free. I'm retired. Remember?"

The next day they sat on a bench together at Sand Island State Park between the city and Waikiki, with burgers and Cokes.

They made small talk as they chewed and sipped. Finally, Clay turned toward Walter, leaned back, and crossed his legs.

"I'm from Elko," Clay said, getting to it. "How about you?"

"South Salt Lake."

"Ever been to Elko?"

"Sure."

"Lotta people pass through, but most don't stop." Clay prompted. "Except for gas."

"Uh huh."

"Did you ever stop?"

"Sure, plenty of times," Walter said.

"What made you stop?"

"Cuttin' cows. There was a cuttin' in Elko and one in Winnemucca, and sometimes at a ranch in the Ruby Valley."

"I worked a couple high school summers at the Winecup Ranch north of the Ruby's." Clay said.

"Did you cowboy there?" Walter seemed to be warming to the conversation a little.

"Nope. I wish," Clay said. "I welded broken machinery and washed cowboys' dishes when the wagon was out."

"I heard that ranch is huge, fifty miles across."

"The name now is Winecup Gamble, and it was almost a million acres, but not quite. Many decades ago, the old Winecup was owned by Jimmy Stewart, or at least I think I heard that. One of those old movie stars, anyway," Clay said. "Way before my time."

There was a pause, and they looked at the ocean.

"What brought you here?" Walter asked. "This is a long way from Elko."

< 132 >

"I don't know. Wanted to see the world, I guess. Elko's a very small town. After high school I had to go somewhere."

"I understand."

"So, Walter, how did you get interested in cutting horses?"

"Skiing and horses were my passions as a kid. Those, and girls. But I was never good at girls. Anyway, can I be frank?"

Clay looked him in the eye.

"You're being awfully friendly," Walter said, "and I've never seen a friendly cop before. So maybe I should limit my history to when I came to Hawaii, about two and a half years ago. My Hawaiian birthday."

"Okay," Clay said. "You're not what I expected either."

"What did you expect?"

"Not sure. Jerky movements, shifty eyes. Guess I was hoping for someone more sinister. Are you packin' heat?"

"Course not. I'm retired." Walter paused, glancing at the detective's loose-fitting aloha shirt. "Are you?"

Clay smiled at Walter. They sat quietly a while.

"One last question," Clay said, "Who knows you're here?"

"You mean from the old days on the mainland?"

"Uh huh."

"Not many. Polanski, of course, and his partner in LA, and back home, he told me, a Kamas Valley sheriff, Marv Thompson, and Jake Oar. Nobody else, unless they spread it around.

"I guess Jake's wife probably knows," Walter sad. "The less the better for me."

"Well, Walter, it's been nice to meet you. Keep my number and call me whenever you like. Good luck with your new life and let me know if I can help."

"You're single?" Walter asked.

"Afraid so."

"Maybe I'll invite you to supper sometime, if you can keep the conversation current. My girlfriend is a pretty fair cook, but she doesn't know I existed before I was re-born in Hawaii a few years ago."

"Well," Clay said, "It's back to work for me. We'll stay in touch."

At his desk Clay put Walter's phone number in a small box with other numbers not related to specific cases in progress.

There was a business card in there that jumped out at him. He looked at it and put it on top of Walter's number. Looking up at him, a naked Polynesian woman was inviting him to call.

< 134 >

## Missing Secretary

Y ou forget how important your secretary is until you lose her."
Jay Paul was speaking to Jif and Sammy. All three shooting
victims sat around the living room in their various bandages,
looking out at a moody ocean pressed under a sullen sky. The
future was way out there, a silver sliver of sunlight at the horizon.

"I really hope she gets back soon. I know I'm supposed to be
doing something somewhere, but without her I don't know
where, what, or when."

"Where'd she go anyhow?" Jif asked.

"Hell, if I know," Jay Paul said. "Sure as hell, I just don't
know. I'd call her mom if I had the number. She might have gone
there. Wherever it is, she's not answering her cell phone and
I can't leave a message 'cause her mailbox is full.

"Fucking mechanical voice doesn't even say 'goodbye.' Just
'click'."

"Could be she's with Buddy?"

"Sure, could be. But his cell phone, you get the same 'mailbox
full', fuck you very much, Click."

Jay Paul looked at Sammy, who shrugged his shoulders.

"Well, shit, she should have check it in."

"Expect they're off the island, one-way or another, because
our shooting was all over the news here and they would have
called to see if we were all right."

Jay Paul looked at the weather. "Together or separately, they
would have called."

"Maybe we should report them missing," Jif said, "It's been ...
what? Three or four days."

"Best idea I've heard lately. I definitely will." Jay Paul said.

< 135 >

# Back to the Big Island

On Hawaii, the Big Island with the temperamental volcano, Jake lolled around all afternoon in one of the Parker Ranch guesthouses wishing Darcy were with him. But by the time he completed a long walk on the beach, it was time to put his boots on and head for supper, a short stroll up the coast. He arrived ten minutes early, but Jeffrey and Allie McCumber were waiting in the bar with Bob Claymore.

After 'howdy do-s' all around, handshaking, and a hug from Allie, they sat around a tiny table chatting over cocktails.

"Suz called us, said you were a hero at a big wave contest," Jeffrey said. "Once again your fame precedes you."

"Hmm."

Jake took off his hat and looked for a place to put it. The table was too small, but he could pull over an empty chair. The others kept theirs on, so he ignored his mother's training and wore it. Chivalry had become quaint.

"So, you-all will be in Texas for The Futurity?" Jake asked.

"Guy with a pistol takin' hostages at Starbucks, and you punched him out." Jeffery said.

"Wasn't a fair fight, a sucker punch below the belt."

"Sounds heroic to me," Bob said.

"Barista was the hero." Jake smiled. "She poured expensive coffee in his face till he surrendered the gun. A team effort."

A waitress helped Jake change the subject.

"Your table is ready, folks," she said.

After supper they talked about young horse prospects that would be auctioned off in Fort Worth.

Allie ordered a dessert and Bob had a fresh Scotch over ice.

"Jake," Bob said, "we'll be beside you at The Futurity two-year-old sales, and I'll get us seats for the final's weekend.

< 136 >

During the days you can tour us around your cutting pals, ranches, farms, and facilities."

"Sounds great."

"Jeffery has sale catalogues for the various horse sales, and maybe you could help him mark potential prospects to watch for. We think we're getting to know bloodlines pretty well, but your knowledge is a lot deeper."

"That could be our evening's entertainment after supper tonight." Jake said. "More fun than watchin' television alone."

"Sounds great," Jeffery said.

"And here's something new to think about," Bob said.

"Maybe we could get a real solid older horse, bring it here, and set up a little daily demo for tourists. Make it sort of educational. Explain the sport and basic rules. Maybe somebody narrates our little demo, step-by-step, as a cow is set up and being worked. Toward the end the rider pulls off the bridle and cuts one like that."

"I could narrate," Allie said. "Ain't nobody seen more cuttin' than me. An I'll do it with an authentic Texas accent."

"Dang Honey, I believe you really could," her husband said. "But nobody's gonna' understand you but me."

"I kinda' think the Texas atmosphere would be more important than the lost information," Bob said. "It'll add a lot to the ambience. Sell more tickets for the trail rides. Probably sell more barbecue also."

"What you think, Jake?"

"I like it," Jake said. "I like the idea and the accent, too."

Later, when the conversation began to wane, Bob said, "We'll meet at my office tomorrow morning and go over our agreement. Then, we'll walk around the village and point and look where we might set everything up — pens, viewing area, parking, and all the rest."

"How early do you want to start?" Jake asked.

"Any time you get there, you must be tired from travel and

being heroic, so sleep in. We usually start pretty early around here."

"Is seven too early?"

"No, we could manage."

"Okay," Jake said. "Sometime before eight."

"You won't need a car, Jake, we'll have one waiting for you."

I'll be ready at seven in front of this hotel, breakfast eaten, with a coffee to go." Jake grinned and they all got up.

Allie took Jake's arm. "Bet aw could narrate an' ride a dang hoss both at da' same dang time."

"I have no doubt," Jake said.

< 138 >

# Torso from the Cold Room

It was during the early morning detectives' meeting when Mikio and Clay were officially assigned to the torso that had been in the cold room drawer.

They were informed that she was now in the hands of the scientists trying to answer the basic questions: who was she, when and how did she die, how long did she spend in the water, and anything else helpful. They would get DNA, X-ray her teeth and check dental records, and try to identify her.

That was about the extent of the meeting's focus on the torso. They moved on to other crimes.

Regarding the attempt to assassinate Jay Paul, ballistics had checked out, witnesses' statements collected, the case was solid. Who had hired the shooter was still unknown. But speculation was on Jay Paul's wife, Beth.

Other cases were discussed, and notes compared. Sharing information could sometimes help in unexpected ways.

Clay and Mikio pricked up their ears when they listened to an officer's report of an apparently abandoned fishing boat. It had been tied in a remote part of a seldom-used harbor and had a parking violation ticket on it, showing that it was first reported illegally tied two weeks earlier. About the time the torso may have gone in the water.

After the meeting broke up, Clay got a copy of the ticket and requested the boat be retained right where it was as evidence.

On the phone Mikio contacted the officer who wrote the ticket. After salutations Mikio asked his questions.

"Did you respond to a call mentioning the boat, or did you stumble onto it?"

"As I recall, there was a lady who called the police about an abandoned boat that some local kids were playing on. She thought it looked dangerous — you know how some mothers are —

and she wanted it removed. It's in an area with very little traffic around. If a kid got hurt, there are no grown-ups to see.

"I checked it out, but it didn't look any more dangerous than the boats we played on as kids. So, I put that ticket on it so the owner would move it. Thought I'd check back in a week and see if it was gone. It's still there, so I turned it in, to get it moved. It's got a number, so it could probably be traced."

"Fine work," Mikio said. "How do I find it?"

Mikio wrote down the information and asked, "Can you give me the name and number of the woman who first called you?"

"I'll have to text it to you when I check in ... or better yet, I'll call in and ask our secretary to find it and text you. That'll be quicker."

"Thanks," said Mikio.


Clay and Mikio took a drive to find the boat. Out the Queen Liliuokalani Freeway they went toward Makakilo City, got off, and headed south. After about twenty minutes of following directions they found the boat, a weathered Bertram 33 Sport Fisherman, tied up with a parking ticket taped where it wouldn't be missed by anyone stepping aboard.

They appraised it from the outside and decided it was probably seaworthy, since it was afloat. But it appeared to have been neglected recently.

"It doesn't sparkle like the boats in the popular harbors," said Clay, the observant dry lander. The haole.

"Yep." Mikio, older and wiser in things Hawaiian. "When they first get 'em they spend every weekend polishin' them. After a few years they get a new hobby, and the boat starts lookin' like this." Words from the kamaaina. The 'old timer'.

"Uh huh."

"It's neglected, but this one still has way too much value to be abandoned. I bet if we leave it alone for another week or two, the owner will come back."

< 140 >

"Uh huh." Clay said again.

"Bet it's worth a couple hundred thousand if it got spruced up a little," Mikio said. "Probably more if the engine starts."

"This could be the murder boat," Clay speculated out loud, "where our torso took her last ride."

"Guess we could step aboard," Mikio said, "kids been playing in there and a couple weeks of wind and weather."

The detectives pulled on plastic gloves, stepped over the side into the stern, and investigated the cabin, careful not to touch anything. It was very compact in there; a tiny head, tiny galley, two tiny benches, and a tiny table. Squeezed into the bow were two tiny bunks covered by aluminum rod fittings and rolled up blue canvas. Probably parts for the upper deck sunshade.

"Pretty intimate in there," Clay observed.

A sloping ladder with handrails led to the upper deck and a mounted captain's chair.

They saw no signs of a scuffle, noticed no blood smears, no damaged railing or torn canvas. No spilled drinks. No bag of any kind. No wallet or personal effects.

This boat was hiding her secrets.


Mikio's phone rang, and he got the name and address of the woman who had reported the boat. Google showed them she wasn't too far away.


She invited them in and offered coffee.

"No thank you, Mrs. Smithfield. We just want to ask you about the boat."

"Well, sure you do. We are going to have a child drown around here pretty soon. Kids are completely reckless these days, and their parents just don't care. I guess they think what the heck, if we lose one, we can always make more."

"When did you first see the boat?" Mikio asked.

"Are you fellows sure you don't want some coffee? I just have

< 141 >

to warm it up."

"No thanks, ma'am."

"Well, I was walking with my friend Jean, and we usually go through the neighborhood, but we decided to go look at the water. We need exercise, so we went the long way and that's why we passed the boat. We'd gone that way before and there had never been a boat there.

"Well, not never, but certainly not often and almost never — and certainly not this boat."

"When was this walk?" Mikio asked.

"Well, I'm not sure. A couple weeks ago, I guess. We called the nice officer right away. Children were skateboarding close to the boat and if one slipped, he could be tangled in rope and in the water under the boat in no time.

"We changed our route so we could make sure the boat got removed, but it never did. It really is a danger zone. Those little fellers go speeding around there every day and we're going to lose one soon."

"On your walks past the boat, have you ever seen people on it, or anything out of the ordinary?" Clay asked.

"No, I'm sorry, sir, not on it. Actually, nobody's ever out there except the children."

"Have you seen children playing on the boat?"

"Well, of course, they play on it! That's what children do. Play on things. You know, play pirates and such. Remember when you were little, weren't you a pirate?"

"No ma'am," Clay said. "I played cowboys."

"But," Mikio said, "did you actually see any kids on the boat, playing or looking around?"

"Maybe I didn't actually see them, but I know kids. They can't resist a chance to get hurt."

Clay nodded, and Mikio smiled.

"What time of day do you make your walks and check on the boat?"

< 142 >

"Well, Jean gets off work about five and is home by nearly five thirty, so we walk about then. I suppose we're looking at the parking ticket just about four minutes after six."

She produced a wrinkled smile and touched her gray hair.

"Sure you don't want some coffee?"

"No, but thanks," Mikio said. "I'm afraid we will have to mark your boat with crime scene tape, and have our lab guys examine it."

"You mean my boat is solving a crime?" She was invigorated by the thought and leaned forward.

"Well, we don't know, but you never know until you look," Mikio said. "Then we'll try to get it removed for you."

"Is it a murder mystery?"

"No ma'am, it's just somebody's lost boat. We're trying to find the owner, that's all."

The detectives stood.

"Thank you, Mrs. Smithfield, you've been a big help," said Mikio. "We need more citizens like you."

Clay said, "Thanks ma'am," and they left.

In the car Clay smiled at Mikio. "She's too old for me, huh?"

His partner laughed, "You bet," he said, "by forty years."

Mikio, serious now. "I could fix you up with a Delta stew if you're getting lonely?"

"No thanks, maybe later."

## Skateboarders

Four minutes after six, Clay was sitting within sight of the boat wrapped in yellow crime-scene tape. This held true for three days in a row, usually arriving about a quarter of six and leaving about six-thirty or seven.

Mid-watch on the first day he got a call.

"Hi Clay, how's it goin' in Honolulu?"

"Jake? Zat you?"

"Yup."

"How's our hero?"

"Fine. I'm stoppin' in your town tomorrow and thought if you're not busy, maybe I'd buy you supper."

"Great. I'm hungry already."

"So, here's my plan. I talked to Suz and she found some slack-key guitar music for our entertainment. Haoles can't usually find it, but she uses the coconut wireless, and it'll be in a residential carport near Kalaepohaku Park, north of Diamond Head.

"I'll take you to dinner somewhere, and you can fill me in on all the adventures in your crime wave and tell me if you dated my barista yet. We can go to your favorite restaurant or decide as we go.

"Then we'll go see the garage band in a carport, and Suz might join us there, if she can. She sounded like she wants to, and my experience with her says she usually gets what she wants."

"I'm up for any food," Clay said. "We can see what looks good with no waiting."

On the second day, hoping to catch the skateboarders, Jake was with him in what the police called a 'ride-along.' When six-thirty arrived with still no kids, they moved on to supper at the Angry Mexican, where Suz joined them for dessert and two hours of Slack-Key strumming and deep raspy singing.

< 144 >

Jake was in his motel bed by ten-thirty and Clay in his own bed thinking of Keilani. It was well after midnight when Clay awoke, riding a subway through heartburn city. Revenge of the angry Mexican.

On the third day watching the boat, a few minutes after six, Clay heard the distant rolling thunder of skateboards. Metal rollers on concrete. As he watched, five kids weaved toward him.

He waved and yelled.

"Hey! Hey, guys," he called, and stepped in their path.

There was plenty of space and they did some clever footwork and tricky swirls and stops as they collected near him. They were pre-teens, four boys and a dark-haired girl.

When he had their attention, he asked: "Guys, what's with this boat?"

"What you mean, mister?" one boy asked.

"Well, kids, I want to know all about it. Like, when did it come here and whose is it?"

These kids seemed curious and almost innocent. Too young to have developed the inner-city hostility and smart mouths reserved for strange haoles.

"Is it your boat, mister?"

"No, I'm afraid not."

"I'd like to go fishin' on that boat," said a boy in a blue jacket.

"Me too," came from two little voices at once.

"Well," Clay said, "first I gotta' find the owner before I can ask him if we can get a ride."

"Oh."

"So that's why I want to know if any of you have seen people on that boat."

"There were two guys on it yesterday."

"When was that?" Clay asked.

"Morning." The little girl looked around. "I skipped school," she said proudly. She glanced at Clay and smiled.

"Two guys, dressed kinda' funny. They had a white van parked right here," and she pointed.

"They were lab workers, gathering evidence," Clay explained.

"Like on TV?"

"Sort of," Clay said. "Did you see people on the boat any other time? Looking at it, or getting on or off?"

"I saw 'em," she said.

Her friends turned to look at her.

"I was far away." She pointed at some trees.

"They were getting out of a car and staggering around, stumbling into each other. Drunk as you could imagine. My dad would say they were wasted. Could hardly stand. Had to help each other onto the boat. There was some falling over, too."

"I didn't know you saw that," said the boy in the blue jacket.

"I told Bobby," she said.

"Why didn't you tell us?"

"I forgot."

"When was this?" Clay asked.

"Let me see," posing like an adult, finger under her chin. "About two weeks ago. About sunset."

"Do you remember anything about them?" Clay wanted to know.

"Naw, too far away and the sunset made it hard to see good ... two men, one of 'em was pretty big and two girls. Sloppy drunk, I could tell."

"Could you hear what they said?"

"Naw, just gruntin' and groanin'."

"And this was about two weeks ago?"

"It was the day after the boat came here."

"They were getting on the boat, not off?"

"They were gettin' on."

"Which way was the boat pointed?"

"At the ocean," she said, pointing at the ocean.

Did the boat leave with the people?"

"I think so, but I went home."

< 146 >

"You think they went out to sea, but you were gone before they left?"

"Uh huh."

"You did not see them come back?"

"Nope."

Clay thanked the kids and wrote down three phone numbers. Two didn't remember theirs. But he had the girl's number and her father's name.

"How old are you, sweetie?" he asked.

"E-leven."

"Thanks. Aloha," ... The kids started rolling away.

"Next time wear your helmets ..."

But they were gone.

< 147 >

## Boatload of Clues

The preliminary lab report on the boat came back before the information on the torso.

Hair samples were found, bagged and recorded. The handrails and the captain's chair, the wheel and everything that people might have touched had been wiped, as well as anything an operator might have handled. However, a few prints were collected in more obscure areas. Places touched inadvertently, mostly partial prints, but a total of five good ones.

No blood was found. No shell casings, bullets or bullet hole. Nothing but some dried vomit in some cracks and crevices.

The registration number led to a Robert Johnson, but the address and phone numbers were not current.

The aluminum rods and fittings, ropes and pulleys and hooks, and the canvas for enclosing and protecting the upper deck had all been stowed on the two bunks in the bow and were covered by a light coat of grime, leading to speculation that they had not been disturbed for a long time. A year, perhaps.

A nearly empty plastic 'bai' antioxidant infusion water bottle was found in a corner of the head that contained more good fingerprints.

The boat was impounded.

< 148 >

## Walter Gets an Offer

Walter Abbott's back was against a palm tree that shaded his sketch on cold-press watercolor paper. The surface was entirely too bumpy for his taste, and he resolved to only deal with hot press in the future. His painting of Koko Head was moderately successful so far. Hoping to save it, he persevered.

Pinky was in the waves with her board.

She was getting toasty tan now that the new Walter liked the outdoors. Looking fit.

Walter saw her catch a reasonable four-foot wave and ride it for more than eight seconds before the curl snuck up behind her. She cut to the top and popped out like a cork in a champagne bottle. It all looked very professional to the country boy. If surfing were bull riding, she would have made the whistle.

Back astride her board she floated, and looked at Walter, grinned, and waved.

He mixed a puddle of ultramarine blue and a bit of emerald green in the metal lid of his paint box. Then his cell phone rang.

"Hello?" he said.

"Walter Abbott?"

"Yes."

"Want a job?"

"Who is this?" Walter asked.

"Never mind who. Do you want a job?"

"I'm a retired man, and I'm not looking for work."

"I have a job you could do easy, and it pays a lot."

"I'm living out my retirement on a beach, and not interested in any job, thanks."

"It's the kind of thing you used to do on the mainland."

"Who the hell is this?" Walter asked.

"Never mind who. Do you want to know what it is?"

"Hell no, I don't," Walter said.

"Want to know what it pays?"

"No, I don't."

"Are you sure?"

"Are you a cop?"

"Walter, I am serious, and I am not a cop."

"Bullshit," Walter said, and hung up.

He watched Pinky surf a while. Then looked at Koko Head, then at his artistic attempt. Pinky was paddling to catch a forming wave, but she was a little late.

Walter picked up his phone.

"Detective Burnam."

"Detective Burnam, this is Walter Abbot."

"Walter, call me Clay. How can I help you?"

"Let's have lunch again tomorrow or as soon as you can."

"Tomorrow's okay," Clay said, "are you all right?"

"I hope so," Walter said.

< 150 >

# That Voice

The next morning Walter got another call from the same voice. "Good morning, Walter, I hope you're thinking about a job," it said, and hung up.

Walter and Clay met at a sandwich place in the Ala Moana Center and ate with the pigeons and gulls in the park across the street. It was typical Waikiki winter weather, comfortably warm, with rain predicted for later.

"So, Walter, what's up?"

"Who around here knows my history?"

"Well, so far as I know, in Hawaii it's only me and my partner. When I took responsibility for you, Polanski said his partner knew, and I probably should let a very dependable closed-mouth person in on it. And so that's Mikio, my partner.

"I think Polanski probably talked to someone higher up in Honolulu to help decide who to be your connection, but that person probably got only a general overview of the situation, without specifics. All I know is when Polanski called me, everything was to be strictly on a need-to-know basis. So, I think the answer to your question is me and Mikio.

"So, Walter, why do you ask?"

"Who knows on the mainland?" Walter asked. "Any idea?"

"That I don't know," Clay said, "Polanski and his partner, and maybe others in the LAPD and FBI, but Polanski told me most of the files on cases that involved you were closed or in limbo somewhere gathering dust."

"And in Utah?"

"The same," said Clay. "Only exceptions are your friend Jake Oar, and his sheriff buddy, Thompson, or Thomas, or something like that. They are not sworn to secrecy or anything, so maybe word got out. I met Oar, who seemed friendly but not much for gossip. Don't know anything about the sheriff."

"Well shit," Walter said, "go figure."

Clay looked closely at Walter's tired eyes.

"Is there something you want to tell me?" he asked.

"Yeah ... somebody's fuckin' with me."

"How's that?"

"Yesterday somebody called to offer me a job." Pause.

"Go on ..." Clay prompted.

"I told him I was on the beach, retired. He implied it was a job like I did on the mainland, and that it paid well. I am retired, and I thought it might be an officer trying to test me or trick me somehow. It kinda' pissed me off. I thought if they didn't trust me, they would have tried that shit before now.

"Anyway, it sort of made me mad either way, so I thought I'd call you and see what you thought."

Clay sat quietly a few moments. "I don't think the FBI or cops would do that, but who knows what people do?

"What did the voice sound like?"

"A mature educated man. Could have been an accountant or a lawyer, or a cop. Not sure. No particular accent. Businesslike, straight to the point without revealing much. I had the feeling it was a local call; you know, didn't seem like there were any delays like you sometimes get over long distance. Crisp and clear."

"Did he give you anyway to contact him?" Clay asked.

"I hung up too quick," Walter said, "but he called back this morning. Asked was I thinking about his 'job' and then hung up before I could say anything."

"He'll probably try to contact you again then ... maybe."

"I guess if he's serious, he will."

"His number's probably on your cell phone," Clay said.

Walter dug it out of a pocket and handed it over. Clay looked at it carefully, pressed a button or two. Then he put it down, pulled out a note pad, and copied the number.

"Probably a throw-away phone," Clay thought out loud.

< 152 >

"Walter, would you be willing to work with me a little on this?"

"I guess so."

"Let me see your phone again, please."

Clay took it and showed Walter what he was doing.

"Here's the app," he said, and downloaded it. He showed Walter how to press 'Record' when a call comes in. Don't forget to press the button and do it right away. He might hang up if he hears a strange click in the middle of a sensitive conversation.

"So, if he calls back, lead him on a little, just enough for the next step. We don't know what that will be. You'll be trying to get clues to who he is, what he wants done, and how.

"Then tell him you'll get back to him, somehow. But stay aware, it could get dangerous, so you have to keep me involved every step of the way."

"Play it by ear, you're asking?"

"Yes. But carefully."

Clay thought for a moment. "I will keep Mikio in the loop, step by step, so if it' s real, we have a witness that you are working with the law from the very beginning. I need to keep you out of any potential legal trouble, and get you credit for your help.

"If it turns out to be a real thing, we can get phone taps and various approvals, but for now let's see what happens next. Do you know how to reach me?" Clay asked.

"I guess so. Like yesterday? I just call your office?"

"No," Clay said, "Too slow. Here's my card; the number written on the back is my cell, always with me. If you have news, call that number any time.

"Okay," said Walter. "You can call me Wal, like my girlfriend does."

"All right Wal. Thanks for getting in touch. Call any time day or night, for sure, whenever your potential employer calls. I'm a lonely bachelor, always available."

"Want me to fix you up?" Walter, in a much lighter mood now, "My girl knows some Delta stews."

< 153 >

# Pretty Good Plan?

Alfred McGriffin and his attorney were waiting in a drab interview room when Mikio and Clay entered. Red-headed Alfred was in a one-piece orange jumpsuit sitting behind the table. Mikio's first words, "Colorful character," were muttered quietly behind a brief but insincere smile.

The lawyer beside McGriffin was in a light gray suit and a cream-colored shirt open at the collar, the tip of a maroon necktie hanging out of a breast pocket. Mikio was in a suit and Clay wore a short-sleeve shirt and slacks. They pulled up chairs and sat down.

Mikio knew the attorney and spoke first. "Morning, Mark; hello, Mister McGriffin. How are you feeling, sir?"

McGriffin's answer was a serious squint and a frown.

"You fellows know Detective Burnam?"

"Hello Clay," said Mark Colfax, the lawyer.

"Gentlemen," Clay said.

"Well," Colfax said. "We've been talking to the DA and after some discussion, Mr. McGriffin has decided to try to help your investigation."

He pressed a button on a device and continued. "We are recording for the record. This is a statement by Alfred McGriffin, given of his own free will. Present are Mark Colfax, attorney for Alfred McGriffin, and Honolulu Police detectives, Mikio Iwasaki and Clay Burnam.

"Mister McGriffin."

"Well, shit, I got a call on the phone asking me if I thought I could kill some guy. I said I could kill somebody and so could you. Just gotta' have the guts to do it. Not that hard.

"So, this guy says how much is it gonna' cost, and I said depends on who you get to do it. So, he says how much if you do it, meaning me. Like how much do I charge. I never done it

< 154 >

before, how the hell do I know what to charge? So, he says he got it all figured out. All I gotta' do is get a gun, and I could throw it in the ocean later. So, I said a gun would cost three hundred and up, what kinda' gun does he want?

"He doesn't give a shit; any pistol will do. Do I have a car? I say I got a motorcycle. He says that'll be just fine.

'So, he tells me get ready and he'll call me and tell me what car, and when. Says he's got a plan. It was a pretty good plat too, by the way.

"So how much is all this worth to him? And he says, 'how about a thousand dollars.' I say that's total bullshit. Tie the guy up and put him in an abandoned warehouse and I'll shoot him for a thousand dollars. You want me to shoot 'em in his car in daylight, shit. I say to do that it's gotta be ten thousand in advance. So, we haggle about the price.

"Finally, he agrees to eight, but I don't get it until he sees it in the papers that this guy is dead. He said he's kinda' important and it'll be in the newspaper for sure. The guy I'm supposed to shoot is named Jay Paul Something-or-other. So fuckin' important he gets two first names.

"So, the guy says, 'Get ready. Surf's up, the first contest in Waimea Bay is coming up and our target is probably gonna' be there.'

"He says he'll call me and tell me what kinda' car and when, and just go by and shoot the driver between the eyes. He said the traffic goin' up would be light and the traffic comin' back would be slow, so when I see the car just slow down and shoot the driver, stuck in traffic. Then speed away and get lost in the crowd.

"Pretty good plan till it went all to hell at the end."

There was a long pause. Mikio smiled at the prisoner.

"So ..." Mikio said.

"So what?" Alfred said, staring at Mikio's eyes. His lips mouthed the words that got him in trouble a few days earlier, but the detective just smiled.

"So that's your story?"

"Shit, yes."

"The detectives may have some questions," Colfax said.

"First, Mister McGriffin," Mikio said, "we'd like to know the identity of the person who hired you to shoot our victims."

"Never met him."

"You never met him?"

"What are you, a fuckin' parrot?"

"Just an officer searching for some truth ... You're suggesting he was just a voice on the phone."

"Yes, that is exactly what I am suggesting."

"All right then, what was his name? What did you call him?"

"He didn't ever tell me a name. 'Hello it's me,' he'd say. I don't think he ever used my name either — don't remember, anyway."

"What did the voice sound like?" Mikio asked.

"It was just a voice, like any voice. What do you want?"

"Deep voice, soft voice, male, female, or in between? Talk fast or slow, any accent?"

The orange suit looked at Colfax.

Tell them, to the best of your recollection," Colfax said.

"The voice was strong like a man, kinda' like a military guy ordering people around, straightforward and direct. Kinda deep, I guess. The other voice was a bitchy woman."

"There were two voices?" Clay sat straight up in his chair.

"The man called first and I did my talking with him.

"The bitch was the one told me it was the fancy car made to look like a wooden car. Like a wooden station wagon surfers used way back centuries ago.

"And she told me where and when. She had me waitin' near the phone for couple of hours. When I called her to ask politely why the fuck were we waitin' all day in the hot sun, she chewed my ass off. She was a highly fucked up broad."

< 156 >

"Did she have a name?" Clay asked.

"Not that I can remember." He glanced at Colfax.

"But I think I remember her using a name when she was talkin' about the other guy, the guy who had told me the plan in the first place. Like she asked me; am I the guy Fletch hired, or Fletch wants me to describe the car, or something like that, you know. Anyway, I think she said Fletch, or Sketch or Retch, at some point. Could have been French, or Fetch or somethin'. I think Fletch."

"What was the last thing she said to you?" Clay asked.

"She said the target started moving, then she'd pause, and says it's stopped, then it's movin' again … shit like that. Finally, she said it's perfect and told me to go shoot it."

"You called her once?" Clay asked.

"Mebbe twice. Or more, I guess. I wasted a lot of time waitin' up there."

"So, you have her phone number?"

"It was on my phone. I just pressed 'recent' and it would call her."

"Can I see your phone?" Clay asked.

The prisoner looked at his attorney, who nodded.

"I think it's with his belt and personal items. I tried it," said Colfax. "I think that phone no longer exists. You can pick up Alfred's cell at my office." Tell 'em I said it was okay."

"What about the male voice," Clay asked, "ever call him or get a number?"

"He always called me," said Alfred McGriffin.

"Here's a question, Alfred," said Mikio. "How did this voice find you?"

"How?"

"What made him select you? He could have called anybody. How come he selected you?"

"I sure don't know. Maybe one of my gang told him I'm not afraid of shit." He looked at his lawyer but got no encouragement.

"Maybe it's because you are such a good marksman?" Mikio suggested.

"Did any of your friends mention anything to you about a guy looking for a shooter … or anything at all?" Clay asked.

The red head in the orange suit looked at Colfax again.

"Not that is in any of my recollections," he said.

When they had no more questions, they stood and the good cop said, "If you think of anything that might help us, please give us a call."

The bad cop gave him a little smile.

Alfred grunted. "Ugh."

"Not that is in any of my recollections," Clay quoted. "Our attempted-murderer talkin' like a lawyer."

< 158 >

# The Futurity in Fort Worth

Jake spent several days in Fort Worth during the National Cutting Horse Association Futurity with his Parker Ranch friends. Low-stress fun. And partway through, Darcy joined them.

In the past when he had competed, there had always been a pressure filled three-week visit. This time he saw old friends, looked at handsome horses, and saw some amazing performances.

For the Parker Ranch folks, it was an intense and expensive shopping spree. Their eight days started quietly, visiting ranches near Weatherford, looking and learning. The pace increased as days slipped by. Sale catalogues gradually filled with notes on horses, pedigrees, and finally, sale prices.

They sat in the packed Watt Arena as bid spotters stood with fingers out and eyes that darted all around, surveying the crowd of big hats, well aware of who meant business and who was just taking up space.

In the little ring full of fresh shavings, the polished colts and fillies reminded Darcy of Easter eggs in a basket.

The auctioneer jabbered and rattled.

One two-year-old sold for over a million, as the elderly owner held the lead strap and cried. The audience stood and applauded.

Some sales lasted all day, as horses and money changed hands.

It was in the last few days of The Futurity festivities when budgets and dreams collided.

For two weeks in the Will Rogers Coliseum, some great horses were washed away, by bad luck, uncooperative cattle, or tiny errors. Six-hundred-eleven open horses that had arrived full of optimism were whittled down to the eighty-two highest scores that would compete in the NCHA open semi-finals.

The Open Semis.

The coliseum was packed to the rafters for a very long night

< 159 >

of cutting. Six sets of cattle. Fourteen horses in each, two-and-a-half minutes for every contestant. During the forty minute or longer cattle changes, most of the audience drifted into the huge Cowboy Christmas auditorium, where vendors sold everything from hats and saddles to jewelry and spurs.

Enthusiasts socialized. Californians or Idahoans greeted friends from Florida or Georgia. Impromptu, once-a-year rendezvous sprouted all around.

Jake reminded his little group to get a snack. The restaurants would be long closed by the time it was over.

Next it was finals night.


The climax.

A cool evening in Texas had the ladies in their jewels and glitzy jackets. Every seat was filled and the space behind the box seats was standing-room-only. Felt hats, boots and creased wranglers, wall to wall. A fire marshal's nightmare.

And this crowd knew what they were watching. Afficionados. A horse, head-to-head with an active cow, would set the audience into a deafening roar. But a lost cow could turn the huge noise to a unanimous groan, ad dead silence.

There were twenty-eight horses in the open finals. Two pens of cattle. About three hours of spectating if you add the hype and shopping. Far-flung friends made dinner plans. The throng was amped like an NBA playoff game.

Everything on the line. This was it. Cliché maybe, but true.

The end came suddenly. The last rider. His score, a two-seventeen. Darn good, but not good enough. There had been an arena shaking two-thirty, a heroic score. Almost impossible to beat.

The winner got his quarter million, an expensive trophy saddle, a belt buckle, and many other goodies.

The Reserve Champion, that first loser, got his two hundred thousand, saddle, buckle, and so on, down through all the finalists. Each one got a share of the huge purse.

< 160 >

Pumped adrenaline calmed, and the mob broke into tiny groups and scattered into the night.

The Old South restaurant, next to I-30, was packed, the parking lot full of cars, Dually pickups, and people in Stetsons standing and talking. Too crowded. Jake, Darcy, Bob, Jeffrey, and Allie went west to Applebee's.

That night all the restaurants in West Fort Worth were packed with people dressed like upscale cowboys and cowgirls. Their conversations about the last two weeks, the last two hours, and the winning two and a half minutes, turned eventually to next year.

An early flight the next day started the Parker Ranch group's trip home.

Jake spent the morning arranging transportation for the newly acquired Parker Ranch horses.

Three prospects would catch rides from Weatherford to Utah's Kamas Valley. They would become Jake's projects. A young blue roan stud colt and two long yearling sorrel fillies.

Three older horses would travel to Moorpark, California, where they would stay until their Coggins tests and health papers were complete, then make the expensive flight to their new home in Hawaii.

# Beth and Fletch

There was a photograph on the living room wall in the beach house. It documented an impossible sheet of water cresting, foam and spray at the sky and darkness turning emerald green below. A tiny crouching surfer was screaming across the center. The image was printed on aluminum and the picture's highlights were silver. The metal was mounted to give the surface a three-dimensional curve inward, enhancing the wave.

Beth carried her coffee into the living room, and sat down on the couch in her T-shirt, and looked at the picture.

"I've been living with that snapshot ever since I moved out of his big house and have never really seen it. It was just always there. But this morning I am examining it and realize I hate it. I want to kill it."

"Whatever you want, Babe," Fletch said from the kitchen.

"I hate the photographer, the disgusting sport, and the stupid wave. The pretentious metal screaming, 'look at me, look at me.' Let's get rid of it."

"Whatever you want, Babe," he repeated.

"Can you bend it into a wad that looks like a big, squished beer can?"

"Whatever you want, Babe."

"Is that all you're gonna' say today?" she asked.

"Repetition breeds retention," he said.

"Can you flatten it so it can fit through the bars on his iron gate, then open it and twist it into a mess so that he can't get it loose?"

"Whatever you want, Babe."

"What would be great, if you could twist it so when he comes home from the hospital really hurting and can't wait to lie down, he can't get the gate open. Can't get home."

"I think the news said he's home already."

< 162 >

"Shit."

"Our shooter was pathetic."

"Dumbo with a gun," she said.

"Probably gave him a good scare, though."

"Hope so. Anyway, maybe we can fix it so he drives his stupid car up to the gate and presses his little button, the gate hums but can't open ... 'cause his fuckin' wave photo has wrapped the iron bars together. That would be really great."

"Well, we'll see." Fletch was looking at the size of the thing.

"I think we can," he said.


Digging around the bedroom Beth found some shorts to add to her T-shirt. With slip on footwear, she was prepared to go.

"Gimme a minute to make the bed," Fletch said. "It'll only take a second." A well-made bed was a visual footnote to his military career.

He found the shirt he wanted and some olive-green well-worn pants. Dressed and ready.

At Denny's, over breakfast, they discussed the day.

"What 'ya wanna' do today, Babe?"

"Well, I want to wrap that piece of shit around his gate some time when he won't see us doin' it. I'm trying to think if he has something he always does at a certain time."

"So, let's put it in my van so we don't scratch the Porsche, plus, he doesn't know the van. We'll be ready when the time is right."

"He usta' always go to lunch with his buddies on Thursdays," Beth said. "I can't remember if it was every Thursday or the first one every month, or every other one. But that's probably a good time. I like doing it when he's stuck out and can't get to his tools.

"So, Babe, what shall we do today?"

"Relax. I'll relax and do some stretching this morning. Read, maybe. Hang out."

"Okay then, I'll go for a run on the beach and later maybe you'll join me at the range, get in some small arms practice. How about that?"

"All right," she said.

"I suppose tonight is yoga night?

"Every Tuesday and Thursday is yoga night," she said. "I never miss one."

"When you yoga, I'll take a long walk on the yacht harbor near Waikiki. Watch the boats returning at sunset. Put my mind to planning my retirement."

Fletch looked at his sister and smiled. Not a blood sister, he knew, an adopted sister. She could be a bitch, but she was certainly a good-looking bitch.

< 164 >

# Yoga Night

J ay Paul's marriage to Beth headed south after their brief
honeymoon. He didn't remember the exact date she moved
permanently to the beach house and had the door locks changed.
It wasn't really on the beach anyway. It was across the street from
the ocean. There were no houses on the beach side; the sea was
too close.

It had been a enormous relief to finally have her gone. The
new security was just one of her ways of saying goodbye. But it
didn't really matter. The back door was old and could be jimmied
with a simple credit card.

It was Tuesday night, and he knew she always went to yoga
and wouldn't be home till after nine.

As expected, the beach house was dark when he passed, so he
parked and walked back, carrying a small satchel. He opened it
and put on a pair of plastic gloves.

Jay Paul's neck was still bandaged and caused a sharp pain if
he turned his head too quickly. The arm on that side didn't go
comfortably above shoulder height. But none of that interfered
with opening the back door.

He moved easily through the semi-dark house, passing the
bedroom into the windowless bathroom. There he closed the
door and switched on the light. Her mess of toiletries was there
on the counter with the sinks, as he imagined they would be.

But there was a surprise.

A man's shaving equipment: toothbrush, paste, and a leather
travel kit were parked next to the second sink. Obviously, she was
not living alone. He stood and stared for a long moment. Then
he turned off the light and went to the bedroom.

Jay Paul used his cell phone's tiny light to explore. The bed
had been made, the cover so tight that, as they say in the army,
'you could bounce a coin on it.' Beth had never made a bed, at

< 165 >

least that he could remember.

Men's clothes were hanging in the closet. They had a military look — fatigues and some green and gray camouflage. No fancy-dress uniforms or anything extreme. A couple of shirts and a jacket that had three chevrons over three rockers, sign of a Master Sergeant. He examined the size. Too big. This guy must be huge. He snapped the light off and stood in the dim light, thinking.

Finally, he went back to the bathroom, shut the door, and turned the light back on. From the bag he removed a small jar of liquefied arsenic and a syringe and needle.

He found her favorite lip balm, Burt's Bee's almond flavor, in a lipstick-style tube. He uncapped it carefully, inserted the needle into the tip, pushed it in deep and released the liquid slowly as he pulled the needle out. Then he touched the tip where the tiny hole remained and smeared it slightly with a finger to hide the puncture.

He left the bathroom just as he found it, and went to his main target, the refrigerator.

Beth was not much for cooking, so besides a few carrots and lettuce it was mostly cans: three six-packs of Coors and bottles of her favorite antioxidant infused water; bai.

With the refrigerator door open, the interior light helped Jay Paul examine the red plastic cap on a bottle. He twisted it and took it off. A telltale red ring remained. He drank some and then some more. Pretty good. He screwed the cap back on and put it in his bag.

Jay Paul crouched, took a leather working tool, an awl, out of his bag and put a fresh bottle on the floor. He poked a tiny hole in the plastic top, filled the syringe and pushed it slowly through the hole in the cap. Carefully. Straight down. Gradual pressure. Then he pushed the plunger and pulled it out and shook the bottle.

There was very small lettering embossed on the red plastic top and the little hole was unnoticeable.

< 166 >

After five bottles the needle broke. He decided five should be enough and arranged them at the front. Before he shut the fridge, he noticed some vinaigrette dressing, partially used, hanging on the door. Taking the top off he poured in a little arsenic, replaced the cap and shook it up. He opened it again and sniffed.

"Smells delicious," he said, replacing the cap.

On a whim, and to see what kind of frozen dinners she was serving lately, he opened the freezer and found a frozen gun.

He wanted to examine it, but it was frosty, and he decided not to touch it. It sort of looked like Buddy's.

He left the house and walked away.

He sat in the car quietly a moment before putting the key in the ignition. Everything he'd taken into the house was back in the bag with the plastic gloves.

The job here was done.

Glancing in the rearview mirror he saw headlights coming. He sat still in the semi-dark waiting for the vehicle to pass. But, he realized, it had slowed and stopped.

Jay Paul sat frozen a few moments watching. In the gathering darkness it was hard to see clearly, but apparently a van was at the curb by the house. Its lights flicked off. A figure headed for the house. It could have been two, but probably just one. It was hard to tell.

When the beach house lights went on, Jay Paul started his car and snuck away.

It had been a close call.

# Negotiations

*Blueberry Buttermilk Pancakes*

Ingredients:
2 cups all-purpose flour
1/4 cup sugar
2 1/4 teaspoons baking powder

1/2 teaspoon baking soda
1/2 teaspoon salt
2 eggs
2 cups buttermilk
1/4 cup melted unsalted butter,
        plus some for frying
1 cup of blueberries, fresh or frozen

*Directions:*
Pinky never followed directions anyway.

Pinky had made pancakes with passion fruit pieces instead of blueberries and tossed in an extra egg. She and Walter ate the results of her experiment at the kitchen table.

A soft breeze moved flower-scented air through the house. Both front and back doors were standing open, and the neighbor's black-and-white feline was in the kitchen exploring the stacked dishes.

Pancakes gone, they sipped a second cup of Kona Coffee and got to their feet. Pinky fed the cat and watched it eat while Walter eyed the pile in the sink. A damp rag hung right there calling to him. He glanced at the kitty.

"Are you trying to steal Tuxedo from next door?" he asked.

< 168 >

"Thou shall not steal," she quoted. "Just helping him fatten up some."

As Walter picked up the first plate, his red cell rang.

"I want you to keep thinkin' about a quick easy job with good money," the familiar voice said, and hung up.

It was a Tuesday and much later, after supper, Walter took his bag with art supplies, and drove to the little blue house at the jungle's edge. He was a little early, first one there. He sat on one of the wooden drawing benches, his board propped up, newsprint sheets clipped in place. With a conté crayon he was drawing leaves he could see outside the big window. Foliage was very forgiving. If the proportions were off, no one would notice or care.

"Good evening, Walter."

Suz had entered quietly and was looking over his shoulder. Walter said, "Aloha" and turned to her.

"It's nice to see you drawing. Do you practice at home?"

"I got a sketchbook, like you suggested."

It was leaning against his art bag.

"Can I peek?" she asked.

"As long as your expectations are low," Walter said.

"Expectations are high," she said, but looked anyway. She saw beach scenes and drawings of Pinky. Lots of Pinky.

Artists started to arrive then, claiming benches and positions and organizing their tools.

A huge fellow took the model stand wearing only a jock strap. He was introduced as Tosh, a sumo wrestler visiting Hawaii from Japan. He dwarfed the platform, then took the chair that seemed to disappear under him as he sat down. Everyone went to work.

About twenty minutes into the session Walter's phone rang. He excused himself, grabbed it, and headed for the door. He pressed the Record app.

"Hello," he said, and then in a few seconds he was outside.

"Hello, Walter here," he said.

"Walter, are you all right?" It was the voice.

"I am. I just ducked out of a class."

"Well, Walter, have you been thinking?"

"Of course."

"Well, Walter, what do you think?"

"I think you are a mysterious voice without a name. Probably you're an April Fool's joke who forgot to check the calendar. That is exactly what I think." Walter paused a beat. "What do you think?"

"I am no joke. I am deadly serious."

"Well, it's your dime. So far, you're just a riddle to me, so if you have something to say, go ahead and say it. Otherwise, I'm going back inside."

"How does seventy-five thousand dollars sound?"

"Sounds like real money," Walter said.

"Did it pique your interest?"

"Sure. Go on."

"All you have to do, Walter, is do what you did in Utah so successfully. That's it."

"You'll have to get a lot more specific, 'cause I did a lot of stuff there. I mowed my own lawn there, for one. Brushed my teeth for another. Want to pay me for mowing your lawn?"

"Don't be coy, Walter, you know what I'm talking about."

"Who's being coy? Tell me your name, you coy bastard."

"Walter, my name does not matter, and you do know what I want."

"Say it out loud, you chicken-shitting squirrel!" Walter sounded a little heated now. "Say exactly what you want or I'm hanging up. Period."

"Don't get excited. I want you to kill someone."

"Now was that so hard? ... So why call me? The world is full of people with guns."

"I want a professional, and I'm willing to pay for it."

< 170 >

"I'm a retired gentleman living in paradise, not interested ... well, maybe a little."

"So, are we talking business then?"

"Not yet. You're too cheap."

"Oh?"

"You're only halfway there," Walter said.

"You're expensive."

"Expensive and also not very interested."

There was a pause, and then Walter said, "Who do you want killed?"

"It's a woman. And it shouldn't be too hard. I know her address and she drives a silver Porsche 911 Carrera."

"How did you find me?" Walter asked. "I really do want to know."

"The short answer is I have my sources."

"What's the long answer?"

"There was a Polynesian boy in Utah who went to prison for killing a cop in a gunfight. He has an aunt in Honolulu. Word was, among other things, he had an assignment to kill a professional killer who had escaped the law and snuck off to Hawaii. Sort of a hero in some circles.

I have a friend who has a friend, and so on, friends of friends, down to a snitch in the courthouse in downtown LA, who knows a lawman who is in loose touch with the retired killer. It took a while, but luckily I finally got the number."

"So, who are you anyway?" Walter asked again.

"Probably best if we never meet in person. I'll gather all the information I can on the woman, and I'll figure out how to get you paid. A money transfer into your account, or I could have laundered money in cash in a suitcase in a locker at the airport or somewhere and send you the key. We can work that out to your satisfaction."

"Double the seventy-five is one-hundred-fifty," said Walter.

"Well, it so happens that could be your two-for-one sale price.

< 171 >

I have a second job for you, and then I promise to never bother you again."

"Let me think about that," Walter said. "Who is the other party you want done?"

"Jay Paul Gottlieb, a local hot-shot."

Walter was surprised. "Holy cow. Wasn't he just in the papers for getting shot in an assassination attempt recently?"

"Yes, that's him," the phone voice said.

"Your amateur failed, so now you want me?"

"No, Walter, that was someone else entirely. I just want a professional job so no one goes to jail, and no one solves the case. If the bodies disappeared that would be fine, too."

"So, if I decide to pursue this, how do I get hold of you?"

"I'll call you in a few days, after I put together all the info I can find on the two people. If you want to talk to me, just write 'yes' on a piece of masking tape and stick it at eye level on the flagpole outside the Davies Pacific Center building in downtown Honolulu. Do you know where that is, Walter?"

"Yes, I do."

"I go by there every day, and I'll watch for it."

"All right," Walter said, "I will think of a two-for-one price, and you think of how you can guarantee I'm going to get paid."

After they hung up, Walter called Clay. "Bingo," he said. They spoke a couple minutes and agreed to meet soon.

Then he went back to the fat man and his conté crayon. Tosh had abandoned the chair, or broken it, and had fallen asleep on his right side.

Suz said that apparently it would be a long pose and she'd try to wake him at the break.

< 172 >

# Wicked Witch

*Folk Wisdom:*
   *"In like a lion, out like a lamb."*

That is an eighteenth-century proverb. It was often applied to the month of March, and sometimes used in reverse, depending on the weather. It could also be used for other things, perhaps to describe a hospital visit.

When Beth Gottlieb arrived at the hospital in Honolulu, she made a rather grand entrance for a horizontal woman on a gurney. As ambulance attendants maneuvered her through the emergency room door, she turned her mouth on.

"You fuckers be careful, she roared. "Sons of bitches. Shit ... Careful, motherfuckers!"

They wheeled her to the check-in desk that still had a Plexiglas Covid shield to protect the innocent.

"Aloha, Ma'am. Can I have your name please?"

"Speak up, bitch, you got fuckin' plastic you're talkin' through!" Beth spat the words as loudly as she could with her stomach pain and sore throat.

Out of the corner of her eye she noticed her ambulance driver looking at her.

"Sit down, asshole," she said, and raised her knees, clamped them to her stomach and vomited all over her neck, wild hair, and sheet.

Beth's skin was red and swollen and she was developing lesions and brown spots. Her stomach was "hurting like fucking hell," she yelled.

"We'll get you in now, ma'am," a voice said calmly, as the woman behind the plastic pressed a button and the interior door swung wide.

Men in scrubs came out and took over. Beth disappeared, trailing the strong smell of her diarrhea.

Even with the woman gone her voice persisted as she was rolled down the hall, leaving a wake of smoking-hot language.

The two ambulance attendants stood to the side, waiting for their wheeled stretcher to be returned. They looked at each other.

"Wow," one said quietly, "amazing vocabulary. That was quite a ride." All the waiting room eyes were on them, and everyone understood.

They put Beth in a little room with a battle-weary nurse who took her vital signs and hooked her to an IV. The process involved some bad language from both sides.

As her skin started to darken and she began retching, a timid young man in a pale green smock tried to ask the usual questions: name, next of kin, any allergies, insurance, and more. It took a while because she had a sore throat, and her anger added many extra words.

By the time a young doctor in a white coat and stethoscope came in, she had been cleaned up three times and had messed up four. She presented a convulsion as he entered.

"Well," he smiled, "how are we doing this evening?"

By midnight in the dimly lit ICU, she was quietly enjoying a morphine drip. By two-thirty-two AM she was quiet as a lamb. By two-thirty-nine she was finally asleep.

The night nurse monitoring the green line with blips noticed the blips had gone away at two-fifty-two and Beth Gottlieb was finally, totally, quiet.

Dead quiet.

< 174 >

## Cancel That Order, Please

H ello Walter," the now familiar voice said.
   "Yes?"

"Walter, this whole thing has been a big mistake. I want to cancel my order."

"Just a second," Walter said. "The cat's trying to pee on the carpet."

He changed hands on the phone and made a strange sound scrunching moisture through his teeth as he pressed the Record button.

"Sorry," he said. "Damn cat ... Now, whatcha' mean, cancel the order?"

"Well, I mean I no longer want what I ordered."

"Hey," Walter said, "you know this isn't Amazon. Be clear. You wanted something and now you don't?"

"That's right."

"But same as before, what you want, you don't want to say."

"That's right."

"You said it before, and I want to hear you say it again."

"No."

"Come on, you can do it. I heard you before ... let me hear you again."

"I wanted you to kill someone, and now I don't."

"Thank you," Walter said. "That wasn't so hard, was it? Can we still be friends?" Walter, having fun now.

"Seriously, Walter, job is over. Do not do anything on my behalf. Okay?"

"Don't kill a lady ... and don't kill this Jay Paul fellow?"

"Right, you got it."

"Can I ask why?"

"You can ask. She died all by herself. Just died, I guess. Anyway, she's gone. That's the main thing."

"How about this Jay Paul guy, he die of old age?" Walter asked.

"I think he's alive, but I don't want to kill him."

"You're not mad at him anymore?"

"I was never mad at him," the voice said.

"I have an idea," Walter said. "Why don't we have a beer together sometime? You sound like a nice guy. I bet you have some stories."

"Well, that's not possible, Walter. I'm sorry."

"I wouldn't even know your name. And I've got good stories to tell also."

"Hmm. I imagine you do."

"Here's what I think," Walter said. "You are some sort of business guy, real serious, probably doesn't have time to relax and have fun. Probably real moral ... by the book. Real straight.

"But you are very curious about me, 'cause I am so different. You're tempted to meet me for a beer. Twenty minutes. Maybe we have something in common and could become the most unexpected friends imaginable. Or maybe we split and that's it. But you're curious.

"Safe. A bar of your choice. We're not plotting crimes, so nothing's illegal. What could it hurt?"

"I am kind of tempted," the caller said.

"Two friends, and I never know your name. A safe friend. You could tell me anything and I could never trap you with it.

"And me? You are almost the only person here who knows I had a previous life. You're somebody I don't have to pretend with. Even my girlfriend thinks I was born three years ago."

They quietly held their phones.

"It's an interesting proposal," the voice said. "I've got your number; maybe I'll get back to you sometime."

"I hope you do," Walter said.

Neither hung up and a moment passed.

"You're not gay or queer or anything, are you?" Walter asked.

"Why? Do I sound funny?"

"No. You sound regular."

"Good. I am ... regular, that is. Not gay."

"So," Walter said. "If I want to call, how do I get a hold of you? More tape on the flagpole?"

"This call is from my actual cell phone. You were correct if you thought the others were throw-aways. They were. So, you've got my number in your phone right now."

"What name shall I put with it?" Wally asked.

There was silence for a few seconds before the answer.

"How about Jack?"

"Sounds good. I'll put you near the front of the J's ... Jack."

Later when Clay heard the recording, he smiled.

"Crime solved before it was committed. Can't beat that."

"Interesting," Walter said.

"Crime solved, but the mystery remains."

They pondered the situation.

"Well, you did a great job, Wal." Clay said. "Thanks."

Clay wrote down the number Walter had given him. He looked at it on his desk for a minute, then wrote "Jack," with a question mark. He didn't know where to file it, so he taped it to the edge of his screen for the time being. Then he pulled it back and put it in his pocket.

Later, on his way to lunch he passed Betty's desk and gave her the number.

"Could you find out quietly who has this number?"

< 177 >

## Lab Results

'Happy Birthday, Janet!' the big homemade sign said. Apparently, it was her birthday.

Janet was from the pool of secretaries who served the detective unit, when she was not on loan elsewhere. She was dressed a little fancier than usual, and her hair looked like it had recently been cut and puffed up.

The party had gotten a bit too noisy and silly for Mikio's taste, so he and Clay slipped into an interview room to find some quiet and get something done.

They took the fresh lab reports and closed the door.

"Birthdays are such a waste of time," Mikio said. "After the age of twelve I think they should be illegal."

"How old do you think Janet is?" asked Clay.

"I bet she's about thirty-five."

"You heard those girls saying after thirty, you start subtracting years, so, figuring like that she'd be back to twenty-five."

"Women are children when it comes to birthdays," said Mikio, "out there wasting the tax-payer's money."

"Mikio, do you think twenty-five is too young for me?"

"I think she's married."

They spread out the lab reports. Three manila folders.

FEMALE TORSO
Summary:
The torso had been in the ocean approximately two weeks. Sharks had chewed it. No evidence of foul play, except for the hands held by a plastic zip-tie which had also probably been in the ocean about two weeks.

DNA from the torso matched samples taken from the bedroom and bathroom used by Carnation Olivetta at the home of Jay

< 178 >

Paul Gottlieb. This had been her residence of record with the US Post Office for at least three years.

Gottlieb had reported Carnation Olivetta missing a few days after the assassination attempt on his life.

The remains of the jaw, although incomplete, provided partial dental information that was consistent with the X-rays provided by Olivetta's Honolulu dentist, Fred Jameson, DDS.

THE DEEP-SEA FISHING BOAT

Summary:
The boat had apparently been superficially cleaned, recently. However, in the cabin the fiberglass floor had been covered by removable wooden mats provided by the manufacturer that conform to the unique shape of the cabin floor and allow liquids to pass through. This is for safer footing in heavy seas.

Apparently, these mats had not been removed for the cleaning, and on the lower floor human vomit was found between the head and the seating area. Composition of the human vomit is not yet available.

Some hair had apparently come out by the roots and DNA samples were taken that matched the DNA of Carnation Olivetta. Other hair and skin scrapings matched Robert (Buddy) Johnson, the registered owner of the boat, who was also reported missing by Gottlieb on or about the same time as Olivetta.

Most of the boat's railings and steering wheel had been wiped clean, as stated in the earlier report. However, on the edge of the roof, where a tall person would have to duck when stepping down to enter the cabin, there were several good fingerprints. No matches had been found. Some agencies have yet to respond.

This file had an addendum on a separate sheet.

It said those fingerprints from the edge of the roof match Fletcher Armstrong, a United States Army Master Sergeant, retired. Current address unknown. Height: six foot eight, two-hundred-seventy-two pounds.

Contact information for Armstrong was included: His mother's address in Kentucky, and his cell phone number.

"Well, there are some of our answers," said Clay.

"You bet."

They sat quietly thinking.

"Remember how that boat was tied?" Mikio asked.

"Sure. It was pointed in, right side against the dock. Tied tip and tail."

Mikio looked at him. "You sound like a man from Nevada." He grinned. "Here we say starboard, bow and stern. But I digress."

"Uh huh," Clay grunted. "I'm thinking the direction suggests it probably came straight in from the ocean into the harbor and pulled up to the dock. Remember what the little girl said about how the drunken people were getting on board at dusk? She said it was pointed at the ocean then."

"So, I speculate they went for an evening cruise."

"Seems likely," said Mikio. "They would have parked like we saw it if they were gonna' leave the boat. Leave it, period. Maybe left in a hurry ... but still took time to wipe it down.

"You'd turn it around facing the sea for another reason too. Waves from the ocean would hit the bow first."

"There was plenty of room to swing it around if they wanted to," said Clay. "Probably thinking more about getting gone, than the boat's welfare."

"Can't prove that without witnesses, but I bet you're right.

"Did you notice how it was tied?" Mikio asked.

The door swung open then, and the party noise flooded the room. A short brown-haired woman's head popped in.

"What are you old fogies doin' in here? There's a party heatin' up outside."

"Hi, Betty," Clay said.

"Get ya' some cake." And she was gone.

"So," said Mikio, "did you notice how the boat was tied?"

< 180 >

"Old fogies?" Clay asked. "Old fogies?"

"Guilt by association," the elderly detective replied.

The door bounced wide, cake was delivered with two forks, a giggle and a smile. Then the door closed. They were alone again.

"How old do you think Betty is?"

"Too young for you," Mikio said, "You need maturity."

"Oh,' Clay said.

"The knots that tied the ship," Mikio said. "Those knots, did you notice them?"

"It was tied, stem to stern, to those little iron things that are bolted to the dock and stick out both ways," Clay said, "like a farrier's anvil, except it goes both ways. Or like the horns sticking out of a steer's head that you want to rope, if you were a cowboy. Most docks seem to have 'em for tying up boats. You gotta' watch out for 'em 'cause you can easily trip and fall in the drink if you're not looking."

"The way they were tied was amateurish," Mikio said. "Looped around the iron deal and tied with a series of half-hitches. I bet it wasn't tied by the owner or anyone who knew about boats. Sometimes one of the lines might have a loop braided into it at the proper length to toss over the iron, then the other end you have a rope you loop over another iron goodie, and you can pull till the boat gets snug.

Then you wrap the rope in a series of figure eights around the iron horns, give it a twist on the last wrap, and that holds the boat. That's the main way I've seen it done."

The older detective was in teaching mode. "But half-hitches ... pure amateur. That looked to me like a landlubber in a rush."

"Probably right," Clay said, "That's how I'd have done it."

"From Elko." Mikio looked at his student. "Last nautical lesson," he said, "The fenders, those bumpers on a rope, are supposed to be between the boat and the dock. They usually use at least four. I saw two in use, badly placed, and the others, one on a seat in the cabin, and one on the floor near the head.

< 181 >

I bet they were drunk or stoned or in a big hurry.

"And I bet the owner was nowhere around."

Then they opened the last folder.

*BETH GOTTLIEB*

Summary:

There was a preliminary report on the death of Beth Gottlieb. The complete toxicology report was not in yet, but the physician who treated her in the emergency room, Doctor Robert Burns, said the symptoms all pointed to some kind of poison, probably arsenic. Most cases involving arsenic are low dose, slow over a long period, and recovery is not unusual. But in big doses it can lead to a very unpleasant death. The doctor noted he had recently read *Arsenic and Old Lace* and hoped that hadn't influenced his diagnosis. Toxicology would have the last word, when it came.

It was common knowledge in Mikio's world that the Gottliebs had been separated. But separation was a long way from murder.

Mikio opened the door, and sounds and smells of the party rolled in. Betty was close, and he stepped near her.

"Thanks for the cake," he said, paused, and then, asked: "Could you do me a real quick favor?"

"Yes?"

"Find out the address of Beth Gottlieb and get a uniformed officer to put a crime-scene tape around it. And get us a search warrant, please. She just died of poison and that's why we need it. Any problems, call me."

He gave her his version of a charming smile. "Soon as the party is over ..."

She saw him look at his watch. It was after one-thirty.

"Clay and I are goin' over there pretty quick to look around," he said.

< 182 >

## Bottled Water

It took the two detectives almost an hour to find Jay Paul's beach house. It was west of Pearl Harbor and the directions got a little confusing. It was in the general neighborhood of the boat full of clues. But once on the right street, they saw the yellow tape. The policeman was almost finished.

"Greetings," Mikio said to the young man. "Mikio Iwasaki and this is Clay Burnam."

They were in plain clothes but wore their identification around their necks.

"Welcome," the cop said. "I'm Chas Brighten."

"Have you seen anyone around here lately, officer?" Mikio asked.

"Nobody today, sir, but I don't get here every day."

"How often do you usually pass by?" Clay asked.

"I try for three times a week, unless there's something goin' on. It's very quiet out here."

"Ever see the owner?"

"Never seen her but I see her car quite a bit. It's hard to miss. Silver Porsche Carrera. Nicest car on my beat."

"But never seen her gardening or taking out the garbage or anything?" Clay asked.

"Only time I ever saw her she was driving with the top down. I wanted to give her a ticket 'cause she was so pretty. That was the only time. I know who she is, though."

"Yeah?"

"She's Jay Paul Gottlieb's wife," he said.

The detectives looked at each other.

"She was," Mikio said.

"You mean their divorce is complete? I had bet money it would go on for years."

"She passed away last night." Mikio said.

< 183 >

"Oh no. ... so now it's a crime scene? Murder?"

"We just don't want anyone going in until we get through."

"The boyfriend?" the uniform asked.

"Tell us about him, please."

"Never met him either but seen him jogging a time or two. He's a real big, fit lookin' fellow. Drives a dark van and parks it in the street. She keeps the silver car in the garage usually, but I see the van a lot. I think he lives in the house."

"How long?"

"She's been living here over a year, maybe two. But the van ... probably about two or three months."

"I suppose," the policeman said then, "you guys don't need me anymore?"

"Thanks," Mikio said. "You can go."

"Think a skeleton key will let us in?" Mikio asked Clay.

"Let's find out."

Inside, wearing plastic gloves and carrying an evidence bag, they looked carefully around. A closet with a large man's clothes suggested a live-in boyfriend. There was one large well-made bed. The bathroom had toiletries for two people. His and hers.

Of course, their main target was the fridge and they saved that for last. Not much in there except beer and 'bai' plastic water bottles.

"Coors, I understand," said Clay. "But what is 'bai'? All lowercase like they were ashamed of the name. Or maybe they are trying to be extra hip."

"I think my wife tried it. Just colored water. She thinks the name is supposed to say 'buy', like, 'buy this water', to encourage sales, but the package designer couldn't spell. Sounded right when they said it, so they just let it go."

Clay picked one up very carefully, using two gloved fingers, and examined it closely. The white label had a picture of three blueberries on it surrounded by the lettering. He looked at the

< 184 >

panel marked Nutrition Facts. Calories: 10, it said. The liquid that could be seen above and below the label was a beautiful transparent reddish-purple, like the ocean right after a Maui sunset.

Inviting, and healthy too.

Clay looked at the red cap sealed for purity. The kind you twisted till the seal broke, leaving the lower red edge on the bottle. Clever. And ... there it was ... a tiny hole.

"A hit!" Clay said, and carefully gave the bottle to his partner.

Mikio looked at the hole, hardly more than a dot. He put the bottle in the evidence bag. They found two other bottles with the tiny holes in the top and collected them too.

In the garbage can there were two empty bai bottles and they found the red caps. Both with the tiny holes.

Outside they took off their gloves and Mikio called the office.

"Hi Betty, could you arrange for an officer to come over here to the Beth Gottlieb beach house and guard it? Get a big officer who's armed and tough. ... Yes, twenty-four-seven.

"Yes, I know all our guys are armed and tough. But if some-one comes and wants to get in, I want him in custody." A pause, then, "Thanks, and tell Janet happy birthday." Another pause as the detective listened on his phone. Then he said, "You too, bye bye."

Clay and Mikio stood next to the house waiting for an armed and tough officer to arrive. After twenty minutes they crossed the street and watched the ocean. But soon a deep blue van pulled up, its windows tinted dark against the Hawaiian sun.

It sat by the curb waiting, as the detectives walked up. Mikio stopped about ten feet away as the driver's window rolled down. Clay moved around to the other side, watching.

"What's up, man? the driver asked. "What happened to the house?"

"Do you mind getting out of the car, sir." It was not a question.

"Are you a cop?"

"Honolulu Police detectives, sir. Please step out."

The van door opened slowly, and a large man got out. He was in a light gray jogging outfit. If he was armed, it wasn't obvious. But there were pockets.

"What's up, officers?"

"Is your name Fletcher Armstrong?"

"Yes sir, it is."

"Let's walk across the street and watch the ocean as we talk," Mikio said. And they did, Clay staying a little behind and off to the side.

"So, what's with our house?" Fletch asked.

"Well sir, it's a crime scene at the moment. We don't want anything disturbed until our lab people go over it."

"But I live there. All my stuff is in there."

"We won't hurt your stuff."

"So, what's the crime?"

"A woman died last night, and we have to look into it. That's all," Mikio said.

"I know," said Fletch. "She was sick last night; I called the ambulance."

"I went to see her this morning and they said she'd passed away in the night. Shit."

"I couldn't figure it out. Bad stomachache. We all get 'em. It was gettin' bad with cramps and all. She had good insurance, she said, so we called the ambulance. But dead? I couldn't figure that."

"What did you eat last night? Anything unusual?" Clay asked.

"Spaghetti and meatballs and ice cream, nothing unusual."

"So, you called the hospital and found out she was gone, what did you do then?"

"Shit, I didn't call the hospital. I went to the hospital. I went to pick her up. That's where they told me ... you know ... she'd passed away ..."

< 186 >

Unable to speak, he folded his arms and stared at the sea.

They gave Fletch a moment with his apparent grief.

"What did you do then?" asked Mikio, the good cop.

"Well, I sat in the lobby awhile trying to think how the hell does a stomachache kill you? I tried to talk to a doctor or nurse to tell me what went wrong, but nobody knows. Her emergency room people had all gone home to bed."

"Then I went to the gym for a while, didn't know what else to do. Sat in a juice bar a while, went for a walk, and then for a long run. Decided to go home, change clothes, and take a shower ... and here I am."

During their conversation a marked patrol car had pulled up behind the van. The driver sat behind the wheel watching the backs of the three figures.

"Well, Mister Armstrong, you can't go in yet," Mikio said. "May we talk to you about another subject?"

"Yeah?"

"Will you go downtown with us? You're not under arrest or anything. We'd just like to talk."

"I'd rather talk here if you don't mind. Then I'd like to go take a shower somewhere, at the gym probably, if I can't do it here."

They were quiet a moment.

"All right," said Mikio. "We'd like to find out if you know anything about an abandoned boat not far from here. It had been tied to a dock. A deep-sea fishing boat."

"Those are a dime a dozen, officer."

"Suppose we drive you there. It's fairly close, and you could tell us if you saw a boat there, and when. It would be really helpful. We're trying to track down the owner. It was so close you've probably jogged past it."

Fletch thought about that for a while. Finally, he said, "If you let me get clean shorts, pants, and shirt, I'll follow you in my van and you show me where the boat was; then I'll go get a shower."

"You tell officer Burnam where your stuff is and he can get it for you," Mikio said.

What actually happened next was that all three went carefully in and Fletch got the clothing he needed and his toothbrush. The detectives made sure nothing else was touched, but Clay hung back and peeked into the garbage under the sink where they'd seen the empty plastic bottles and red caps and noticed the remains of a spaghetti dinner.

They were back out quickly.

Mikio drove and they led, the van next, followed by the patrol car, to the wide-open area, cement and grass, where the deserted dock floated. The tide was out, and the dock was lower than the cement. They stopped and got out.

"That's the dock," Mikio said.

The wooden structure looked naked without the boat, its iron things, exposed and lonely, with their horns sticking out.

"Well, I've run by here several times, might have seen a boat."

"You're sure," said Clay, the bad cop.

"Yeah, I think maybe there has been one here, but I don't remember when."

"So, you never got on a boat here or looked in into one?" bad cop asked.

"Shit, officer, when I'm runnin', I'm focused on where I'm goin', not lookin' around. But I guess if I stopped to look at a boat, I'd remember stopping."

"And you didn't stop."

"No sir."

"Well, thanks, Mister Armstrong, you've been very helpful," said Mikio, "and we're very sorry for your loss."

He pulled out a business card. "Please contact me if there is any way I can help."

"Thank you," Fletch said. He got in and drove slowly away.

Clay jotted down the license plate number.

"Mister Fletch Armstrong being cute with us," Clay said.

"I bet it was right at this dock when he put his fingerprints

< 188 >

on our boat," said Mikio.

"Maybe he could have been on this boat when somebody pushed our torso, Miss Carnation Olivetta, in the ocean."

"Attached to an anchor, maybe? Do you remember seeing one on that boat?" Mikio asked.

"No, I don't remember an anchor. It might have been up front with other nautical stuff I didn't understand," Clay said.

"I remember one," Mikio said, "but lots of boats that size have two, one fluke-Danforth style and a plow-scoop."

"The more I hang with you the more nautical I feel," Clay said. They walked down and stood on the dock.

"I wonder what they call those things," Clay said, pointing at the iron fittings with horns sticking out.

"Not sure," his teacher said. Then: "Cleats ... I think."

They stood, and the dock rocked slightly. They looked across the harbor. There were a few little houses nestled in some trees. It was a long way across.

"Well, Clay, who do you like?"

"For the torso? Too early to call, I think.

"But for the wife, our boy Fletch had opportunity, but I don't see a motive yet. But for motive you gotta' consider the husband, especially in a divorce situation."

"Word on the street is that the divorce has been ugly," said Mikio, "so the husband is a consideration."

"How did you like Fletch's story about last night and today? Seem sincere to you?"

"Seemed genuine at first glance. Or maybe he's a good actor. We already know he is a good liar."

"Truth runs for daylight," Clay said. "Keeping it in the dark is difficult, if not impossible."

"Poetic."

"I read it somewhere." Clay smiled.

"Let's hope it's true." Mikio said.

# Freedom

Jay Paul awoke to a new day. Yesterday had been a wild ride of emotions. Joy, guilt, sense of duty, filling out papers, calling lawyers, more guilt, relief, and more guilt. But yesterday was past and Jay Paul sprang up like a kid with a new Christmas surfboard.

A free man with a stiff and sore neck.

He made some calls and gathered a little crew of close friends, including Jif, with a bandaged thumb and elbow in a metal brace, and an ear covered with salve. He also had a headache. Sammy came with his jaw wired shut, a bandage-wrapped head, and his girlfriend. Her body seemed to be struggling with the smallest bikini Jay Paul had ever seen.

There were also three other surfing buddies to help crew when the sails were up. And a few more guests including a reluctant John Silverman, full of Dramamine.

The fifty-foot Hinkley motored carefully from her slip in Ala Wai Harbor and out past the forest of masts and rigging. She was indeed a classic beauty and turned heads as the powerful engine deep in her bowels purred like a big kitten.

As the channel widened, the noise took on a throaty growl.

Once out of traffic, the three friends with crew duties attacked the canvas, and as the sails went up, the engine was silenced, and the thrill of sailing took over big time.

There was the sense of rapid acceleration as the ship leaned port at an angle that put the edge of the deck into the waves. Nature ruled this world. Nature and nautical engineering.

Spray in faces. The sound of the rushing hull dominating the waves. The wind and the exaggerated sense of freedom and speed.

The only communication was shouts among the crew as the lesser sails went up. When everything was ship-shape, Jay Paul gave a scream to the wind.

"Freedom!" he yelled at the wind. "The bar is open below.

< 190 >

Let's drink to freedom."

And so, they did.

Most with cups.

Sammy used a straw.

< 191 >

# Return to Paradise

That last step from terminal to sidewalk is the step that says 'Aloha' best.

Travelers with bags over shoulders, under arms, gripped by hands, or following on leashes, their rent-a-car envelopes clenched in teeth, flowed like a human river. Out through that invisible wall, from cooled air, recycled and conditioned, into the sweet warm humid embrace of Hawaii.

With luggage and a bellboy who had the room key, they smiled like the honeymooners they had recently been.

The boy demonstrated how the sliding glass doors worked and pointed to the kitchen, the toaster, and the coffee machine. He got a nice tip to stop stalling and left them alone. In the islands where the air is sultry, when the heavy lifting is done, further assistance is unwanted and unneeded.

Jake and Darcy were naked before the boy hit the ground floor.

They were still naked an hour later, relaxing, when Jake's cell phone rang.

"Aloha," said the voice of Suz. "You guys settled in yet?"

"Yep. Your timing is good."

"I talked to your friend Clay, and he'd love to join us for supper."

"That's great. How are you, Suz?"

So, at dinner they all filled each other in on their busy lives.

Suz had a show scheduled in about two years at her old school in San Francisco and was working on some new directions. She had been trying to focus but seemed to have misplaced her mojo. The ruined painting haunted her.

Jake gave her an overview of their time in Fort Worth,

< 192 >

spending other people's money, and trying to adjust client's dreams to fit reality.

"Can horses really survive a flight over the Pacific?" Suz wondered.

"I sure hope so," Jake said. "Jeffrey told me they landed and took a barge the rest of the way. He said they made it safe and sound. I'll see for myself tomorrow."

"How long will you be at the ranch, this trip?" Clay asked.

"Well, not sure. Till we get everything underway."

Darcy spoke a little about the open space business, and Keilani showed them her flower and gave Clay some smoky soft eye and her sensuous smile.

Clay brought them up to date on the assassination attempt, and the death of Beth Gottlieb, the public knowledge part. Conjecture with his partner was off limits.

After supper and more conversation, they wound down, gradually.

Outside, everyone enjoyed Suz's special goodbyes, and they broke up into separate cars in the parking lot.

Clay walked up to Jake and suggested they meet for an early breakfast at his hotel the next morning.

"I met a friend of yours, and need to ask you something," he said.

"Wally?" Jake asked quietly.

"Yup."

"Okay," Jake looked at Darcy. "Honey, I'm meeting Clay for breakfast tomorrow before we fly."

"And Darcy's meeting me," Suz said. "Separate but equal breakfast meetings." She looked at Darcy, who grinned.

"Sure."

< 193 >

## A Whole New Vibe

When Clay entered, the restaurant's clock said six-twenty-five. Most tables were empty and four or five people were eating at the counter. Near the big window a cowboy hat was pointed at the view.

"Morning."

Clay's word caused the hat to swing around.

"So, Howdy," Jake said. "Sleep well?"

"Yes, sir."

"Great to see our pals last night. And it looked to me like Keilani might be flirting with you."

"You noticed that?"

"Hard to miss," Jake said, as he took off his hat and put it brim up on an empty chair.

"Darcy looks great," Clay, changing the subject. "I was really glad to see her."

"She's meeting Suz here pretty soon. They want to talk about art, I think."

"I understand," Clay said. "Separate but equal meetings, as I remember it."

"Anyway, Jake said, "I don't think she wants to hear about Wally. She's not sure how she feels about him. And, come to think of it, I'm not sure how I feel either."

Jake's eyes darted around and found Darcy and Suz just sitting down, being handed menus. It was a big room, and they were far away.

"As a friend I'll let you in on a semi-secret," Clay said. "It's not really an official secret, but here it is.

"Walter did some very bad things in Utah, Wyoming, and Idaho, and ultimately got away with it. I think you know the story and I'd like to hear it.

"I'm involved only because when Walter came to Honolulu,

< 194 >

law enforcement knew he was guilty of stuff they couldn't prove. Some of the files were never closed but got tucked away. Finally, they let him sneak away.

"Also, there was a gang of killers after him, and the law thought maybe they would do the job that justice couldn't."

A waiter interrupted, so they ordered breakfast and coffee as Jake tried to juggle Wally and Walter in his mind.

"A lawman from LA was sort of keeping in touch with Walter, but it became apparent he was going to stay here and might be trying to go straight. So, they handed him off to us. Because I was close, and the low man on the totem pole, I got the job.

"Basically, Walter had given them a little helpful info on some cases they were working on. Enough so that they overlooked some things, but not good enough to get him into an official witness protection program with a new social security card. So, he lives a shadow life now.

"I've met him and talked to him," Clay went on, "and we had a little adventure that sort of leads me to think he really is trying to change his life ...

"Of course, all this changes if he makes any mistakes. We'd be all over him like a Doberman on the mailman.

"To help him, we're not spreading news about his previous life, so almost nobody here knows his history.

"But you know him, ... so there it is."

Story over, Clay checked Jake's expression and sipped some coffee. He glanced toward Darcy and Suz, seriously engrossed.

"I knew him for a long time," Jake said, back on subject.

"Any history will be helpful," Clay said.

"Well, he had cutting horses and I'd see him at contests and banquets."

Their food arrived. They had a few bites and Jake drank some orange juice. Clay, the bachelor, was reveling in his breakfast. Cooked by professionals, and the dishes would be skillfully cleaned by someone else.

< 195 >

"When I first started with cutting horses," Jake said, back on his story, "we were at a party, just friends talking ... and a couple weeks later our host died in a hunting accident. That was over thirty years ago, when we were young.

"A hunting accident, but much later it turned out to be a murder they couldn't prove. But all the circumstantial evidence pointed to Wally.

"But there's more.

"A few years ago, we were at a competition and a friend of ours was shot getting out of his horse trailer.

"Bang. Just like that.

"I got there quick and so did Wally, and we're watching him die. Turns out it was Wally who did it. We were talking about it at the guy's funeral, trying to figure out what happened and why. Well, Wally knew all along."

Jake paused his story a few seconds for dramatic effect.

"So, then there were some drug runners thinking I might know something I shouldn't and hired their favorite killer to shoot me.

"The guy they hired was Wally."

Jake tried some more orange juice.

"I thought we had been friends, but here he comes with the crime boss and his partner, and we hold a little shoot out, right there in my barnyard.

Wally's pointing the gun at my coat. Point blank. If he sensed I wore a Kevlar vest and a wire under there, he might have sensed a trap. Otherwise, he was getting ready to shoot a friend. Or pretending to.

"But anyway, he — real quick — swung around and shot the crime leader. Then the other guy shoots him, I shoot the other crime guy, the sheriff popped up and shoots him some more. The only one killed is the kingpin. Wally's quick and accurate first shot.

"Pop, pop, pop, pop, one dead, two hurt. All in about two

< 196 >

quick seconds.

A sip of coffee, and Jake finished his story.

"I have been trying to decide if Wally is a friend or a danger, 'cause of the history I know. I thought he was in prison by now, till I actually saw him feeding pigeons."

"Quite a story," the detective said. "Maybe we have two Wally's. A Wally with a criminal history and the new Wally named Walter Abbott."

Jake finished his orange juice. A waiter poured more coffee.

"I have his phone number," Clay said, and he handed the card to Jake.

And at another table Suz confided her worries about painting and her mental block.

"It's like I'm in a dry period. No inspiration or motivation. My efforts seem confused and tentative. My ideas trite. That picture with the head cut out has been haunting me. I have nightmares about it. It has left me unproductive."

Darcy didn't know what to suggest beyond throwing the ruined painting away. But Suz was clinging to it like a mother elephant to a stillborn calf. It probably just takes a little more time, Darcy advised, and suggested a vacation to the Big Island.

"You'll join our little gang, all friends of yours, and see new things and get a fresh perspective. Every one of us will be happier with you there," she said.

"Come surfing with Allie and me, go sketching. There will be horses and cows to draw and a whole new vibe. Trade the big city for the rural life, for a little while."

Hmm," Suz said, thinking it might be a good idea.

## To Sing a Worried Song

Old folk song: "It takes a worried mind
to sing a worried song. I'm worried now,
but I won't be worried long.

Darcy and Jake had a short flight from Honolulu to Waimea/Kohala, a little airport on the Big Island.

The plane was small and fun. There were eight rows, three seats in each. The left side had one seat while two were on the right. Passengers on the aisle could lean in and look forward over the pilot's shoulder and see what he saw. When the tiny runway appeared, it seemed no bigger than a cell phone lost on the lawn.

Some first timers might have closed their eyes and clenched their fists, hoping for the best. It definitely was a little target, seen from above while bouncing through the turbulent trade winds.

But the more common reaction was to watch it grow and become something to actually land on. The thrill came when the crosswinds caused the plane to come down sideways, nose to the wind, until the last possible moment, when the pilot did a whoop-de-do to get it straightened out just before touchdown.

And that was how Jake and Darcy arrived near the Parker Ranch, avoiding the long drive from Hilo.

A ranch employee met the plane and handed them a map, and keys to a ranch-owned Jeep, and to a guesthouse by the ocean in Kawaihae.

The next day work started with a meeting that included Jeffrey and Bob. By midmorning, things were underway. Some of the paniolos set up a temporary panel fence, gates and pens. This would be the classroom for the potential cutting horse riders.

< 198 >

After lunch Jake went to look at the new horses. They had arrived less than a week before, and all seemed fine. Swollen ankles and normal problems expected from such a long trip were gone. Loose in a small pasture they were frisky and working out their pecking order and making friends.

Then Jake, Bob, and Jeffrey staked out the tourist seating on a gentle hillside and the arena that would be carved out just below. Spectators would look down into the pen instead of through a fence. The action would be up close and personal.

Hammered-in stakes and stretched string told the story of the future arena, cow pens, and loading facilities.

Allie and Darcy had been touring somewhere, and arrived in a noisy red dust cloud, laughing and singing behind their wire framed sunglasses. They turned the motor off, cleaned there dirty eyewear and dismounted to admire the layout of tiny posts and twine.

"Gall darn good," Allie said, "gonna look a lot like Texas pretty soon."

"Fetching," Darcy winked at her dusty pal.

Things were moving fast. One day stakes and string. The next day a bulldozer. When Jake said it's time for cows, they showed up early the next morning.

But what was not moving fast was Jake's mind.

He knew this tourist trap was going to be an ongoing project that threatened to spread him too thin.

He needed the time at home to maintain a training schedule for the young horses and work his ranch. Darcy needed to keep her office running.

Jake needed to find, or train, someone here to hold things together in his absence. He sensed a solution was hiding somewhere.

Each dawn found Jake on the beach, walking with his worried

< 199 >

mind. But he wasn't alone. The heavens had sent him a lifetime of clouds. Puffy little storytellers that came in all sizes, shapes and colors. Soft friends bringing wisdom and weather predictions.

If he were a surfer, the sea might have something to say. But for Jake's early walks, the ocean was just a stage for the sky and her whimsical dancers.

These strolls were a diversion. The crystal days were for getting things done; the gracious evenings, for Darcy. But the morning walks were for wrestling with Wally.

To forgive and forget?

Or to fret over the past. Wally, sentenced to life in paradise. Where was the justice in that? But who decides justice anyway?

Walter had been able to move on. Maybe Jake could too. Forget. Maybe even forgive.

Could he welcome the new Walter?

Walter could keep the horses tuned and be knowledgeable support when small problems arose. Jake had planned to train someone to do that. But it had always been the weak link.

Wally could. That was the point, but also the problem. Could he be trusted?

After five dawns on the beach, he decided to share his dilemma with Jeffrey. The time seemed right, and they happened to be near the ocean.

"So, Jeffrey, when was the last time you walked on the beach?" Jake asked.

"Last Christmas, I think."

"Well, let's take off our boots. I want to have a quiet meeting with you."

So, they did.

Walking and talking.

Explaining his need for a hands-on helper was easy. Jeffrey and Bob had been to Texas on the edge of the sport, studying, so Jeffrey had a solid idea how important the right person could be.

< 200 >

In any precise sport, sloppiness is the creeping danger. A full-time coach would be a great asset. Jake would get things started, and visit now and then, but he needed to spend most of his time in Utah.

Explaining Wally was much more complicated. A reformed professional killer in a semi-official witness protection program. Reformed? Jake hoped so. That was a complex story.

The secrecy to protect Walter meant most people wouldn't know. Bob and Darcy would have to be told, and agree, and maybe others.

"If he'd paid his debt to society," Jeffrey said, "we'd give him a second chance, for sure. Heck, I bet some of our paniolos have been in jail. Actually, I know at least one has … "I'm tempted to give him a break."

"We could meet him and see what you think," said Jake. "See what I think myself, too. A couple of his victims were friends of mine."

Jeffrey thought, and then they turned and started back down the beach.

"I think you should invite him to come see us."

The weekend is coming and maybe we could meet him for lunch and toss it around."

Jake sighed.

"All right," he said.

< 201 >

**... Forgive, and you will be forgiven. Luke 6:37**

... Give us this day our daily bread
    and forgive us our trespasses
    as we forgive those
    who trespass against us ...
        – *Expert from the Lord's Prayer*


After his talk with Jeffrey, Jake gave each of the three new cutting horses a long ride. Then there were meetings and other chores, and soon most the day had been spent. At supper he shared some thoughts with Darcy.

That evening Jake stood on the guesthouse porch, thinking. Darcy was inside, reading.

He looked at the ocean, sat on the top step, and pulled off his boots. The sun was sliding through some dancing clouds on the horizon before sinking into the silver sea.

He moved to the canvas chair and watched a family wandering up the beach at the surf's edge. He pulled out the piece of paper Clay had given him and studied the numbers.

Finally, with resolve, he picked up his phone.

The conversation with Wally, or Walter, or whoever the hell it was, needed to be a long one. And deep. A real dialogue leading to an understanding of some sort. Philosophical, maybe.

It should be an exchange that parts the clouds and reveals the sunlight.

This would be a discussion far too heavy for now. Probably it could come later. Or maybe it would never come. Just evolve non-verbally, a collection of actions and events over time.

An understanding.

Jake dialed the number.

< 202 >

"Walter?" Jake asked.

"Yes?"

"Walter Abbott?"

"Jake? Zat you?"

"Yup."

"Are you here? You sound close."

"Pretty close, the Big Island."

"Aloha then," Walter said.

"What are you doin' with yourself now days, Wal?"

Calling him Walter sounded dishonest somehow.

"Well, right now I'm trying to paint a beach scene."

"How's that going?"

"I'm polishing another failed attempt, I think. Sinking sun is right in my eyes. Color changes faster than I can mix paint."

"Ridin' any cutting horses lately?" Jake asked.

"No. I don't know of any around here," Walter said.

"Miss it?"

"Yeah ... some."

"So," Jake said, getting to it, "I may have a proposition for you."

"You do?"

"Maybe. Are you working? Do you have a job?"

"No job. I'm an art student. Retired, living close to the vest, as they say."

"Well, here's what I've got. I'm riding some young horses for the Parker Land Trust, and I'm also helping them put together a cutting horse tourist attraction. We're setting up an arena and little bleachers and cow pens and so on. We've got three solid horses, and I'm trying to teach a few folks there to ride them."

"Shit," Walter said, "I never thought you'd give up your non-pro card."

"Marriage does funny things to a lonely old widower," Jake said. "So, as you might imagine I can't be here and home riding their colts at the same time. When I get this setup going, I need somebody to keep it in gear while I'm gone."

"You have always been lucky, Jake. Wow." Walter said.

"I noticed," Jake said, "you've been lucky, too." He let that sink in. He was having trouble with this new Walter old Wally bullshit. The old Wally was the luckiest killer he knew.

"Hmm."

"Anyway, Wal, if you're interested, I could introduce you to the Parker Ranch folks and show you what we're up to."

"Of course, I'm interested, Jake. What's next?"

"You'll have to fly over here, and we'll meet for lunch tomorrow or Sunday. Would that work?"

"Yes sir." Wally was enthusiastic.

"Fly to Waumea/Kohala. Tell me your flight number and I'll pick you up."

"Saturday?"

"Saturday."

"See you tomorrow," Walter said. "I'll text you the flight."

< 204 >

## Fletch Armstrong

The iron-barred gate swung wide, and the maroon Subaru-woody rolled through. The bullet-riddled rear and side windows had been replaced, and Jay Paul was driving his colorful surfing car again.

Down the curving driveway he went. The view to his left included rooftops and ocean, while the steep, brush-covered hillside rose on his right.

A dark blue van parked on the street above, came to life as he passed below and followed him down to a Walmart parking lot. He waited twelve minutes, then followed to a residence in Makiki Heights where the wait was twenty-seven minutes. Finally, west to the coast where the Subaru-woody went north and pulled off the pavement between Nanakuli and Maili onto a wide dirt shoulder.

As he passed, Fletch watched his rearview mirror and saw the woody gets smaller and two men get out.

Once out of sight, he doubled back, going south.

Traffic was very light, and as he approached his target, he drove slowly, assessing the situation. The Subaru was in an area widened for parking comfortably away from traffic, next to the hillside vegetation. No homes were visible, and no other cars were around. The two men from the Subaru had crossed the highway and were climbing down a trail to the beach.

"This is it," Fletch muttered to no one. "Finally, a good spot."

When he was out of sight, he turned around again and parked behind the little woody.

Its passengers were down on the sand watching the surf.

There was a hand grenade on the seat beside him, and a roll of wire, an eye screw, some duct tape and hardware, all hidden under a towel. Fletch moved the cloth and picked up three items.

He checked that he was alone. Foliage partially obscured the two men who sat on some coral rocks studying the waves.

The road was clear.

He moved between the parked auto and the bushes, knelt, then lay on his side and wired the grenade to the underside of the car near the gas tank. Then he twisted a six-inch eye screw into the ground as far under as he could comfortably reach. He attached one end of the wire to the grenade pin and the other end to the eye of the screw.

Whichever way the car went, it would pull the pin.

It had taken Fletch less than a minute to set his trap. When the car moved, it would take about five seconds to end a life.

Back in his van, Fletch drove past the woody and on up the road to Kaneana Cave, where he got out and sauntered to the big hole in the cliff. Killing time.

He went in a little way. It wasn't deep. Dark stone walls, cool and uninteresting. Fletch stood with his back to the wall and studied the gleaming ocean. Bright and welcoming. Just like his future.

Thinking of his future took the wrinkles off his brow and animated a smile. He missed Beth, of course, but the unfamiliar loneliness that had been clouding his spirit fell away. Now he could finally shake it off and look to a shining tomorrow.

Sooner or later, someone would kick him out of the beach house. Probably the Gottlieb family's attorney or maybe a realtor. But that was not a serious worry.

His work — revenge, really — was done. An explosion erases all fingerprints.

Freedom from his obligations and a fresh start.

He sat on the sand and looked out at the day, then laid back and saw the stone ceiling above. His eyes closed.

He liked sailboats. He might become a sailor.

Fletch got in his rented van and headed back down the way he'd come. When he approached the Subaru-woody, it was gone.

Orange cones had been placed, directing traffic onto the

< 206 >

shoulder, allowing the slowed traffic to slip past the crime scene tape and police cars. There were flashing red and blue lights and some law around, talking, directing traffic, and scouring the site.

South-bound traffic was stopped when he arrived, and he sat behind six cars waiting for a string of north-bound vehicles to pass. North and south, taking turns.

He smiled as he passed. A dangerous souvenir from his army days had been put to good use.

A crime scene, without evidence. Disappeared in a big bang. Gone with the wind.

< 207 >

# Big Bang

When Mikio and Clay arrived, the lab fellows were already at work. The detectives maneuvered around patrol cars, parked, and got out. Their identification hung around their necks.

They stood behind the yellow tape and looked.

"Somebody was serious about getting rid of Jay Paul," Clay said.

"Jay Paul?"

"Look over there," Clay was pointing. Chaos that it was, the passenger-side door had been blown off and still retained some of the woody look decal on it.

"Well," Mikio said, "could be. Hard to tell for sure."

The car was just a blackened skeleton of its former self. It had been tossed several feet and was upside down.

"This is an explosion, not a car wreck."

"I bet you're right," Mikio agreed. "The frame's turned over as though there was dynamite under it."

Stuff had been scattered everywhere. Blood and guts. Glass shards, bits of metal. A real mess.

"Probably wasn't going very fast. Looks like the blast was right there," Clay pointed to the black smudge of a serious crater in the dirt."

"Look on the hill where burning bits and pieces fell into the bushes and started little fires," said Mikio.

"Yup. Some of it traveled quite a ways, too."

Mikio knew one of the patrolmen working traffic. He and a partner were slowing people down and keeping them in line until it was their turn to go.

"Were there any witnesses, Jim?" Mikio asked.

"Two," the cop said. "One had just passed, and the blast scared the shit out of him. You can see his skid marks up the road about sixty feet away. Admitted he'd wet his pants. Didn't

< 208 >

want to be interviewed standing up, so we talked through the window." The officer smiled. "I've got his phone number if you want to talk to him. Nice guy but confused. Sounds like the car had been parked. Starting to leave when it exploded."

"Did he see any people around?"

"He figured there were people in it because it looked like it was getting ready to move. He said there wasn't much traffic, so it probably was waiting for him to pass. No pedestrians he could remember. He said all his attention was on the road. Claimed he was a slow, safe driver."

"Maybe looking for a place to stop and pee?" Mikio asked.

"Just trying to be a good driver," Jim said.

"What about the other witness ... you said there were two?"

"Too far away to see much. She said the blast was huge. Stuff flew very high. Fireball and everything. She loves to talk, and I have her number, too, if you want it."

"How old is she?" Clay asked.

The officer looked puzzled. "I'd say mid-thirties if I had to guess. Nice-looking, but loves to talk, if you know the type."

Jim took out a cloth and wiped his glasses. He glanced at Clay with greenish eyes. "I asked her how many people were in the car and she said she didn't know. She was coming south and stopped near the other witness, and got out, but she saw blood and body parts and started shaking, she said, so she got back in. She called 911, and when we got here, she was still shaking ... talking and shaking."

"We?" Mikio prompted.

"Liz and I. She's my partner." He gestured to the officer handling traffic.

Clay glanced over at her.

"Did the ambulance find anyone to pick up?"

"They came, they looked, they left," said Jim.

The two detectives walked around the perimeter of the scene, even into the bushes above, where the burning debris had caused

< 209 >

little fires. Some had burned themselves out in the green foliage, while others landed on dry grass and started to spread. It was apparent where someone had stamped them out.

"I'd sure like to know who was in that car. Do you think DNA will let us know?" Clay asked.

"Bet on it," said Mikio.

"Will we be able to find out what kind of explosives were used?"

"I'd bet on that too. The FBI lab is amazing. They will probably be able to discern the type of explosive, and their data base will tell us all about it. We will probably be able to find out where it's sold, and the store can usually tell us who bought the stuff, how much, and when.

"It won't solve our case, but it'll help us a lot, and narrow things down."

"Let's leave this smoky smelly mess, and speculate a little on the beach," Clay suggested.

It smelled like crime. Explosives, blood, and burned flesh.

They crossed between Jim and his partner, through a bunch of north-bound cars. Past some bushes and down a narrow path to the surf.

"Just thinking," Clay began, "I'm wondering how some of our cases fit together."

"Um hum."

"We know our torso was working for Jay Paul. We think she was probably murdered on a boat, probably our boat with a parking ticket. We know our friend Fletch is lying about being on the boat, and he might have been at sea when the crime was committed on that exact boat. He could have done it. If he were innocent, why would he have lied about never touching it?

"We know, or think we know, that somebody hired that red-headed amateur assassin to shoot Jay Paul. He mentioned a 'Fletch' in his conversation."

"Now it is possible Jay Paul was in that car, alone or with others, in what looks like a successful, probably professional, attack.

< 210 >

"We're pretty sure somebody poisoned Jay Paul's wife but don't know who. Could have been Fletch, but we don't really think so. No motive so far. Keeping an open mind on that.

"And there's Jay Paul's friend Buddy. Missing. But where? I think the lab report said the boat was registered to a Robert somebody, Johnson, I think. No current address."

"That name went missing at the same time as our torso," said Mikio. "He was on our boat, his boat, but we don't know when. That might explain why he didn't move it. Could be he helped with the murder, then skipped town. Or wasn't even there. He could be the murderer. Or he could be another victim."

"We should talk to Buddy," Clay said. "I wonder if our office found him or knows where he is?

"... Just thinkin' out loud here, Mikio, but our Army friend Fletch might know about explosives. I wonder where he is?"

"You make a good point," Mikio said. "I'll call the patrolman who covers that beach house and see if he'll keep closer tabs on that blue van. The yellow tape on the house is gone by now, I suppose. He could tell us if house lights are on in the evenings. It would be nice if Fletch would stay where we can find him."

Mikio watched the ocean and called the office while Clay looked at the traffic above the bushes.

They sat down on a rock and watched the waves, as a jogger ran south on the beach past them.

A family wandering north on the sand, saw the traffic delays up on the road, and sent their teenage daughter up to investigate.

"I don't get a motive for Fletch to kill Jay Paul," Clay said, "if it is Jay Paul. Or to kill our torso either."

"So, here's another angle," Mikio said. "It was pretty well known that Jay Paul disliked his wife, and she felt the same. It's a big step from hate to murder, but they say their hate was extreme. She tried to hurt him every way she could and made lawyers rich trying to break him.

"I heard she killed his dog," Clay said. "That alone could

push a husband over the edge."

"You bet." Mikio said, trying to lighten up.

"Hard to imagine someone that would kill a dog."

"Possible she'd kill his live-in secretary, too?"

"Our torso ... could be."

"She could have hired the dynamiter?"

"Could have ... but of course she's dead."

"So, do you think Jay Paul could have hired someone to kill his wife?"

The tide was coming in, threatening them. It was ten feet away, but sneaking up.

"So," Clay said, "remember I told you about the killer from the mainland? His name is Walter Abbott. Some mysterious guy named Jack wanted him to kill both a woman we presumed was Beth and Jay Paul Gottlieb. Both.

"Then he changed his mind."

"Maybe got suspicious that Abbott was working with you? Got cold feet?" Mikio wondered.

"Maybe, but I don't think so."

"Do you really think this Abbott is being straight with you?"

"Emotionally, I think I do trust him, but his history is hard to overlook. I want to believe in him ... trust but verify."

They sat still but the water was lapping little silver foam cords closer, and they would soon have wet shoes. They stood and headed back to the crime scene.

"Fletch was living with Beth," Clay said. "Sleeping in her bed, it looked like."

"Kinda puts him on her team, maybe," Mikio said as they went up the narrow trail.

"Probably dynamite on a remote mechanism?"

"I'll bet." Mikio said.

< 212 >

## Meanwhile, Back at the Ranch

When Walter Abbott got off the plane at the little airport, Jake realized the first problem with his potential helper was the outfit. Walter didn't appear to be a tourist exactly, but he certainly didn't look like a cowboy.

Sartorial splendor aside, he could talk the talk. Bob and Jeffrey recognized a cowboy even if they couldn't see one.

After a long lunch, all three agreed to give Walter a try. He would consult Pinky, and, God willing, they would rent or lease out her Honolulu house and move to the Big Island.

For the time being they could use a ranch-owned apartment in Kawaihae. Walter would be on the payroll.

Bob went back to his office, and the horsemen took Walter to check out the cutting pen. Some of the paniolos had brought in a small bunch of black cattle. One had a white face, suggesting traces of the ranch's history with Herefords.

One of the youngest paniolos came over eagerly.

"Hola, mister Jake, aloha."

"Aloha, Little Juan. This is Walter, a cutting horse guy from the mainland. He'll help us with the horses," Jake said.

"Nice to meet you, sir." Little Juan's grin had grown into a huge smile of bright teeth as he sized up the newcomer.

"Nice outfit you're wearing, sir."

"Thanks," Walter said with a straight face.

"Your riders should be here by three," Jeffrey said," but I imagine Allie will be early. She's pretty excited."

At the big red barn Walter admired the three new horses, and the tack purchased during The Futurity. They spread it out and looked it over.

< 213 >

There were cutting style saddles, split ear and one ear head-stalls, stiff grazing bits, one with movable parts, a Tom Thumb, and a snaffle. There were sets of Jake's favorite reins. Narrow but heavy, double stitched, and well oiled.

"They feel like expensive leather instruments," Little Juan said. "Makes our reins feel like spaghetti. Jake's reins act alive."

"Your reins pull the bit, pull the head ... pull, pull, pull. These reins send a signal with just the movement of your hand. You can pull if you need to, but this kind of horsemanship is so subtle there is usually no pulling involved."

Jake grinned at Little Juan. "I'll teach you."

"What we're missing," Jake said, "is chaps. Be best if tourists don't see Walter's knees or sneakers."

"No problem," Jeffrey said, "I've got a Leddy's catalog. When we know for sure who our demonstrators will be, I'll order their leggings. Shotgun with fringes, and conchos. Maybe a pair of bat wings, to suggest the old days."

Jake strapped a coiled rope to the right side of the horn as they saddled one of the ranch horses they would use for turn back, "In case one of the cowboys wants to do rope tricks, or a wild heifer attacks the crowd. Plus, it just looks Western."

After saddling, they headed back through the sun and heat to the little practice pen, full of hot sand.

They loped the cutting horses in easy circles, stopped, backed up, walked a little with some bending and collection, then loped the other way. Horses and riders were soon perspiring.

"This clown outfit is getting old," Walter said to Jeffrey. "Do you know a store on the islands where a person can get boots, Wranglers, and a real hat?"

"I'm afraid the feed store on this island is your best bet. I'll draw you a little map when we finish here."

< 214 >

A tan car arrived in a careless little dust cloud, and Darcy and Allie jumped out. They were early, as predicted.

Jake thought they might as well start.

"Gather round, cowboys and cowgirls," he said. "Little Juan, would you send us some cows?"

"Yes, sir." And in a couple minutes they had cattle. Five-hundred-pound heifers, as ordered.

First Jake demonstrated how to settle the herd, telling them what he was doing as he did it.

He also talked about the cow's 'bubble:' how close he had to get to cause her to move. And where he'd have to be to make her stop or turn.

"A cow with a large bubble," he said, "I can control from a distance. With a small bubble, I must get right in her face. As she gets used to the horse, her bubble gets smaller. When it's too small, we call that a sour cow, no longer fun."

After a few questions and when the cows relaxed, Jake rode into the herd and quietly maneuvered one out. He sat on his horse about twenty feet from the herd, the cow about fifteen feet farther. She was in the middle of the pen looking at him.

"The idea is to slip her out and keep her right there, as close to the center as you can," Jake said, looking at Little Juan. Then Jake squeezed his legs and the horse danced nose to nose with the cow.

She was quick, the horse quicker.

Deep stops, balanced bending turns. Again, and again.

After several seconds the heifer stopped still. Confused.

The mare was crouching, ears up, eyes bright, watching for the next move. Jake pinched her neck with his free hand. She relaxed and backed a step.

"So that's really all there is to it," he said. "When it works right, it seems so simple."

They all had a little practice, one after another. There were questions, and over the next couple of hours Little Juan, a good rider, had a horse leave him in the sand. Twice.

"That happened because you took your eyes off the cow," Jake explained. "You have to watch the cow every second. The cow tells you what is coming. Watch her ears, eyes and body language."

They all practiced, and there was as much talking as riding. Riders traded mounts at Jake's direction.

Before the lesson ended, Jake had a good idea of the abilities and personalities of his students, human and equine.

"Anyone want to try again tomorrow?" he asked.

Unanimous enthusiasm.

At the airport Walter called home.

"Hi Pinkaroo," he said. "Gettin' on a plane in five minutes, I'll be in Honolulu in forty-five — twenty more to get the car, twenty to get home, maybe thirty, so we'll go out to supper. How's that sound?"

"What we celebratin', sweety?"

"I got a job on the Big Island."

"Wow. We gonna' be rich?"

"Naw, but it'll be fun. We'll live near the beach, and you can surf every day. That sound good?"

"Sounds like the Lord works in mysterious ways," Pinky said."

< 216 >

# The Attraction

At top speed, a modern American Quarter Horse can run up to fifty-five miles per hour.

In the nineteen-forties a common attraction at county fairs was for a local car dealer to challenge a quarter horse owner to a match race. And, depending on the length of the race, the horse usually won. The earliest ones were a quarter mile, but as automotive technology improved the distances got shorter. Four-hundred-forty yards, a quarter mile, is the distance that gave the Quarter Horse breed its name. They also race three-thirty and two-twenty.

These horses are very quick. For longer distances, a mile, for example, the Thoroughbred is faster. But those big horses need a pasture to stop or turn themselves around.

A Quarter Horse, so the story goes, can stop on a dime and give you some change.

The blood in these athletic sprinters goes back to match racing horses in the colonial days. Horses with names like Traveler, Zantanon, and Steel Dust.

The exceptional intelligence and ability to 'read' cattle started in Texas in the late eighteen-hundreds, and cutting contests were quite common by the nineteen-thirties. Pedigrees of today's cutting horses go back to Poco Bueno, Ed Echols, Peppy San, and others. Contemporary cutters refer to their mental ability as 'cow sense'. And they are very smart.

An experienced rider, comfortable at speed, working a cow on a solid horse for the first time is due for a thrill. The violent quickness, shocking speed and the magic of an animal so focused, provides a memorable experience.

That was the fate of Allie, Jeffrey, and Little Juan. Hooked.

Jake and Walter smiled. Old hands. Still hooked.

## The Addiction

For a horseman interested in the pursuit of cutting, the adrenaline rush of that first ride remains, but evolves over time. If the horse and rider are focused together on this unique art form over hours, weeks and years, they may begin to meld together. Part human, part equine. Reading each other's minds and moods. Muscles, balance, spirit, all unified in a creature larger than the sum of its parts.

That possibility provides the carrot.

Like a surfer's quest for the perfect wave, the cutter seeks that unique harmony. The complete run.

Nothing is ever perfect, of course. The tides, moon, reef, waves, and cows all see to that.

< 218 >

# Explosive Details

The lab report is back from the FBI on that explosion the other day," Mikio said. "Wanna' see?"

"That was fairly quick," said Clay.

He had endured a second date with wild Keilani, and he had to put her out of his mind. Tired as he was, he began to focus.

"Let's get some coffee and take it somewhere quiet and go over it," he said.

"You bet," and Mikio picked up the file. They found Janet's office empty. She was on loan upstairs this week. Her personality was bright, and she had been a popular target when someone up there needed help.

Her desk had been left neat and clean, the computer screen dark. It faced two chairs with a low table between them. The detectives sat there, respecting Janet's space and leaving her seat empty in case she suddenly appeared.

Mikio opened the file and found the summary.

The lab had determined that residue from the explosives was not one of the usual suspects: black powder, dynamite, TNT, cordite, or any others.

The residue found at the scene suggested it had been a hand grenade.

"Suggested?" Mikio said.

"I bet they meant: showed it was a grenade ... You know, like almost proved it was a grenade," Mikio said. "Semi-proved it. Almost a grenade, or maybe it was a grenade, almost proven."

Regarding the DNA the lab report suggested there were at least two victims and maybe more. There was a match with Jay Paul Gottlieb.

"Are you thinking what I'm thinking?" Clay asked.

"You bet I am," said Mikio as he stood up. He opened the door and stepped into Betty's cubical.

< 219 >

"Could you join us for a second?"

"Sure, big boy," and she followed him the seven strides to Janet's door.

"You guys workin' for Janet now?"

"Nope. We just wanted a door to shut so we could think."

"What's with Janet anyway?" Clay asked. "How come she spends so much time upstairs?"

"Some of us have a pool goin'. Sally thinks she's having an affair with Mister Big, but I believe that's just wishful thinking. I think they need her 'cause she's so smart. Their main girl up there is on maternity leave, so I guess they're shorthanded."

"Hmmm ...," said Clay.

"I can't figure why they need her so much," Betty said. "What do they do up there anyway? We do all the work down here."

She looked at her detectives for a moment.

"What you fellows want, anyway?" she asked.

"Well," Mikio said, "we'd like you to find out a couple things about our Master Sergeant, recently retired from the army. Like get pictures of him and whatever you can find. What was his specialty, and was he ever in trouble? Any war experience? Stuff like that."

"And where was he when he mustered out, what base? And were there any hand-grenades missing when he left? And when? If they keep records on that sort of thing," said Clay.

"This guy got a name?" she asked. "That might help."

Clay wrote it on a legal pad. "Fletcher Armstrong," he said.

"Betty, this guy is big and dangerous, and I think he is a flight risk, so that's why you see us so nervous, panicky, and twitching."

"You're asking me to hurry?"

They both gave her their best smiles.

"Uh huh," they said.

Betty found them an hour later, back at their own desks.

< 220 >

"I'm still waiting for details," she said, "but I know a couple things.

"Master Sergeant Armstrong mustered out at Fort Hood in Texas, and they are doing an inventory of hand-grenades for me, although it might be pretty iffy, because they use them in training. I got the sense they might not watch things like ammo and grenades too closely, although they did not say that. I imagine they spend a lot of their time blowing things up.

"The mission there is to provide a combat-ready ground fighting force.

"How's that, boys? Enough to get you started?"

"Thanks," Clay said.

"You're a dreamboat," said Mikio.

"Oh, so you want something else?" she asked, looking at Mikio's eyes.

"You really are in my dreams; but yes, I do want something."

"Pictures of Fletcher Armstrong," said Mikio, "circulated at the airport in case some employee spots him. Especially at check-in or where ticket sellers are. Probably we should circulate his picture and alert the highway patrol and the Honolulu cops also. Have them stop dark blue vans, check driver's IDs. We really do need him. Emphasize big and tough, and a flight risk. Mention to get back-up, if possible."

"More coming, they told me, including pictures," Betty said.

"I can imagine him going back to the mainland quick as possible." Mikio said.

"I'll keep you posted, you guys through with me?" Betty asked.

Clay looked at her.

"Betty, are you too young for me?" he asked.

"Clay, I'm too married for you."

## Closing In

The detectives drove to the beach house, but it was locked up tight. No answer to their knock, no blue van out front, nobody with in sight. The garage door was shut, and Clay wondered if it was big enough for the van to drive in. It had been a tall van.

The closest house was about fifty yards away and they discussed visiting there. But they didn't want to alert Fletch to their search.

Mikio got on his phone and tried to get a warrant so they could search the little beach house. It took three phone calls to find that the judge was out of town and would be gone for two days. They would have to wait or find another way or another judge ...

They drove through the immediate neighborhood in case Fletch was parked and jogging.

They went past the open area near the water where the ticketed boat had been. The place was deserted.

They returned to the beach house, drove past, and parked about a hundred yards farther. They sat. They got out. Walked on the beach. Sat. Frustrated.

Nowhere.

< 222 >

## Outta' Here

Fletch saw the flashing red and blue in his driver side mirror. He started to pull to the right to let the fellow pass. No luck. It was on his tail.

He slowed, looking for a place to get safely off the pavement. He was headed north on the Farrington Highway near Pokal Bay. He crossed a wide canal and turned right on Ala Hema, pulled over, and started to get out.

"Stay in the car, please."

The voice was amplified, a bullhorn of some kind. "Both hands on the wheel, please," it said.

Fletch sat quietly, waiting.

There were two churches a block ahead on the right. A new subdivision, its trees still wired to stakes, lay across the street. No traffic or people were visible. Children in school, their parents at work. A few cars were parked behind one of the Churches.

The ocean and the patrol car were in his rear-view mirror. The sky was cerulean blue with soft white pillows floating by.

He pressed a button and the window rolled down. He waited. Then he turned the engine off.

He heard an organ and choir practicing somewhere.

Finally, a young officer came up.

"May I see your driver's license, sir?"

Fletch rolled onto one hip to get the billfold from his back pocket. He opened it and handed the license to the patrolman.

"Just one minute, sir."

In the rear-view mirror Fletch watched him go and get in the patrol car. It had been warm, and without the air-conditioning it was hot. Time was moving slowly. Even the clouds were faster.

Finally, the lawman returned, and handed back the license.

"Was I speeding?"

"No sir, you had a tail-light out."

"You're kidding."

The young man seemed to blush. "You're from Texas," the officer said.

"Yes sir, you read my driver's license," Fletch said. "Out of the service and ready to see the world."

"Army?"

"Yes. Now I'm searchin' for something beyond Texas."

"I was at Lackland for basic," the officer said. "And I thank you for your service."

"So, you were in the Air Force?" Fletch assumed.

"Air National Guard."

"You going to write me a ticket or what?"

"I have to wait till I hear the radio screech," he said, "In a minute you'll be on your way."

"Well, I remember a scene in a TV show," Fletch said. "Maybe it was a movie. Anyway, the officer stops a guy, and the guy asks why did I get stopped? And the cop says 'taillight out, and the guy says it is not, and the cop says, come back here and I'll show you. They go to the back of the car or truck, whatever it was, and the cop picks up a rock and smashes the taillight. See? he says."

"It's not that, Sergeant. We're supposed to stop dark blue vans today, something about a kidnapping or something."

"No shit," said Fletch. "There must be ten-thousand blue vans on this island. Most full of surfboards, I expect."

Fletch stared straight ahead at the quiet street. It looked deserted. It could be Orange County, California. It could have been anywhere USA.

There was a loud squawk, and the officer went back to his patrol car.

In his mirror Fletch saw him talking on his radio microphone. More time was passing. Wasting ...

At last, the young man got out and approached the van. His pistol was in his hand, not pointed, but ready.

Fletch moved the door handle down, so the door was

< 224 >

unlatched but still closed. He held it like that.

The officer looked in at the passenger seat, then at Fletch, and spoke slowly and carefully.

"Put both hands ..."

The door opened so fast there was no time to dodge, and it slammed into the patrolman. Fletch had all his substantial weight and strength behind it.

It was not a fair fight. The officer staggered as Fletch burst out and kicked his legs out from under him, then kicked him in the crotch, kicked the gun away, and kicked him under the van. It was over quickly. The officer was overwhelmed.

Fletch grabbed the gun and stuck it in his pocket. He started the engine and left, his wheels crushing the man's legs in the process.

There was a Taco Bell on the south side of the canal, and a couple of customers had witnessed the patrol car with flashing lights stopping the van.

In about the time it takes to eat a couple of tacos and relax over a milkshake, they heard the bullhorn, and looked over in time to see the van drive off, leaving the officer thrashing around on the ground. But it was too far away for them to do much good. They were, however, able to call 911 and get some help for the crippled patrolman.

As Fletch drove away, he spotted the cars behind one of the churches. Most had their windows left open because of the heat. The sound of singing voices came from inside as he quickly traded his van for an older gray Honda he could hot-wire easily.

He grabbed his duffel bag and a few things from the back of the van. A couple of shirts on hangers, a backpack, a pistol, and some ammo. Knife, his brogans, whatever might be handy living in the jungle.

The aluminum surfing picture was still there, but he left it. He didn't like it any more than Beth had.

In the gray car Fletch passed the red and blue lights and the

< 225 >

uniform on the ground with a banged and bloody head, and a smashed leg.

As he drove back down the highway toward the airport, he passed two patrol cars, lights flashing, heading to help the officer on the ground.

For Fletch, the highway soon widened into the Farrington Freeway and then became part of the metroplex freeway system. His mind was buzzing.

Just follow the signs to the airport and get the hell out of town. First flight available. Avoid the big carriers. A short flight would be best. Disassemble the gun and put the parts in different bags. Check bags. Find a cash machine.

A mantra: shortest lines, shortest flights, smallest carriers. Get gone quick, before the cops get the word out.

Think smart.

Disappear.

< 226 >

## Well-made Bed

At the office on the morning after Fletch slipped away, Betty was showing a little cleavage. Nothing serious, but just enough to make a lonely bachelor wonder if she'd been in hurry getting dressed.

The bachelor turned to Mikio. "Did you watch TV last night?"

"I saw our show, if that's what you're asking. It was just before the weather report. They got the picture up and made the point that we need the public's help. They could have kept the phone number up longer, and I thought the announcer could have read the number slower and maybe said it twice."

"How much time you think we got?"

Mikio appeared to think about that.

"About fifteen seconds," he said.

"If that," said Clay. "They give those three goofs five minutes at the end of a newscast to vamp, and chat like idiots, and laugh hilariously at stupid non-jokes. Exhibiting their fun personalities, I guess. Wasting time before the national news. And we get maybe fifteen seconds for our friend on the loose, with a van full of hand grenades."

Mikio noticed Betty passing by.

"Betty," he said, "did you watch TV last night?"

"No, why?" She stopped and put her elbows on the top edge of the cubicle's short wall.

"Good morning," Clay said. "You look fetching today."

"What I meant," Mikio said, "our Fletch Armstrong's image was on TV for about fifteen seconds last night, thanks to you. This morning too, I hope. Although I didn't see it."

"I saw it again this morning," said Clay. "On CBS."

"He looks good in that army uniform," Betty said.

"Is that the only picture you've got?"

"It was, but it looks like I've got some more on my computer that came overnight."

"I wish you had one that made him look more sinister," Clay said. "We really do have to stop this guy quick before he escapes. It's a time the public could really help."

Mikio grunted — a positive sound, emphasizing the point.

"Here's a suggestion:" Clay said. "Maybe you could call the different news channels and get a reporter to film you holding the picture or talking on a split screen. You could recite the Hotline number slowly so even old people could write it down. How's that for an idea?"

"Me?" Betty said.

"You."

"You mean like a news conference? ... We have people for that."

"Not a news conference. Just you and Fletch, inviting the public to keep an eye out."

"Clay, I don't get it. You could do it."

"I just wish they didn't slip it in so quick. This is very important, and I think it would get more attention if it had some sex appeal."

"Shame on you, Clay Burnam. That is sexist talk. We females can't put up with it." She sounded stern, but leaned forward on her elbows, and rolled her eyes across him. Self-satisfied.

"Especially in the workplace," she added.

Mikio had been paying attention.

"Stop by any time you're in the neighborhood," he said. "We'll work on political correctness with our country boy here."

"But," Mikio paused and wiggled his moustache, "he might have a point."

Betty grinned at them. She stood up, flirtation over.

"I'll look and see if they sent something more sinister," she said, and glided away.

"So much for show business," Mikio said. "But she gave me an idea. ... Why don't we get Mister Big to give a press conference? Or maybe Mister Biggest. That would make some news and help

< 228 >

get the word out."

"Sounds premature from a news point of view, but to ask for the public's help? I think that sounds good. Suggests we're on top of things. Acting fast."

"Politically, I hope it doesn't sound like we're not capable, or whatever. Mister Biggest has to run for office now and then."

"You know, I think I'll run it by Betty and see if she wants to try to sell it," Clay said. "Invite the politicians to decide."

"I'll get someone to tell us how it's goin' at the airports, make sure they're still watching the travelers."

"I'll get a car and meet you in front. Our search warrant is ready, and we can grab it as we pass the Federal Building."


In a slightly worn green Cadillac, the two detectives picked up their search paperwork and headed for the beach house. They pulled up and parked about fifty yards away, on the beach side. The house appeared to be deserted, but they were both wearing concealed weapons.

When they were close to the house, a light blue sedan moved toward them and parked nearby. A young man got out and approached.

"Mikio, I thought that was you."

"It was, and is," Mikio said. "Clay Burnam, this is Frank Sear."

"I relieved Edwards about three hours ago. He told me it had been quiet, and so far, there's nothin' except you two officers. You here to search?"

"Yup."

"How long do you want me to keep watch?"

"He must know we'd watch his place, but we really need to catch him. So, let's keep lookin'. If it looks like he's moved out, we'll rethink that, but for now let's watch. If somebody shows up, be sure to try to get some back-up help. But, for sure, try not to lose him."

"Roger that."

< 229 >

They knocked and let themselves in.

They inspected slowly and carefully around the living room.

"At first glance it looks shipshape," said Clay. "Shades not drawn suggests he left in daylight.

In the kitchen, breakfast dishes had been washed and stacked in a wire holder on a plastic drain board. One juice glass, one plate, one coffee cup, and one saucer. One everything. A man living alone.

In the bathroom a cardboard box stood on one end of the counter. Its contents included some of the items supposed to ease a modern woman's drift toward middle age, health-wise and beauty-wise. Once necessities, but no longer needed.

The other end, Fletch's area, had a man-sized-bottle of Listerine, a toothbrush, shaving equipment, deodorant, and toothpaste, all lined up, side by side, equally spaced, square with the counter's edge. In basic training, that was referred to as "in a military manner."

In the bedroom the bed was not only made, it was ready for inspection. The top surface was tight, no wrinkles, and tucked in with those military corners that fold at a 45-degree angle. It was the polar opposite of the bed Clay left at home.

Fletch may have left the army, but the army had not left him.

"I'd say when he left, it was not in a hurry," Clay observed. "Probably yesterday morning after coffee. Wandered out to see what the day had in store."

Clay stuck his head in the shower. No fancy shampoo or conditioner. Just Head and Shoulders and a well-used bar of dried soap with a hair stuck to it.

Women's clothes were still on hangers, but things that had probably been in drawers were in three cardboard boxes.
Bras and underthings. A box with a lot of lady's shoes.

Fletch's clothing was on hangers or in drawers. The collection seemed to describe a man getting ready to explore civilian life.

"My guess: He has the clothes on his back, and not too much

more. But he might well have had a change or two in the van. I can't see any weapons in here except the two hand grenades in the sock drawer," said Clay.

"Wow," said Mikio, "I just saw socks."

Mikio went back to look. They were there, under the cloth footwear.

"I wonder if the gun is still in the freezer?"

"The fridge will be our next stop," said Mikio.

"Frozen fingerprints, maybe?"

"Bet on it."

Mikio got a phone call and listened to some news from their office. Finally, he said, "Better get some officers out to the airport and see if it's there somewhere. Where it's parked will give us a hint as to which carrier he might have used. Find a carrier, find a manifest, find a name, find a destination."

Pause.

"Yes, sure."

Pause.

"Yes, I'll tell him."

Pause.

"Okay, Thanks."

Mikio hung up and looked at Clay.

"Betty said you're a sexist pig with a cute ass and she likes you just that way."

"A five-minute phone call about my ass?"

"Well," Mikio said, "there was more to it than that.

"She said a car had been reported stolen at a Wai'anae Baptist Church meeting about an hour after Fletch drove over the officer that stopped him. The church was only a block or two away, same street.

"The car was a gray Honda and the lady who owns it gave us the license number. And the minister reported a dark blue van, apparently abandoned, in his parking lot. He'd noticed it after the choir practice, and again this morning. It is now on the back

< 231 >

of our tow truck on the way to our garage so the lab boys can examine it. I bet he traded the van for the Honda.

"And we might want to take a look at the van, too," Mikio said. "Maybe get an idea what was inside. It's owned by a leasing company, and Fletcher Armstrong had a six-month lease. Officers are going to search airport parking lots for the Honda. If they find it there, we'll know he beat us out of town. And where it's parked might give us a clue as to which airline he left on, and maybe we can nail down his destination."

"If he's on a manifest maybe we could have a cop cuff him as he stepped off the plane," Clay thought. "But I'm sure that' just wishful thinking."

"Or he could be right here on Oahu, just trying to throw us a curve. Anyway, the Highway Patrol and the city cops are all watching for the Honda."

Mikio took a long, thoughtful breath. His cheeks puffed out.

"So aside from your ass, that's pretty much the crime news I got."

"That's a phone call full," Clay said.

"If it were me who just drove over a cop, I'd wanna' get a different car as soon as possible. And if I'd exploded a well-known local rich boy, I'd want to get off the island before the law plugs up the airport with my picture," said Mikio.

"He probably left last night," Clay said. "We probably missed him."

"Yeah," Mikio said, "I know."

< 232 >

## Gone


"Well, boys, did 'ja get anything useful?" Betty asked. She tended to hang out where the action was, and Mikio and Clay had the most interesting challenges at the moment.

"We talked to the officer with the crushed leg. Poor guy, only eight months out of the academy and he meets Fletch Armstrong, who could be a handful for any cop ..."

"Go on," she said.

"He was a sad sight. Happened so fast he had a hard time remembering. He got a concussion and a squished leg. Could be broken, but the muscles and sinew and tissue and veins and arteries — everything a mess." It was Mikio telling the story.

"He was headed for surgery when we were there, and he was full of painkillers ..."

"Go on."

"Let's see ... he said Mister Armstrong was kinda' chatty and pretty friendly, showing his Texas driver's license and joking around a little about the traffic stop. But when the radio said he had a dangerous character and he went back with his gun drawn, it was slam bam. He was caught by surprise, and Fletch smashed him down.

'He couldn't remember what happened next. All he could say was the sun was hot and his leg hurt like hell. He could hardly stand the pain. He tried to roll but it hurt worse, so he lay there in the sun, sometimes conscious, sometimes out.

"When he finally woke up, he was being moved from the ambulance into an emergency room. Then out again, and he remembers waking up to a cop standing by his bed, asking him questions.

"What questions?"

"Like, 'where's your gun?'"

Mikio stopped his story, so Clay continued.

"That's absolutely all he could remember." Clay glanced at Betty's eyes. "Then they wheeled him away toward surgery. And that was it."

"The poor kid." Betty said.

She was leaning, an elbow on the half wall.

"I'm not too busy right now. Want me to help solve your crimes? You guys have all the juicy stuff."

"Fine," said Mikio. "Grab a marker and some paper and let's find a room."

In an empty interview room, they went to work.

"Let's do it like on the TV. Put names on pieces of paper and move 'em around," Betty said.

"Sounds like fun." Clay, playing along.

"Might help us remember something," Mikio said. "Least I hope so. We're in trouble here; our perp has slipped away, and we don't know where. We could really use a clue or two."

Betty put the paper and marker on the table.

"Start with Jay Paul. He's our most famous customer," said Mikio, "and all our murders seem to revolve around him."

"Betty ... Are you okay?"

"Sure."

"But you're not writing?"

"Why me?"

"But you're the one who brought the paper and stuff."

"Came from my drawers, is all."

"Yeah ... but?"

"I'll do it," Clay, the reformed sexist pig, said.

Betty squinted and raised her eyebrows. "A modern man. Nice goin'."

Clay printed 'Jay Paul' on a sheet in bold letters.

"I can hardly read your writing. Here, let me do that."

She moved the paper close and snatched the felt-tipped pen.

Mikio sent them a 'tend to business' look. "Fletch," he said, "our probable killer. Put that under Jay Paul."

< 234 >

They agreed. Fletch, currently at large somewhere in the wide world. Probably.

Betty told them the gray Honda had been found at the airport near the inter-island terminal. And further news that Fletch had been on a flight to Hilo on the Big Island. He had two big pieces of carry-on luggage and three checked bags.

Hotels and motels in Hilo had been called, but no one with that name had been registered. Other Big Island lodging was being checked; rental car companies were also contacted.

So far there were no leads. He was probably not using his real name.

"You were going to keep this a secret?" Mikio asked gently.

"Course not. It was on my computer and that's why I came this way. I got distracted 'cause you guys were late, visiting the hurt highway man, you know. Now here we are and I'm tellin' you. The news isn't complete yet. They're checking banks and everything we can think of, to see if he's withdrawing money, or whatever."

"Okay," Mikio said. "We still love you."

"Oh, good."

For an hour they made their notes, marked the papers, and explored possibilities. Reviewed and discussed evidence. The felt markings told the highlights:

DEAD: Jay Paul.

    KILLED by Fletch, fairly sure. Hand grenade.

DEAD: Sammy Smith.

    KILLED. Probably collateral damage in the explosion that killed Jay Paul. DNA evidence puts him at the scene.

DEAD: Beth Gottlieb.

    KILLED by Jay Paul, we think, or possibly by Fletch.

        No motive for Fletch. Yet.

DEAD: torso; Carnation.

    KILLED by somebody probably on a boat, we think.

        Likely suspects: Fletch, maybe Beth, maybe Buddy?

< 235 >

MISSING: Buddy.

Suspects include Fletch and maybe others.

Buddy could be okay, gone somewhere unknown.

ARRESTED for attempted murder, evading law enforcement, and more: biker Alfred McGriffin.

OPEN QUESTION: who hired McGriffin.

Possibilities include a man and woman unknown, voices on the phone to McGriffin.

Probable: those voices were Fletch and Beth.

Also possible, the man "Jack" who approached Walter.

QUESTION: Who is Jack? Jack first wanted to kill a woman; we presume was Beth. Phone number for Jack proved to be out of service. Probably another throw-away.

THE MOST IMPORTANT QUESTION: Where is Fletch? In Hilo? Or maybe he just wants us to think Hilo?

"Hey guys," Betty said. "A foot was found on the beach near Makaha, and they assigned it to Detective Furgeson. I wonder if it could be our Buddy's? Or Carnation's?"

The room was silent a while until Clay said, "Wow."

"Gone to the lab, I suppose," Mikio said.

"Yes, I think so."

"Could be nothing,' Clay said, "or it could be Buddy was on the boat with Carnation and Fletch. Maybe he was tied to the same anchor as Carnation. Maybe chomped loose by the same shark that ate our torso. As I recall they were reported missing at about the same time."

"They were," Mikio said, "both reported missing in the same phone call from Mister Jay Paul."

"Maybe DNA will tell us."

"I bet it's a male foot." Mikio said. "And I bet it's our missing Buddy."

It was almost time for lunch, and they were thoughtful for a while.

"Well," Clay said finally. "That was a hell of a way to end a marriage."

Mikio moved his chair back and they all stood up.

"Let's go to Hamptons," he said, "I'll buy."

After lunch Betty went to her computer but bopped back to the pair of detectives like a flash.

"DNA said that was Buddy's left foot," she said.

< 237 >

## Part Three


## Three Months Later


Pinky was in bloom. Walter sensed it when she jumped him. She was also no longer pink. As brown as his leather boots. It had been two hours since he'd last gotten off a horse but his spurs were still attached.

"I just realized I always wanted a cowboy," she said.

"I must smell awful," he said.

"You smell great, Honey, like a cowboy."

"I smell like cows."

"Nice."

She was unbuttoning his shirt.

"Finally, Hawaii has a smell I recognize," said Walter.

"Cow shit is the official smell of Texas," said Pinky. "Did you come from Texas?"

She stopped with the buttons and performed a little striptease. She made a little rhythmic "ka-thump noise as she pulled off her T-shirt. "Ka-thump ... Ka-thump ...ka-thump," and soon her shorts were gone.

The color contrast between the brown skin and the freshly exposed pinky was rather striking. Too much for the old cowboy. He sat on the couch and pulled off his boots.

She pushed him into the depths of the couch and worked on his belt.

"Smells kinda' sexy down here."

"Probably more sweaty, Sweety, than sexy," he said.

"Sweaty can be sexy sometimes, Sugar," she suggested.

An hour later Walter could see the sun sliding toward a cloud bank somewhere way out there.

< 238 >

"How do you like it here, Pinky? Are you getting used to it?"

"Sure am," she said, "and the best part is, you seem happy being a cowboy. When you're happy, I'm happy."

"You know I'm not really a cowboy. Over here the Paniolos are the closest we've got to cowboys. I'm more like a horseman, I guess."

"Smell like a cow makes you a cowboy for me."

Walter's focus changed from the ocean to Pinky, her legs crossing his chest.

"Is your pal Jake a cowboy?"

"Closer than me. He actually ranches his own cattle. But, you know, he's mostly an excellent horseman."

"Nice guy?"

"Yes. Straight shooter. Kind of quiet, but the longer I know him the better I like him."

He looked at her intense eyes. She was a frisky little thing. A Border collie pup to his basset hound.

"Are you makin' friends?" he asked. "Do you like Darcy and Allie?"

"Sure. They're nice. I surf with 'em when Darcy comes over here. The only problem with Allie is I can hardly understand her. I can't believe they really talk like that in Texas. But she's fine. Pretty sure of herself and dang proud of Texas."

She poked Walter's tummy with a finger.

"Are all Texans like that?"

"Confident and proud?"

"Uh huh."

"Yep. ... Well, mostly they are. But they got all types."

"I think if she ever went to church, she'd be a Southern Baptist."

"Is it different from a regular Baptist?" Walter asked, mildly curious.

"More fire and brimstone, I think."

"You like your new church?" he asked.

"Tell you something, Wal, I love it. And I bet you would too. Kinda' old style prayers but the preachin' is pretty informal and not too long. God loves you no matter how bad you've been. That's the style.

"There's some guitar playing and singing and once a month they've got communion with a little wine and wafers that melt in your mouth ... Think about that Wal. Wine, strummin, quiet preachin' with no yellin' or scoldin'. All the people are friendly.

"In and out in an hour."

"Sounds nice," Walter said, "What kind is it?"

"Episcopalian."

< 240 >

## Three Months in the Jungle

Fletch dug through his little cache of valuables and found the only money he had been able to get quickly when he left Honolulu. Grab what you can and disappear. That had been the plan.

Leave no tracks.

He took the envelope of paper money and spread it on his mat and counted it.

Three single-dollar bills. He glanced at George Washington's face. It was a quiet face. No smile, of course, probably because of all those wooden teeth.

He stacked them neatly and put a pebble on top. He had twenty tens. Hamilton on one side looking toward the future, the White House in green on the back. A pile with a stone on top.

There were seven twenties with Jackson and his wild hair, the White House on the back. Realizing his mistake, Fletch looked back at the ten-dollar notes. That was not the White House, it was the U.S. Treasury.

So what?

The last stack had Ben Franklin on one side, Independence Hall on the other. Each bill had the number 100 repeated seven times and the words spelled out twice more. One Hundred Dollars. Fletch counted these bills. He had fifteen of them.

Fletch realized he'd spent quite a while examining his money.

While he had lots of time, he did not have much cash. He wondered how much of either he had left.

Counting the eighty-nine notches he'd carved on his little shelter, he realized it had been almost three months he'd spent in this jungle. Except for 'Aloha' and 'hello' when he went down to the valley to gather food or fish, he had spoken to no one but himself.

He pulled on some Army-issue fatigue pants with lots of

< 241 >

pockets. His feet felt too large for the tennis shoes, but he put them on anyway.

He put his identification and some of his money at the bottom of a tin box with his other treasures. Then he buried it in the floor of the cave and covered it with a scrap of mat he had found on one of his fishing trips.

With his backpack and a black T-shirt, he went down the winding trail to the valley floor, and out to face civilization. Besides clean underwear and an extra shirt and toothbrush, he had half his money and his smallest pistol.

It was a long walk to the bus stop in Honokaa.

Waiting, he bought his first hamburger in three months.

## Three Months to Create a Legend

Shortly after the public was encouraged to help find the explosive killer on Honolulu's televised news shows, the strange sightings began.

On Kauai a blue and green tour bus made a pit stop between Barking Sands and Kekaha. A passenger saw a huge shaggy figure and pointed.

Partly human, it stood at the jungle's edge about two-hundred yards from the highway. Someone screamed and eight credible witnesses had time to shoot cell-phone pictures before it picked up what appeared to be the corpse of a dog and moved into the dense undergrowth. The driver reported the sighting and officials were able to interview several of the tourists.

It was reported in the *Wailua Observer* and *Advertiser*, available at the supermarket beside the real estate brochures.

About the same time, over on Maui, on the almost endless curve-fest that make up the road to Hana, passenger cars were stopped and harassed by a naked man.

He had jumped out of the forest in front of the autos. Over four days, several travelers were accosted by this hairy guy. Usually loud horn honking drove him away.

However, at least once a car with four young women reported they were exposed to things they would rather not have seen. The windows were rolled up, doors locked, so they were not particularly frightened.

Interestingly, later, under intense questioning by officer Taki Wakayama, as he was writing up his report, they revealed that two of the girls thought showing their breasts would drive him away. It didn't.

And there was a folk song, *The Ballad of Fletch Armstrong*,

< 243 >

which played in a few bars but was never recorded. It was written and usually performed by a local guitarist in and around Kihei and Wailea. A modified version was performed by a cute third grader with a ukulele. It went viral and aired on a local newscast.

Legends of the Kauai Big-Foot, the Naked Man of Hana, and others persisted a while, but finally faded away, until a family of hiking buffs from Minnesota came to the Big Island and were camping and hiking in the Waipio Valley.

This valley is north of Honokaa at the end of Route 240. Largest of the Big Island's north shore valleys of the Kohala Mountains, it's the least accessible. It's about six miles deep, a mile wide, with the open end at the sea. The other three sides are steep cliffs with the Hiilawe Falls plunging down thirteen-hundred feet.

The faint remains of terraces and fishponds suggest that in ancient times it was home to thousands of people. But the population dwindled to about five thousand by the time Captain Cook arrived, and is down now to under a hundred self-sufficient residents.

The valley floor is lush with avocado, banana, taro, coconut, and wild fruit. The ocean is full of fish, and rain provides plenty of fresh water.

It had been three months since Fletch departed Honolulu and the law, when the Minnesota family, the Leggersons, made camp in the Waipio Valley.

While his wife, Joan, and the youngest girl searched the black sand beach for tiny white shells, Ted and his fifteen-year-old daughter, Laura, took a tough hike on the Muliwai Trail, a steep zig-zagging path up and over the top toward Waimanu Valley, seven miles away.

Pausing to rest their burning legs after the exhausting

< 244 >

switchbacks, they sat on the trail, sweating, and looking over the jungle and valley below. Heavy breathing evolved into conversation and relaxation. Father-daughter bonding.

Laura saw what might be a path splitting off the trail into some dense vegetation. It was hidden, but discernible on close inspection. When they finally did get up, Laura had a suggestion.

"Dad, let's bag the trail and see where the path leads."

"Probably a jaguar den," he said. "Wanna risk it?"

"Sure."

About seventy feet down the path, which was hardly visible, they discovered a tidy lean-to shelter and a shallow cave. It appeared to be a permanent survivalist's home. A duffle bag and a little grid of sticks, tied together with pieces of vine, corralled a supply of fruit: avocados, coconuts, bananas, and more.

There were two jars of water.

A large homemade mat with a small, folded blanket where a pillow might go, dominated the cave's floor. They saw a blackened area where there had been a cooking fire, and a few simple pots and utensils. Everything looked tidy and homey.

"This is somebody's residence," Ted said. "Let's go and leave it alone."

His observant daughter looked at the food storage arrangement. She reached over and squeezed an avocado.

"Too squishy for my taste," she said. "And look at the dark spots on the banana. Dad, the over-ripe fruit ... seems the owner has been gone a few days.

"I think he went fishing."

Laura was kneeling by the mat where the stone ceiling was low, but as she scooched back to stand up, she accidently scuffed a smaller mat to the side, revealing the corner of a buried tin box. The lid was flush with the dirt floor.

Being a curious teenager, she pulled off the lid, and peeked in.

"Look!"

The surprise in her voice brought her father.

The little cache included a Lugar pistol partly hidden in an oily rag, an envelope, and other things. It was hard to tell what was down there without poking around.

But the most obvious item was right on top.

The warning could not have been more clear, whether the messenger was a crouching black panther or a crocodile.

You don't belong here, was the message.

The messenger was a hand grenade.

"Honey, don't touch anything. Let's get out of here."

Ted put the lid back on, carefully pinched a corner of the little mat, and pushed it back in place.

And they left.

Back at their campsite Ted gathered the family. They packed up and headed out.

"Don't worry, girls, we'll find plenty of new places to pitch our tent. I'm taking us out to supper tonight. Maybe we'll get a motel room and take a bath and sleep on soft beds."

He was moving a little faster than the average father.

"Whatcha' think, girls?" he asked. But it had not been a question.

In Honoka they were able to contact a highway patrolman and Ted and Laura told their story.

The story made its way to the Honolulu Police Department.

Clay headed for the Big Island early the next morning.

< 246 >

## Three Months and Finally a Clue

Clay met Ted and Laura Leggerson in Hilo, and they drove north to Honokaa, while Joan Leggerson and the younger daughter went shopping.

Past the town they continued north on 240 to the Waipio Valley, where they parked, walked a mile on the black sand beach to the cliff, and then started up. It was a cruel hike, and father and daughter, fit hikers, were not eager to do it again.

Clay's legs were pathetic noodles after the first few switchbacks. By the time they reached the top, they were all out of breath, with hearts pounding.

Sitting in the trail, looking down at the green view, they were quiet for a while, sucking air.

"You are a very fit family," Clay offered. "How do you do it?

The Leggersons both spoke at once.

"Youth," Laura said.

"Vitamins," Ted said.

When they were all breathing normally, Clay popped the question.

"So, where's this little path?" He didn't see one and guessed there was more hiking to come.

"Right there." Laura pointed.

Clay thought about it.

"I think you two should stay here and let me go alone, in case someone comes back."

They agreed and remained seated, as Clay got up, touching the pistol at his back.

Sure enough, the path itself was hidden under a carpet of low ferns, but it could easily be followed once away from the trail. After twists and turns through deep foliage, the little shelter and cave were as described. Neat, clean, and deserted, for the time being. Waiting patiently.

Clay looked under the small mat and saw the tin lid. Peeking in, he saw what Laura and Ted had seen.

It was certainly Fletch's calling card.

He left the primitive home just as he had found it.

Back in Hilo, Clay thanked the vacationers profusely and bought their suppers. Clay excused himself, gathered some supplies, and headed back north in a rented car.

"Hi Mikio," he said when the ringing was answered.

"How's it goin' down there?" his partner asked.

"Well, Mikio, I think it's our best lead in three months. The campsite is terribly remote and very, very well hidden. It has the neatness of Fletch's room at the beach house and it's as shipshape as you might expect from a master sergeant whose job had been teaching combat and survival skills.

"His cache includes weapons and at least one hand-grenade.

"I'm driving back up as we speak.

"I have a room reserved in the little town of Honokaa and want to get there before dark.

"Tomorrow I'll go back up and set some little thread traps that will show me if he comes in or out. Of course, an animal can break my thread too, so ..."

"Better be careful," Mikio said, "he could set a trap for you too, you know."

"Okay, for sure," Clay said. "I'm tempted to gather all his shit in evidence bags and get it out of there. I'm sure there are fingerprints all over stuff, and I'm pretty sure they'll be his. But I'd rather he didn't know we're on his tail.

"If someone stumbled into the grenade or whatever, it could be really bad. On the other hand, it is nearly impossible to find. So, what to do?"

"It's in the jungle," Mikio said. "You don't need a search warrant. If you want, you could bag stuff and split. But you'd lose the element of surprise, and probably send him running."

< 248 >

They both thought a while. The sunset flickered through passing trees as it spilled onto Clay's left shoulder.

"Assuming I'm left to my own devices, I think I'll sneak up there early and set some little traps to get an idea if he is still around. Hope he doesn't discover me while I'm at it.

"Then I'll spend a couple days with a long gun in my lap watching the switchbacks on the cliff face. If he wants fresh veggies or fruit or fish, it's all on the valley floor and in the ocean. He'll have to go up and down. It would be a good place to trap him.

"My fear is he's gone, and we missed him again. But maybe he'll come back. His duffle bag is still there, and it's full of his stuff. He could just be out fishing.

"How long you figure he's been gone?"

"His things are neat and clean. In time I expect leaves will fall and animals will disturb stuff. But not yet. Duffel bag is worn but in fine repair. I guess he's been in it recently ... maybe a week or two ago. The fruit is not fresh, but not yet rotten. Maybe a week in this heat?"

"We can get you some back-up if you want it."

"I'll stay in touch. But for now ... I don't know, probably just get in the way. I think I'll get some sleep and figure things out tomorrow."

"OK," Mikio said. "Good luck."

< 249 >

# A Rolling Stone

In a little beer bar on the coast road, several locals were leaning on elbows looking at their nearly empty glasses. The sun had slipped over the mountains and the dark sea looked grim. The neon beer signs interrupted the ocean view and furnished a warm coziness to the room.

"Well, I'm outta' here," one fellow said as he stood.

"Me too."

"Bye, Gurtz."

All three shuffled across the floor and out the door.

The woman was in her mid-thirties, in tight jeans and a black tank top with a scooped neck. Her dark hair had been pulled into a no-nonsense ponytail, but some strands had escaped and slid across her vision or stuck to her brow. The curls and tangles suggested it had been a long day. Her neck and arms glistened with sweat. She was hot and tired. Done.

She glanced around the empty room. There had been one more customer alone in a corner, but he must have gone to the men's room. She hadn't seen him leave and his large backpack was still beside the chair.

Gurtz sighed and began wiping tables and setting up chairs. She turned off the electric 'open' sign.

A noise distracted her. It came from the kitchen.

"What the hell?!"

A large guy with a three-month-old beard was standing with his hands in the sink holding beer steins.

"What the hell are you doing in my kitchen?"

"Washing dishes?" He said it like it was a real question.

"I noticed," she said. "But we're closed now."

"We're closed? Who's this 'we'?"

"Me, myself and I. We're closed."

< 250 >

"That's what I thought. You were my waitress at lunch, you were the cook that made my burger, and you fried the fries I ate. Now you served as bartender, waitress, and cooked the hot dog and probably made the potato salad and soup, too.

"So, I figured you could use a little help with the dishes."

"Who are you?"

"I was your lunch customer about two days ago and about four days before that. Twice today."

"You're a repeat customer then? Makes you think it's okay to come into my kitchen now?"

"Well, I figured you could use some help."

Gurtz pulled a chair into the doorway and sat down.

"Who are you, mister?"

"Joe. Who are you?"

"Gertrude, but the locals call me Gurtz. Now that you're a repeat customer, you can call me that. I'm the owner and proprietor. I guess you noticed."

Fletch went back to the cups and glasses. As she watched, she noticed he was doing an efficient and thorough job.

"All right, Joe. If you insist, you can do the dishes while I make tomorrow's soup and salad."

They were quiet while they worked. The bar area was semi-dark, lit pinkish by the neon signs. The big man finished the dishes, wiped them, and put them away.

Then he put her salad into Tupperware.

"So, Joe, my repeat customer, I suppose you're a local, then?"

"No ma'am. I'm a rolling stone."

"Where do you sleep?"

"Wherever I find myself at bedtime. Indoors or out. This is Hawaii, you know."

"I saw your backpack. Sleeping bag and jammies in there? Your surfboard probably outside?"

"No board. Not a surfer."

"Oh?"

< 251 >

"I can swim, but never surfed. I'm playing tourist right now."

"Oh?"

"Just a tourist till I meet some friends and we go sailing.

"How about you, beautiful woman alone running a bar in paradise?"

"Running a lonely bar ... running ... and running from a previous life, I guess."

She glanced at the cupboard, and then the refrigerator. Her anchors.

"I am so tired," she said.

Fletch moved to go.

"Where are you sleepin' tonight, Joe?"

"Hmm, dunno. Under a fern of some sort, I guess."

"You can sleep on the couch in the bar. It's by the front door. It's kinda' short for you, but not too uncomfortable," she said. "Use my shower in the morning if you're quiet about it. I usually sleep in a little."

"Great, if it's no bother," he said, and took his pack toward the couch.

"Light switch is right by the door. Will the neon bother you? I can turn the beer signs off if you prefer the dark."

They said goodnight and she went through a door marked 'private' and into her bedroom.

Fletch laid on the couch in his skivvies with his knees up and closed his eyes. The electric signs made a slight humming noise. The beach was close enough he caught the sound of the surf.

And then he heard her shower running, as he drifted off.

When sunlight finally lit the room, he sat up, confused. A window was open, and the moving air smelled like gardenia. The slow cadence of the surf was omnipresent, and he listened until he sensed he was being watched.

The woman's face that had seemed worn-out the night before was soft and fresh. Her chestnut brown eyes were looking at him.

< 252 >

Watching. Keeping secrets.

"Good morning," she said. "Do you have plans?"

"A rolling stone," he said, again.

She moved a chair up and sat down.

"Would you sit still for a hair trim? Nothing personal, but you look rather scruffy. Like the legendary Kauai Big-Foot."

"Oh yeah?"

"First tell me your hopes and dreams," she asked lightly.

"Hmmm ... well, I wanna' sail," he said.

"Do you know how?"

"Not really." He glanced in the direction of the ocean. "I took lessons in a Soling, so I got the general idea. But I want to go on a big boat. Maybe a ketch or a yawl. Something with lots of sails to put up and take down. Lots of ropes to pull and knots to tie. I'd like to be part of a crew, going island to island, or maybe even farther."

"That sounds like freedom," she said.

"Yes ma'am. Wind and waves."

She sat quietly, looking at his hairy face.

Finally, she said, "You could hang around a yacht harbor, and you'll find a ride. Ask around, and check the bulletin boards in the grocery stores, and you'll find someone needing crew. Tell 'em you're strong and willing to learn, and you'll have an adventure and make a little money."

"Without experience?"

"They'll teach you. Almost all the big boats are different. And each owner wants things done his way."

"Good idea," Fletch said.

"Meantime, get up and put a chair on the deck. I'll trim you up before I go to the grocery store."

When the hair on his face and head looked tidy, and the rest was in the foliage, he showered, and put his backpack by the door.

"Will you be back tonight?" she asked. "Just wondering."

"I'm going to take your laundry basket and my clothes to the Wash-n-Dry behind the gas station, use a machine, and read a magazine, if they've got one. Then make your bed. After that I don't know. I might hang around a yacht harbor, check out the boats, and ask around. I think you've given me some ideas."

"Good luck, Joe," she said. "You're a nice guy."

"I might be a rolling stone on the rolling sea when tonight rolls around. Or I might roll in here and try your couch again."

"That would be okay," Gurtz said.

< 254 >

# Three Days in the Jungle

Clay pulled a fern leaf toward the hidden path and tied it with a thin black thread to another from the opposite side. And he repeated the process several other places.

He took cell phone photos of the exact position of the duffel bag in the cave, bracing the phone just so, against a post of the little shelter. He took careful note of the positions of the mats and documented anything else he noticed.

And then Clay spent two days watching the trail zigging and zagging its way up the cliff. Dawn to Dark.

He did not see a soul use the trail.

Nothing.

On the third day he inspected his little thread traps and compared his photos. Nothing had been disturbed.

He had a room rented in Honokaa and had been spending a few hours there after dark, trying to sleep. But he was out before dawn, back to the Waipio Valley with his binoculars and weapon.

Although the little campsite felt deserted, Clay had a very strong sense that Fletch was not too far away.

He decided to change course.

He would ask around, make some friends, chat a little, all unofficial, just to see what might turn up. Farmers in the little valley. Retirees on vacation camped on the beach. A cleaning lady that had worked at Cliff House. One old hippie. More farmers, and some craftsmen.

"Yeah, seen him go up the cliff trail a time or two." ... "Never talked to him." ... "Never close enough to see any details, 'cept he was a haole" ... "Big" ... "Haole." ... "Tall haole" ... "Seen him runnin', kinda' like" ... "a jogger," ... "Sometimes he ran past our place," ... "Runnin' from something." ... "can't figure why any-

< 255 >

body'd run for no reason." ... "Kinda' scruffy lookin', is all." ... "A month ago." ... "Gosh, maybe a couple months back." ... "A while back ... a week ago."

Then Clay started asking outside the valley.

He was unsuccessful in Honokaa but kept going further.

In the Laupahoehoe Public Library a lady remembered spending time talking to a large whiskered stranger who carried a hulking backpack and seemed friendly.

"He surely could have used a bath," she said, "but he spent a long time talking about books, among a lot of other things."

In answer to some of Clay's questions she said, "He seemed very smart and well-read. He was interested in sailing and had plans to crew on a big yacht. I would have liked to see him again, but when he left, I knew he was moving on. Gone."

She didn't have his name. He did not check out any books.

It could have been Fletch.

It could have been anybody.

Clay began to think he might be wasting his time: and then he stopped at the Papaaloa Community Center Gym.

"Sure, I remember a guy like that," said the man in charge. "Nice guy. Real big, maybe six-five or six. Looked a little scruffy, but fit. Seemed to know his way around the weight room and the machines.

"He was here about three hours on a Thursday and again even longer the next day. Figured he'd sign up for a month, but only paid one day at a time. Paid cash. Said his name was Joe. Guess he was just passin' through."

"When was this?" Clay asked.

"Probably a week ago or less. I haven't seen him since."

"Did he talk to anyone who might remember him?"

"Mostly he just worked out; you know the type. Serious about his body. On Friday he talked to Dave a long time."

< 256 >

"Do you know what they were talking about?"

"No. I was mostly working the desk. Except at one point, I know they were talking about sailboats, the biggies that go inter-island. But they probably solved most of the world's problems as well. I noticed 'cause they sat on the machines for a kinda' long time just talking. I didn't say anything 'cause Dave is a regular member, and we weren't too busy."

"Could I talk to Dave?"

"Sure. He comes on Tuesdays and Fridays."

"Is he here?" Clay asked. "It's a Tuesday."

"He was earlier, but he's gone ten minutes ago."

"Oh?"

"He'll be at the juice bar now. On the coast road near the Royal Palm Estates. Called Juice-a-Rama or something like that."

"Think I'll try to catch him," Clay said. "What's he look like?"

"Yellow T-shirt and red nylon pants. Bald head. Can't miss him. Drives a tan Chevy crew cab pick-up."

Clay got his cell phone, found Google maps, and was gone.

Dave was getting into his car with his juice cup half empty, when Clay cornered him.

"I'm trackin' my old friend, Joe," Clay lied, "and I think you talked to him at the gym."

"Big dude? Trimmed beard?"

"Middle aged, about six-foot-six."

"Yes. I saw him."

"I'm trying to catch up with him. You get any idea where he was headed? What was he driving?"

"You're a friend of his and you don't know what he's driving or where he's goin'?"

"We haven't seen each other in years, and I want to surprise him. His cell doesn't answer."

"Maybe he doesn't want to talk to you."

"Impossible."

"Well, if you say so. So how can I help?"

"What did you talk about? Where's he headed?"

"Mostly we just talked, where ya' from, nice weather, 'cept when it rains. Stuff like that.

"We did talk about boats some. Sailboats. He was hoping to catch a ride on a yacht. Workin' as crew, make a little money and see the world, you know."

"Did he say how he was going to do that?"

"Nothing specific. I told him the nearest big marina was in Hilo. He'd seen yachts in Honolulu and Waikiki, but those are big harbors, nothing like that on this island."

Clay realized he'd come on a little abrupt with Dave, so he relaxed and chatted. He learned Joe traveled on buses and hitch-hiked with a large pack. And that was about it.

Clay wasted a day between the O'okala Fellowship and Laupahoeahoe Harbor, more a raging sea and lava-peppered shoreline than a safe haven for boats. Few people, fewer chats, nothing productive. The misnamed harbor with no boats.

The next day he stopped for an early lunch at a little beer joint near the ocean. The parking area was empty, except for a well-used greenish-gray BMW. A lighted sign by the door said 'open,' so he went in.

A woman sitting on a bar stool got up, put her magazine aside, and smiled.

"Have a seat anywhere you like," she said brightly. "Coffee?"

"Yes please."

Clay sat at the bar close to where she had been sitting. He watched her efficient moves behind the bar, as she poured and passed him a menu.

Clay picked up the magazine.

"Strange literature to find in a bar in Hawaii," he said.

< 258 >

"How's that?"

"*Western Horseman Magazine* usually goes to horsemen in the West."

"Out here we're so western, we're west of the west. Harder to get further west than here."

"A western girl?"

"I was once."

Clay looked at her chestnut-colored eyes. She had dark hair tied at the back of her head. She was wearing tight Wrangler jeans; the brand real cowboys usually wear. They were extra-long, just right on horseback, but providing a little stacking around the ankles when on foot. They fit just right.

"Well ..." Clay picked up the magazine and looked at the mailing label, "... Miz Gertrude Lambsul, I see by your outfit that you are a cowgirl."

"And you, mister what's-your-name, are an authority on cowgirls?"

"Yes ma'am, I am,' Clay grinned. "You see, I'm from Elko, Nevada. You can't get more cowboy than that."

"Can't argue there," she said. "Want to order lunch?"

"What soup are you selling today, Gertrude?"

"Please call me Gurtz. I like it much better. The soup is asparagus mint cheese."

"Well, I guess I'll have the burger with potato salad."

"Good choice," she said. "I tried a bite of the soup this morning and it tasted like a failed experiment. I kinda' hope nobody orders it, and I can give it to the mission. They're not real fussy."

They were talking over the counter as she turned to the stove and got to work. Her movements were animated, and she wore a loose white T-shirt with a scooped neck. Sleeveless. She was fun to watch.

"You're the cook AND the waitress?"

"I'm the entire act," she said. "Dishwasher, too."

"It's your place then?"

"Yes, it is."

"How long?" Clay, making conversation.

"About five years, mister who-are-you. And while we're on the subject ... Who are you?"

"Clay. Nice to meet you, Gurtz. Where are you from?"

"Came from California," meat sizzling in the background. "How do you like your burger? There's avocado, lettuce, bacon, cheese and tomato; you can have all or none, your choice."

"Everything 'cept bacon, please."

He saw she had two buns cut, and two chubby paddies cooking. "Are you joining me for lunch? My treat if you are."

"Sure, unless the lunch crowd rushes in and upsets my plan."

In waitress mode, she delivered the food to one of the small tables by the window where they could eat and talk.

The lunch conversation was pleasant, but before long their date was cut short when three locals arrived, thirsty and hungry. And they were soon joined by two more.

As Clay paid his bill, Gurtz took the remains of her burger and salad behind the bar to finish it, one bite at a time, as she poured beers and cooked burgers.

Clay called Mikio after lunch to check in.

"Mikio, it's me. Anything shakin' in Honolulu?"

He listened to a rundown of progress on some of their cases. And there was office gossip. But there was nothing that demanded he fly back. Not yet.

Finally, Mikio asked, "So, how does Fletch look in handcuffs?"

"I'm afraid I'm not quite there yet. This is all hearsay, Mikio, but people have seen a big, bearded guy around here. In the valley for two or three months, and more recently farther from his hide-a-way. I set traps and checked his cave from time to time, but he hasn't come back.

I'm pretty sure he's going to the Hilo Yacht Harbor and wants

< 260 >

to crew on a sailboat. My plan, if you can spare me, is to move out of my little room in Hinokaa and go to Hilo and sniff around the harbor. I'm pretty sure that's his direction."

"If you think you're gettin' close, keep goin', Clay. I think you're the best hope we have to clear this disaster up."

"All right. Tell everybody 'Hi' and that I miss 'em, especially Betty, and that I'm staying politically correct."

"Yeah," Mikio said. "I bet you are."

< 261 >

# Three Hours Later

Three hours later, Clay was still thinking about his lunch date. He remembered Gurtz fondly. A hard worker and responsible, but sort of lyrical in quiet moments. Her secretive eyes.

So, at an early hour, he returned for a beer.

"Is it too early for supper?" he asked.

"Wow. Nice to see you, Clay from Elko. Where ya' been?"

"Out riding the range in my rent-a-car, lookin' for cowboys," Clay said, talkin' nonsense. She looked every bit as interesting as he remembered.

"Paniolos is what we offer here, I'm afraid. Close as we get to what you're used to is at the Parker Ranch, where I heard about some horsemen doing cow cutting for the tourists."

"Ever see it?" Clay asked.

"Not yet, but I know what it is. Horse dancing with a cow. If I ever get a day off, I'm goin' over to see. I bet it's cool."

"I hope you do. I know a couple of those guys."

"You really are from Elko. I believe you. What are you doing here?"

"Being a tourist." Changing the subject, he asked, "You get much time off?"

"Not much. Sundays I'm closed, but busy with everything I should have been doing during the week. The rest of the week is catch-as-catch-can.

"Friday nights usually run late, and Saturday nights we've got music. Sometimes country, sometimes Hawaiian cornball, and sometimes Slack Key. On Friday and Saturday, Sally, the queen of flirtation, and Elsie work too. Elsie cooks. I mean she's a pro, and so we have Mahi Mahi and pork roast on the menu then.

"Saturday nights are always fun. You should stop by."

Gurtz pushed her hair back. It had been sneaking out of containment. Then she pulled the little elastic circle off the tail

< 262 >

and shook her head.

"Beautiful hair," Clay said.

"Oh yeah?"

She re-gathered it all with both hands and pulled it back tight on all sides and fastened the device on a fresh ponytail. It seemed like a quiet, rather intimate moment.

"I feel like you let me in on a secret," Clay said. "Beautiful and free for a moment, now slick and ready for business."

She inspected Clay carefully. "You are a bit deeper than you appear," she said. "Let's sneak out on the back porch and check the ocean till the regulars start to bother us. ...

"Want a beer?"

"Well, I came for a cold beer, but I'd rather just talk to you without one. At least for now."

They went out and sat side by side on the little bench.

"We're looking straight at California," she said.

"Do you get homesick?" he asked.

"Sure. Sometimes. But I love it here. I was from Los Olivos, a nice part of America. And if I rode to the top of the hill, I could see the ocean. I would imagine Hawaii, just over the horizon.

"Do you notice the ocean often looks like a gentle giant? But sometimes it seems to get angry and hostile."

"Yes. It's got a million moods," Clay agreed, "and a mind of its own."

"I think there's bad weather coming," she said. "That was on the extended weather report.

"She can get angry ... the ocean, I mean. But here it won't last very long. In Hawaii the Chamber of Commerce designs the weather."

They sat still for a long while. In a tree below the deck a small gray bird ate a bright orange berry. Then it flew away.

"Ever get lonely out here?"

"I'm pretty independent," she said. "Probably too much so. Basically, that's a lot of why I left California. Here I'm in charge of my life. This bar has taken away my freedom in a way, but it's made me stable, I think; it's given me a home."

"Hmm," Clay said.

"I just took out a mortgage about three months ago," Clay said. "I'm still getting used to that 'freedom exchanged for a home' idea."

"You must be married then," she said.

"Nope. Not married, but no longer homeless."

"Gosh, an unusual man. Most of them I've seen don't want to settle down; first they want to sow wild oats. Seems to me you're smarter than your average guy."

"I don't think it's smarter, just that my oats aren't so wild anymore."

Clay studied her. He hadn't intended to make his debt public.

"Putting some dough into real estate is usually a good move. Planting roots financially and emotionally."

"Life is a series of trade-offs," he said. "You make a decision and try to live with it. A door opens and you step through ... or you don't."

They heard tires crunching gravel in the parking area.

Gurtz got up. "Want that beer?"

"Sure."

She was headed in when Clay called to her: "Can I call you some Sunday?"

"Wish you would."

She returned with his beer and her business card. 'The Jump Off ... Beer, Burgers, and A California View' it said. Then: Gurtz, proprietor. She had written a phone number on the back.

Clay sat alone with his brew looking at the sullen sea and darkening sky. He could hear the jabbering of locals inside. The clinking of glasses. A cacophony of sounds, none of which fit his mood.

"I bet she's thirty-five," he said to himself. "Same as me."

< 264 >

# Terry Cloth

The sky and sea that had looked sinister from the porch of the 'Jump Off' to Gurtz and Clay was a calm orange sunset for Jake and Darcy.

They were back on the Big Island to see how the equine tourist trap was going.

The sliding door was open to the humid air and the view. They wore matching terry cloth robes they found in the closet.

Their wedding was many months behind them, the time in between had been busy. Sometimes frantic. But here, the islands seem to bring them back to those first peaceful days.

As the sun settled into the sea, the honeymoon was back.

Terry cloth fell away. The sound of a guitar far away mingled with the rhythm of the waves.

It was as though they'd never left.

< 265 >

## Tourist Trap

Reactions differed of course, but for the average family what started with, "Lookie here. See the cute horsie?" ended with, "Just incredible, what those animals could do."

As a small crowd started to form at the cutting demonstration the next morning, Darcy and Jake slipped in with them. Jake wanted to see the performance like the tourists saw it. They sat in the last row, the third, and hoped not to be noticed as the riders loped circles and the cows were settled. And precisely at ten o'clock the riders moved away and Allie rode in and took over.

"Aloha Everyone. Welcome to Texas." she said.

Allie narrated from horseback and set the educational tone. Her colorful commentary and personality added the entertainment.

Three cutting horses worked twice, with informal narration in-between. When the last horse to work went into the herd and the rider, Walter, leaned forward and reached between the horse's ears and pulled off the one-ear bridle, people gasped.

"Oh, my hell!" Allie's voice shifted into high gear. "This could get dangerous, y'all. The dang pony is free as a Texas meadowlark. Let's see how this is gonna' work out."

Walter held the handful of leather; bridle and reins, in one hand and rested the other on the saddle horn.

"My heavens, folks, the dang pony is settin' the cow up perfect, all by his lonesome. Walter ain't doin' shit. Damn, I'm sorry. Ex-cuse me. Walter ain't doin' nothin' but tryin' ta stay on ... My mamma told me swearin' is a crutch for a weak mind."

When the horse and cow were nose to nose darting back and forth, Allie would be offering little shrieks of encouragement with a "Whoop, whoop, whoop."

When the cow finally stopped, Walter pinched the little bay gelding's neck. The horse backed a step. Walter stepped off and

< 266 >

walked out, the equine following, as though being led. The crowd, all twenty of them, erupted in applause.

The heifer trotted to the herd and Allie rode to the center, talking.

"Wow-wee, folks, that was something to see! A horse named Metal Toy and our cowboy Walter working a young Aberdeen Angus cow named Bossy, right here in Hawaii. It coulda' easy been Texas!

"We're gonna' walk these horses around to cool 'em and you can feel free to ask questions or let the little tykes pet one. These equine athletes are plumb gentle and getting usta' folks. But don't let the kiddies get stepped on, 'cause it hurts worse than a stubbed toe."

"Don't forget to visit the cutting horse kiosk to the right as you leave. It's got a cutting saddle you can sit on and pictures of them old time cuttins' in Texas. And stories and history galore.

"And don't forget to sign up for a trail ride. You can do that at the little museum while yer lookin' around.

"Shur thank y'all fer comin' — We all wish you happy trails.

"I'm Allie, signing off and sayin' aloha. We'll see all y'all in Texas. Click." Her voice was gone, and the silence was golden.

Jake was happy and decided to suggest some background music on the sound system as the crowd gathered and the cows settled. Maybe Ian Tyson's cutting songs, or Corb Lund's *Cows Around*. He went to chat with his performers and their horses.

Darcy, Pinky, and Allie went surfing.

< 267 >

# Vacation

The next day Suz came. Darcy had mentioned to Jeffrey that Suz could probably use a vacation. It had been his invitation that brought her to spend some time at the ranch. She'd have one of the guest rooms, and she arrived in time to join her friends for lunch. The Oars, McCumbers, her art student Walter, and Pinky.

It was about two in the afternoon when she gathered with a little band of tourists to watch the afternoon cutting demo and listen to Allie's play by play.

Suz wore a blue and white baseball style cap with a Bolt logo. She was attentive and when Allie finally invited people to "Enjoy the rest of y'all's day, y'all. ... Aloha." Suz reached into her little canvas bag for her sketchbook.

That was when she realized Bob Claymore had been watching too, sitting in the row behind her. Higher, and a little to her right. The visitors got up to leave and left. But Bob remained seated.

"Hi, Bobby," she said. "Very interesting, isn't it?"

"It is." His eyes met hers, "People seem to like it."

Then: "Jeffrey said he'd invited you. I'm glad you'll be with us a while."

Suz leaned back so her back and elbows rested against the row he sat on. She squinted up at him and into the sun shining over his shoulder.

"You know," Bob said, "you started all this with your phone call that connected Jake to us, way back last fall."

Suz stood, then stepped over and sat next to Bob.

As they watched, people were departing, some into the arena to meet the riders and horses, others headed for the little museum or the parking lot.

Walter had a three-year-old child on the saddle in front of

< 268 >

him, the gleeful mother standing close, holding on to a tiny ankle.

"His first horsey ride," she said, as her husband took their picture. They were not alone; several others were asking questions or posing for selfies.

"Bobby," Suz looked at faded blue eyes under a big hat. "How long have we known each other?"

"Forever, I think. Remember when you were here painting landscapes. That's when we first met, I think. I was fixing tractors. We've been acquainted for what? ... probably thirty years or more."

"Forever. I like that. It does seem so."

"Every time you're here I've been too busy to really talk."

"I know." she said.

"Everybody on the ranch is happier when you're around."

"Oh? ... I've always felt comfortable here," she said.

They sat side by side for a rather long time. The cattle were let out, horsemen went to the barn to unsaddle, and the spectators drifted off.

"Bobby," Suz said, looking at him closely. "Old friend, how are you?"

"I'm good. Kinda' tired."

"Are you okay? I mean, are you sick, how's your health?"

"I'm fine, I think, but I am getting old and have the aches and pains that come with it. Can't help but feel it. I usta' could get going with piss and vinegar in my veins. There was always plenty to do and I was ... am ... always here to do it.

"Are you alone?" she asked.

"I'm here with you."

"But I mean generally. Have you been married? Have a girl-friend? Children?"'

"Gosh, Suz, I've always been alone. Married to the ranch, I guess. I should be lonely, but never had the time to worry about it."

"Bobby, you sound like a man that needs a vacation."

"Interesting point. Can't remember ever having one."

"Why not take one right now?" she asked.

Bob looked at the attentive little lady.

And she looked at him. Somewhere in that sea of wrinkles his eyes showed a little spark.

"Let's do a little test," he said at last. "Watch this."

He pulled out his cell phone and punched it.

"Hello Mary, ... What's on my calendar this afternoon? ... Okay, tell him let's do it next week, same time ... sure, Mary ... Call Carlos and tell him I'll be gone the rest of the day, unless it's an emergency ... okay. Thanks, Mary."

He closed the phone and squinted at it.

"Wow," Suz said. "That was easy."

"Seriously." Bob looked rather amazed. "Maybe I just learned something. It was easy. So, what do I do now? Go fishing?"

"Sure. Fishing."

"But I don't care much for fishing. Boats bore me."

"Go for a walk then."

"Where?"

"Over there," Suz pointed to some shade and a bench.

"It's gotta' be a huge project," Suz said, "running this ranch. How did you get to be in charge?" she asked.

"When I met you, I was a mechanic in the shop. Every time something needed to be done, I volunteered to do it. That's really how I got here. I got raises and promotions, but never thought about a vacation."

"I bet it was interesting," Suz said, "more and more responsibility means consistent learning and growth. Life doesn't get boring."

"No time to get bored. When the day ended, I went to bed. Sunrise to sundown on this ranch there was always something to be done. Hardly ever saw TV. Socialization and city culture; I missed most of it. War protests, drugs, the sexual revolution and

< 270 >

Women's Lib all passed me by.

"But now days I get tired earlier and try to read a little."

The continued talking, relaxed and calm. It was their longest conversation ever. Finally, the bench got hard, and Bob proposed they take a drive.

He talked about moving into management, going to conferences and learning about agronomy, ranch management, animal husbandry, and everything else.

When the car stopped, they were at the beach near Kawaihae. Bob parked and they took off their shoes and walked in the sand.

"Suz, you probably don't know, but I have three of your original paintings in my house, and two prints in my office."

"I didn't know. The galleries are awfully possessive of the collectors. Thanks for telling me. It is always good to realize some actual human has the paintings, and cares for them. They are like my family, and I worry about them."

She reached and squeezed his warm, wrinkled hands. It was probably the first time they had ever touched.

"I love those paintings," he said.

"Polynesian women?"

"Yes."

They found some coral rocks to sit on.

"Jeffrey said you are changing your painting style."

"Well, I really don't know exactly what I'm doing. I guess I am experimenting.

"Trying to get my head straight.

"Someone cut up one of my children. Killed her. Not really, of course, it was only a painting. But that's what it felt like. So, it sort of left me confused. Off balance. Unmotivated. Adrift.

"That's kinda' where I am now. Maybe I'll draw the same subject, but I'll paint looser, with fancy brushwork. Or maybe I'll apply my regular style to landscapes. For artists, our paintings are our teachers, and as we learn, we change."

< 271 >

"Grow?" he asked.

"Change and grow or fade away." She angled toward him. "I guess we'll see."

And with that, Suz used her toe and drew a question mark in the sand at their feet.

As they looked at their toes Bob pulled a plastic wrapper out of his pocket and showed it to her.

"Suz, would you like a cigar?" he asked kindly.

"No thanks, Bobby. But you can, it's your vacation."

He just held it a moment. Suz was watching it too.

"Reminds me of a friendly doobie I met fifty years ago in San Francisco," she said.

Bob gave her a crinkled smile, and put it back in its plastic wrapper, then into his pocket, with two others just like it.

"While I was sinking roots here, I think I missed a lot of life. Too focused for too long. My horizons ended at the volcano mountains and Highway 18, the Belt Road.

The sky was a fading rose color, and they had eaten fish skewers and chips on a small pier. They walked to the end and watched the clouds showing a silvery afterlife, far out on the horizon.

The ocean's breath brought the smell of salt, and with it a slight chill. Bob put his arm around her shoulders as they started back.

"Are you ready to retire?" she asked.

"I wouldn't know what to do if I did. I'm only seventy-seven. I think I need the ranch as much as it needs me. As a little kid, I wanted to be a cowboy, and this is as close as I'm ever going to get."

"You could retire and ride cutting horses in the tourist demonstrations with Jake, Jeffrey, and Wal."

"I could try to hang on, but it would be ugly. Maybe if I was younger. To ride like those guys, you need to start young, and

< 272 >

develop a good seat. Too late for me, I'm afraid."

"Tonight, I know you better than I thought I ever could," she said, and put her arms around him and held tight.

"Suz, when you leave, I'm gonna feel lonely."

"I'm not leavin' yet," she said.

"I've seldom felt lonely, and if I did, I'd forget it and go to sleep. In the morning I'd wake up with too much to do. But the last few years it's like the ranch runs without me.

"I sometimes think I started this cutting horse demo thing to help me stay busy."

"Oh?"

"Invigorate me. Make new friends and create more fires to put out. Drive loneness away. Most fun I ever had was with Jake and our pals at The Futurity in Fort Worth."

"Bobby, do you feel lonely now?"

"Not with you ... I feel relaxed. It's a new feeling."

"You like it?"

"Gosh, I don't know, it's too new."

"Maybe it's 'cause you're on vacation."

"Could be ... but it wouldn't be the same without you."

"Sort of feels to me like we're on a date," Suz said.

"My first date in forty years."

"Oh?"

"Do people go to bed on the first date nowadays?"

"I guess it depends ..."

"Do you go to bed on the first date?"

In soft light on Bob's bed progress was slow and gradual. Unhurried. Suz, a quiet, generous guide. Bob, a kind, respectful, curious explorer.

"It's been a very long, long time," Bob said. "I don't know if it still works."

"I guess we're trying to get a wiggly noodle into a button-hole." She stared into his eyes and delivered her comment

< 273 >

like a scientist.

Looks, then smiles suddenly erupted into sidesplitting laughter. They rolled apart and doubled over. Tears in their eyes. And they roared hilariously.

Not really so funny, but it released the tension.

They lay still a while then, trying not to laugh. But gradually they found their way.

Next day, his vacation over, Bob went back to his office and his schedule.

And Suz drove around sketching landscapes, paniolos, and horses. Making little paint studies. Taking pictures.

And she had suppers with her friends and sometimes Bob joined them.

But however she spent the languid days, she was with Bob when darkness fell.

Every single night.

## Almost

When Clay got to Hilo, he was close. He sensed it. He felt it in his bones.

The town, Hilo, was the biggest on the island, so random conversations with strangers would be useless.

There was a Yacht Club, and Clay looked there for a message board or a yachtsman. But he didn't find either one, and it felt more like an aging tennis club. The ocean was nowhere to be seen.

The old men he found were more interested in their goiters and gastritis than boats or yachts. Any sailing news they furnished was ancient history.

"So-and-so got a new hip ... a new shoulder ... a stent ... or had his prostate removed."

Talking to these old guys was an organ recital.

But they did mention the weather ... "I know it's gonna' be a storm, 'cause my joints hurt ... storm brewing ... dark sky ... it's gonna' be gettin' bad ... weather coming ... keep a jacket handy."

But closer to the real boats at the actual Yacht Harbor, he did discover fliers pinned or taped up in several places. Some were old, faded, and torn, but Clay tried a fresh looking one. He saw it several places, a market, a telephone pole, a hardware store and on a fence.

Dale Hargraves, it said, had a new boat, and was planning to sail to Maui. He was a top-notch skipper and wanted to assemble a small crew to help him. And it gave a number to call.

Clay called.

"Mister Hargraves, this is Clay Burnam, and I'd like to ask you about the crew you're assembling for a trip."

"Sure, ask away. But you're too late, we've got our crew-roster filled. We're on a thirty-seven-foot Hunter Cherubini on a little shakedown cruise right now, so we can talk till I lose cell service.

"That loud noise you hear is a plane coming from America ...

sorry for the noise ... that's better, can you still hear me?"

"Yes, sir, I can. Go on."

"We're passing the airport about half a mile from shore. Headed south. When we pass Kapoho, I'll probably lose you. We're gonna' circle the island and see how we work together and how the boat goes. I just got the boat, a thirty-seven-foot Hunter Cherubini — maybe I told you — and she's a beaut."

He paused for breath.

"Sounds like a nice boat," Clay said.

"Damn nice. She really is. Upgraded and outfitted in 2020. New sails in 2016. Even my wife is excited. She's not with us. Waiting at home till we head for Maui ... Are you a reporter? I could talk slower if you want."

"I'm a mumble-mumble and want to ask about your crew. Who else is along?"

"I got my son Jer — Jerry — with me. He's sailed before. Not on this boat, of course, but on my old boat. And we got Chip, who's sailed on a lot of fine yachts, so we've got our bases covered. We picked up a new guy, big and strong. He doesn't know much about sailing, but he will by the time we get back. His name is Joe. Joe Jenson, I think, somethin' like that."

"When do you expect to get back to the marina?" Clay asked.

"Shit, who knows? That's sailing for you."

"Your best guess?"

"A week maybe, if we go all the way around non-stop. We might stop in the small boat marina on the west side near Keahole, but probably not."

"I sure wish I could watch you come in. Watch you get off."

"Just get in touch with the Coast Guard. They spend taxpay-ers' money tracking boats. Mine is named 'The Merry Widow'."

"Thanks for your time, Mister Hargraves," Clay said.

"Always glad to talk to a reporter," he said, "Who did you say you were with?"

Clay hung up.

< 276 >

# A Boat to Meet

Clay touched base with the Coast Guard.

"Well, Detective," someone said, "I hope your guy knows what he's doing. There's some heavy weather coming up from the south-southeast. Be wise if he put off his little sailing adventure a couple days."

"Can you keep track of the boat for me?" Clay asked.

"Are you reporting it missing?"

"No. Not yet."

"If it goes missing, we can notify Search and Rescue, and they'll get after it."

The conversation continued, but it began to sound like bureaucratic bullshit to Clay. So, he checked in with Mikio and explained the situation.

"Sounds to me like we may have him cornered on a sailboat at sea," Mikio agreed, "so you better stay there and watch him land. You'll probably need back-up."

"Yes, we sure don't want to lose him now. If it really is him."

"Maybe there's no absolute proof, but let's not take a chance. Sure or not, we've got to talk to this guy ... Joe."

Then Mikio said: "I'll talk to Betty, ask her to arrange a couple of back-up cops to be waiting for your call. Want 'em in Hilo?"

"Probably Hilo, in a week, more or less. Might be sooner in the Small Boat Harbor near Kailua-Kona."

"Small Boat Harbor? That's its name?"

"I guess so. That's how the map refers to it. Maybe there's a real name. Shit, Mikio, it would sure be simpler if the Coast Guard Search and Rescue would get involved and keep track of the boat for us."

"Hey, partner, let me talk to Betty; she has a good way of cutting through inter-jurisdictional red tape."

"Roger that, Mikio, and thanks."

## Coast Guard Search and Rescue

The next morning Clay got a call from the United States Coast Guard. They told him 'The Merry Widow,' a big sloop, was being towed to the Little Harbor near the airport on the West side of Hawaii. North and west of Kailua-Kona.

The caller told Clay the boat's owner, Dale Hargraves, reported his boat had been damaged in a heavy squall rounding South Point.

Apparently, someone was hurt, and the west coast harbor was the closest.

"Estimated time of arrival?" Clay asked.

"Probably about four hours. They are putting the people on the Coast Guard vessel and giving them medical attention, and starting north right about now, sailboat in tow."

"Thanks."

Clay, in his rental car, headed out of Hilo to the harbor on the western edge of Hawaii.

He was in a hurry.

< 278 >

# Landing

... Clay would walk up to Fletch as he came down the gang-plank and stepped onto the dock. The two backup officers would be there, one close and one back. They would all be armed and ready. Waiting.

That was how Clay imagined it.

"Hi, Fletch, we've been waiting for you ..."

But that's not what happened. The Coast Guard ship anchored the crippled sailboat where it would be out of the way of other traffic, then came into the dock.

First off came a gurney maneuvered down by two young Coast Guard medics. Their passenger was a groggy man with a face that registered some serious pain. Clay showed his badge to the medics, so they stopped and let him take a peek.

The eyes were glassy, and the mouth formed a grimace.

"Shoulder hurts," he said, and the bandages confirmed it.

"Sorry," Clay said.

And the stretcher moved on.

A young man in shorts and deck shoes, tattoos, and wild hair came next. He looked sober and tired, but unhurt. The experienced crewman. Chip.

The ambulance shut its doors and pulled away. The medics and their wheeled stretcher went back on board. An official police van replaced the ambulance. A dark suit with identification and a long serious face got out. The Medical Examiner.

"You're here for the sailboat wreck?" Clay asked.

"Yes. You're from Honolulu?"

"Yes."

They waited, and in about ten minutes the gurney came back, covered by a sheet. When it rested on the cement near the back of the van, Clay lifted the sheet. Fletch was sleeping face up.

< 279 >

Clay took a deep breath and looked closely. With a thumb he pushed an eyelid up. The white was the only thing visible. Fletch was looking outside in.

Clay pressed the edge of the jaw feeling for a pulse, but there was none.

"Well, he was mine and now he's yours," Clay said to the medical examiner. "DNA and fingerprints will show he was the legendary hand grenade bomber.

"The what?"

"A legend only to the Honolulu Police, I guess. But just another dead guy in Hawaii, to you.

"His name is Fletcher Armstrong." Then Clay corrected himself. "Was," he said ... "his name was."

Clay sent his two backup officers away with a handshake and a "Thanks, guys. Sorry it wasn't more exciting."

Then he went up the ramp and found Dale Hargraves.

The boat owner was probably sixty, suntanned, wrinkled, with unruly white hair. His eyes were bloodshot and wet.

He was sitting slumped on a built-in bench, in a small passageway, looking at nothing. He had a plastic cup near his foot. Almost empty, it might have contained bourbon or scotch. Maybe it was a urine sample, but probably not.

"Mister Hargraves, can I talk to you?"

"Do I know you?"

"No sir, I'm a police detective from Honolulu."

"Am I in trouble?"

"Not from me. I've been trying to talk to one of your crew."

"One of my crew?"

"Yes. Joe."

"The nicest guy ... I killed him ... My fucking stupidity killed him. He saved my son's life and drowned. I am so sorry ... My fault ... I killed him. My fucking fault." The pauses were long. The storyteller devastated.

The man was crying unashamedly. He held his head, elbows

< 280 >

on knees, sobbing.

"Joe died a hero. ... No way around that. ... My stupidity killed a great hero."

"Could you tell me about it, Mister Hargraves?"

Clay sat down on the bench beside him.

"Yeah. Tell you about it? ... I can't stop thinking about it."

Clay waited a while, then gently, "Can you tell the story?"

"Sure ...

"Mind if I record it?"

"If you want."

"Thanks."

"We wanted a shake-down cruise, like a little sail around the island to get to know each other and study the new boat.

"Down the East side, turned southwest and went past the volcano where the lava goes into the sea. Below the Ka'u Forest. On down-a-ways. The island was kinda' in the way of the sunset and the sky was getting dark behind us, so we thought we'd stop and anchor for the night. Which we did.

"We opened some champagne, to celebrate our first night on the ocean, together.

"Chip thought we should go on and at least get past South Point. It's as close to the equator as Hawaii gets, you know. But I wanted to take our time and check everything out in the daylight.

"Well, we didn't get to sleep much 'cause it started getting mighty windy, and then a downpour hit us. We were rockin' and rollin', I'll tell you."

He paused then, looking at the cup on the floor. The amber liquid rocked slightly. He seemed transfixed by the cup for a moment before he continued.

"At first light I saw we'd got our sails messed up when we put everything away last night in the dark and wind and rain.

"We tried to get the sails up and fumbled around some. Made a mess of it, so I'm thinking, take a deep breath and start over.

"Release the sheets, mizzen, mainsail, headsail. I'm at the tiller trying to aim the thing at the wind, to release pressure on the rudder. I want to return the helm to parallel the center.

"Then my son Jer is trying to trim the headsail first, then the mainsail, and he gets knocked overboard.

"The sea is thrashing all around, I'm struggling with the wheel and yelling at Chip, and I didn't see Jerry go, but I see things in little glimpses, you know, between spray and flapping canvas and ropes and shit. Somewhere in there Joe jumps in and grabs Jer.

"We're all in our life jackets, so that should help. Chip's watchin' everything, and Joe got Jerry near enough Chip could grab him by his shirt and haul him in. Jerry has a broken shoulder and can't be much help. But Joe is a really big boy and grabs the root of something mounted on the boat and shoves him aboard.

"Now during all this, nothing is calm. Half the time I don't know which way is up. Fuckin' spray everywhere, burns your eyes, and wind, and the boom is not tied down, swinging wherever it wants to go. Complete fuckup. Disaster.

"Anyway," Hargraves continued, reliving it all, "Chip starts yellin' somethin' I can't understand because the wind is howling through the stays and ropes, but what it was, we lost Joe!"

"So, we're trying to get him. His vest is orange, and we glimpse it now and then.

"We got no control of the boat. Sometimes we're up and down, backward or forward, sometimes rolling side to side. Usually, we're doing all of that at the same time. Scared and cold — we thought we'd die for sure."

The defeated captain just sat quietly a while. He was again near tears. And Clay waited.

"Finally, there was more light coming and the squall was moving on. Still raining but not so hard. Our sails are a tangled mess. Something is torn, I'm not sure what ... staysail, I think.

< 282 >

Ropes and cables are broken and loose.

"The cabin is full of floating debris, champagne bottles, our bags, and dirty dishes.

"Our radio still works, so I call the Coast Guard. We were floating in a mess. Sails and ropes floating.

"Joe was floating. Tangled in a floating rope. Poor Joe. Chip hooked him and we pulled him aboard."

Hargraves peered at Clay, his eyes: wet, red and dull.

Clay didn't say anything, waiting.

Sometime during the story, the captain's foot had tipped over the cup on the floor. The remains of the amber liquid made a small puddle headed for a drain.

"Sir," Clay finally said, "I'm sorry for your loss. Thank you for the story, I appreciate it."

On his way off the boat, he spoke to a few Coast Guard officials, and then went down the ramp.

He sat quietly in the rental car, looking at the marina without seeing it. His mind was watching a dark storm thrashing a big man floating in an orange life vest.

Clay was waiting for that sense of elation and satisfaction that follows a successful conclusion.

But the best he could find was some relief.

At last, he turned the key and started the motor.

"Case closed," he said.

< 283 >

## Epilogue

North of Honokaa, Clay hiked the exhausting switchbacks up the cliff. At the top he caught his breath and gazed into the lush Waipio Valley. It would be the last time he'd ever have to make that ascent. He relaxed an hour until he heard the sounds of someone on the trail below. Two men and a black box.

"I called for one and got two," Clay greeted them.

"We were having a slow day, so we both came. This is the most excitement we've had since Christmas."

"I'm Clay, and I assume you're the Hilo Bomb Squad."

"Tim and Bobby. We're the squad for the whole island."

After they talked and rested a while, Clay led the way down the hidden path to the little shelter and cave. Under the mat they dug out the tin box. The grenade got special treatment and went away with the Hilo officers.

Clay carefully took pictures on his cell phone and gathered the other contents in plastic bags and made notes. Cash, dog tags, and some personal objects. A picture of Fletch's sister and another of his mother.

The huge duffle bag held only clothes, so Clay repacked it and left it near the rotting fruit.

He got back down to his rental car and stowed the evidence in the trunk in time to catch a beer and supper at the Jump Off.

No longer the quiet little bar and burger shop, this joint was jumping. It was Saturday night. Sally, the flirt, was dressed for tips, helping with deliveries and taking orders. In the kitchen Elsie was sweating as she kept the food moving. Gurtz was everywhere doing everything.

A long-haired guitarist was softly playing slack-key. He hunched over his Gibson, watching his own fingers, as though mesmerized by their performance. When a song ended, he seemed as surprised as everyone else.

< 284 >

Roast pork and mahi mahi were on the menu, and the little crowd of friendly locals filled the place; and a few more waited on the porch.

Clay quietly ate alone at a tiny corner table, his mind moving between a stormy sea and the happy pub. Between right and wrong. Between life and death.

"Tomorrow will be Sunday," Clay told Gurtz, when she brought his dessert.

"It sure will."

"Want a date?"

She turned to face him directly and smiled.

"Yes, I do."

"Ten in the morning too early?"

"Ten tomorrow is perfect," she said. "Gives us time for breakfast and see the cowboys."

"I'll pick you up," he said.

On the west side of the Big Island, Jake stood beside a sweaty bay horse, unbuckled the rear cinch, and let it swing free. He put the stirrup over the seat and pulled the latigo loose. Looking across the saddle he saw his friend hook the cinches into their leather keeper.

"Jake," Walter said, "I hope you have a good flight tomorrow. I'll look forward to your return."

Their eyes locked for a long moment.

"And Jake ... thanks."

"Walter," Jake said. He realized the new name came easier now. And strangely, it seemed to fit.

"You're welcome," he said. "And thank you."

Jake looped the latigo on the 'D' ring, neat, ready for the next rider, and put a hand on the horn and his right on the cantle.

His eyes met Walter's again.

< 285 >

"You're going to be a great help here," he said.

"Jake, you are saving my life. You have no idea how important this is. I can never thank you enough. I owe you, and you can count on me." Walter's eyes reflected the truth of his words.

"I'll get this and put the horse up," Walter said, as he pulled off the saddle and pad.

"Thanks," Jake said again.

He left then and went to find Darcy.

O n a golf course in Honolulu two men played eighteen holes and decided to relax in the clubhouse. They called it 'the nineteenth hole.'

The pair started with a Budweiser, and soon a second. Then one moved on to a martini and the other went for Makers Mark. Over time they had several more rounds.

"Did you see the story in Sunday's paper?"

"Story?"

"Story in the *Honolulu Star*."

"Saw the paper, but we had company and I didn't read it. What was the news about?"

"Long story about Jay Paul Gottlieb. Wasn't he an old friend of yours?"

"Gosh, I hope nobody threw the paper out. Is it in the *Home Section*?"

"In *Living*, I think. It was all about his short marriage and divorce and all the related murders. You knew him, right?"

"I certainly did know Jay Paul. In fact, I'd known him since he was a youth. I was his first lawyer, his accountant and friend. I handle his trust fund."

"I thought you were friends but had no idea you worked for him. You must have known him inside and out."

"I was a good friend of his mother. She hired me to set up the trust and be his everything. Help him with his money and

< 286 >

be his advisor. We became good friends."

"So, John, you advised him to marry that girl?"

John chuckled. "No. He made that choice on his own. Apparently, it was a sperm of the moment decision."

"Sperm?"

"Uh huh."

"The story made it sound like he should have picked his secretary, Carnation."

"That would have been my recommendation if he'd asked. I worked closely with her on his accounting, taxes, and all that. She kept his books and ran his schedule. She knew everything about him, and if he'd married her, she could have been his mother too."

"Pretty?"

"Pretty as Beth, probably prettier. I thought so, anyway," said John. "Beth was a classic beauty with a filthy mouth. Carnation was warm and smart. Loyal to him, but I think he figured she was too old. Actually, she was a wee bit older. Year or two."

"Did you know his surfing pals?"

"Just Buddy. He was a permanent fixture at the house. I don't remember much about the ones that were shot. I had met them once, on a boat ride."

The two men sipped their drinks as a waitress came up.

"If you gentlemen are staying for dinner, I'll be glad to make your reservation," she said with a twinkle.

"No thanks, just give us one more round, Margaret. We'll leave soon," John said, glancing at his watch. He looked at her eyes and made a little signal with his finger that was code for 'on my tab.'

Then he said, "Marge, do you have any copies of Sunday's paper back there anywhere?"

"I'll look, Mister Silverman," and she disappeared.

"Big story?" John asked.

"I guess it was a full two-page spread at least."

"Jay Paul's divorce was a big portion of my life that I certainly won't forget."

"Sounds like it got pretty ugly."

"You don't know the half of it," John said, leaning close and lowering his voice. "Jay Paul told me he wanted to kill her."

"No shit?"

"Yes."

"He must have been kidding."

"He asked me to find a professional to do it."

"No."

"Jay Paul was obsessed with it. At one point I wanted to kill both of them."

"Can't kill your own client."

"I can't kill anybody, but I was at my wit's end. Beth and the divorce lawyers were in no hurry, billing by the hour. They were draining the trust fund. Just for a second, I thought if they both got killed, how nice and quiet it would be."

"But you'd be killing your chicken that laid the golden egg!"

"Nope," John said. "The trust goes on. Without Jay Paul, the money goes to his mother's favorite charities."

"And you're the well-paid administrator?"

"I am. Yes."

"So, who are the charities his mother wanted?"

The Honolulu Hospital and NPR are the main ones. There is also a tiny bit for Doctors Without Borders and some group that saves puppies.

"So, John, after all the smoke clears, who comes out on top ... you and National Public Radio?"

"I guess that's one way to look at it," John said.


The End

< 288 >

< 289 >

## Author's note

As I wrote this book, the Hawaii I most vividly remember is the innocent paradise it seemed to be in the late 1960's and early 70's. In those days, the construction crane was considered the official state bird. The nests the cranes left are full of people now.

'If you build it, they will come.'

Apparently, they came.

Detective Clay Burnam quoted to Mikio: "Truth runs for daylight, keeping it in the dark is difficult if not impossible." It was originally from our late friend Ron Gossling. I can only hope it's as true tomorrow as it was when he said it in 1977.

Speaking about truth, you won't find it here. This novel is fiction. The places exist, but none of the characters or activities are real. They were only imagined. Any resemblance to people living or dead, or events past or present, is purely coincidental.

The Parker Ranch is an important part of this story. Because it is a large piece of the Big Island's map and history, I used its real name. But in this book, nothing that happened there is or was real.

This is my second novel about the adventures of Jake Oar and his friends. If it left you curious about what happened before, feel free to read *Snap Chance*.

Thanks for coming to Hawaii with me.

D.W.

< 290 >

## References

If a curious reader wanted to know more about cutting horses, I recommend googling nchacutting. You can see some videos of great runs, and find the National Cutting Horse Association web site.

If you want to get in a Hawaiian mood before or after you read, just listen to a little slack-key guitar music. You could start with *Aloha 'Oe*, played by George Kahumoku Jr.

And if you want to see what Suz's paintings might have looked like, you might check out the work of Peggy Hopper.

Made in the USA
Monee, IL
08 May 2023

32882049R00173